Rose Rappoport Moss was born in 1937 in Johannesburg, South Africa, of immigrant parents and was educated locally. In 1956 she made her debut in the first issue of the city's *The Purple Renoster* review, edited by Lionel Abrahams, together with others of the Johannesburg school like Jillian Becker, Ruth Miller, Riva Rubin, Barney Simon and Rose Zwi. While a student at the University of the Witwatersrand in 1957 she won an Arts Festival Prize, judged by Nadine Gordimer. After emigrating to the United States in 1964, as 'Rose Moss' with Scribner's she published her first novel, *The Family Reunion* (1974 – shortlisted for the National Book Award). This was followed from Harvester with *The Terrorist* (1979 – featured by the New Fiction Society), issued in South Africa in 1981 under the title *The Schoolmaster* and subsequently reprinted by Ravan Press, to whose twenty-five years of publishing celebration in 1997 she contributed 'A Gem Squash'. In 1990 for Beacon Press in Boston she put together the documentary work, *Shouting at the Crocodile*. After its inception in 1977 she kept a watching brief for *World Literature Today* as a reviewer of key new South African works. She has contributed articles to *Leadership* in South Africa, and also to *Atlantic Monthly*, *The New York Times* and to *The Boston Globe* in Boston, Massachusetts, in the area where she has lived for many years.

As a short story writer she has contributed to several prestigious outlets, including *The Massachusetts Review*, *Prairie Schooner* and *Other Voices*. Her 'Exile' won the Quill Prize in 1971 and was included on the Roll of Honour of *Best American Short Stories* in the same year, and several other stories included here have been nominated for the Pushcart Prize ('Good Friday', 'This Balkan Woman' and 'In Court'). Translations of her short fiction include 'Mulberries' (into Spanish) and 'Exile' (into Nama). Stories of hers have also frequently been anthologised – for example, in *The Penguin Book of Southern African Stories* (1985), *The Penguin Book of Contemporary South African Short Stories* (1993) and *Modern South African Stories* (revised edition, 2002). This is the first collection of her short stories, initially published over the period 1970 through to 2004. This gathering comprises her personal history of those years.

Currently she teaches creative writing at the Harvard Law School in Cambridge. For further information visit 'Rose Moss Writer' on the website www.rosemosswriter.com.

André Brink in *Rapport* (9 March 1975):
> '*The Family Reunion* is surely one of the most notable novels yet written by a South African, and how magisterially she goes to work in it. In her structuring and style one must recognise one of Joyce's heirs, something even Nabokov could be proud of. She manages to be lively, too – plastic, moving and a virtuoso.'

Pat Schwartz in *The Rand Daily Mail* (17 October 1978):
> 'The voice might be lazily gentle, the heavily lidded eyes may be sleepy, but underneath the quiet exterior is a sharp mind belonging to a determined woman. Her name is Rose Moss and once she was a South African. Still is, in accent and roots, but in lifestyle and profession she is American – our loss.'

Lionel Abrahams in *English in Africa* (September 1980):
> 'At Wits I had befriended Rose Rappoport and other student writers. It is no mean thing for *The Purple Renoster* to claim her name as among those it introduced to South African readers.'

Peter Nazareth in *World Literature Today* (1980):
> 'Rose Moss's achievement is in giving words to action, making it enter living history.'

The New York Times Book Review (30 December 1990):
> 'Rose Moss, who has lived in the US since 1964, has written a revealing book. *Shouting at the Crocodile* offers an optimistic glimpse of the new South Africa waiting to be born.'

Michiel Heyns in *The Sunday Independent*, Johannesburg (16 January 2003):
> 'Rose Moss's masterly "A Gem Squash" is exemplary in its unsentimental assessment of an ageing anti-apartheid activist marooned in liberal-capitalist America.'

IN COURT

AND OTHER STORIES

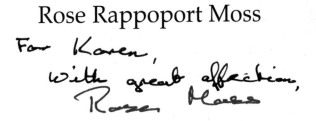

Rose Rappoport Moss

For Karen,
with great affection,
Rose Moss

PENGUIN BOOKS

PENGUIN BOOKS

Published by the Penguin Group
Penguin Books (South Africa) (Pty) Ltd, 24 Sturdee Avenue, Rosebank,
Johannesburg 2196, South Africa
Penguin Books Ltd, 80 Strand, London WC2R 0RL, England
Penguin Group (USA) Inc, 375 Hudson Street, New York, New York 10014,
USA
Penguin Group (Canada), 90 Eglinton Avenue East, Suite 700, Toronto,
Ontario, Canada M4P 2Y3 (a division of Pearson Penguin Canada Inc)
Penguin Ireland, 25 St Stephen's Green, Dublin 2, Ireland (a division of
Penguin Books Ltd)
Penguin Group (Australia), 250 Camberwell Road, Camberwell, Victoria 3124,
Australia (a division of Pearson Australia Group Pty Ltd)
Penguin Books India Pvt Ltd, 11 Community Centre, Panchsheel Park, New
Delhi – 110 017, India
Penguin Group (NZ), 67 Apollo Drive, Mairangi Bay, Auckland 1310, New
Zealand (a division of Pearson New Zealand Ltd)

Penguin Books (South Africa) (Pty) Ltd, Registered Offices:
24 Sturdee Avenue, Rosebank, Johannesburg 2196, South Africa

www.penguinbooks.co.za

First published by Penguin Books (South Africa) (Pty) Ltd 2007

Copyright © Rose Rappoport Moss 2007

ISBN 978-0-143-18552-9

Typeset by CJH Design in 10 on 12.5 pt Palatino
Cover image: Tommy Motswai
Cover design: African Icons
Printed and bound by Paarl Print, Cape Town

Acknowledgements

To the editors and publishers of journals in which stories first appeared, with grateful acknowledgements:

New Voices (1974) for 'Spenser Street' and *Antioch Review* (2006) for the present revised version; *Confrontation* (1986) for 'Lessons' and *Sesame* (1989); *Echad* (1982) for 'Light/Dark'; *Cimarron Review* (1976) for 'Twice Her Size'; *RE:AL* (2000) for 'The Sisters' House'; *96 Inc* (2002) for 'The Night We Talked'; *Shenandoah* (1973) for 'The House is Full of Cars This Morning'; *The Massachusetts Review* (1970) for 'Exile' and also to the last issue of *The Purple Renoster* (1972); *Other Voices* (2001) for 'Good Friday' and for 'The Man of God' (2004); *The Writer in Stone*, edited by Graeme Friedman and Roy Blumenthal (Cape Town: David Philip, 1998) for 'The Widow's Widow' and *Southwest Review* (1999); *Agni* (2002) for an earlier version of 'Mulberries', for 'A Gem Squash' (1999) and for 'In Court' (1991); *The Southern African Review of Books* (Issue 34 of November-December 1994) for the original extended version of 'Stompie' and to *Venue* (1998); and *StoryQuarterly* (2001) for 'This Balkan Woman'.

The 'Author's Note' first appeared in the 'South African Voices from Abroad' section of *Momentum: On Recent South African Writing*, edited by M J Daymond, J U Jacobs and Margaret Lenta (Pietermaritzburg: University of Natal Press, 1984). The interview included here was originally entitled 'Telling the Truth' (*Contrast*, Cape Town, Number 47 of June 1979) and was conducted by Jean Marquard. Reproduced by courtesy of the estate of Jean Marquard.

Rose Rappoport Moss in 2007

Contents

Acknowledgements   v

Author's Note   ix
Interview (with Jean Marquard)   xiii

Spenser Street   1
Lessons   4
Light/Dark   15
Twice Her Size   22
The Sisters' House   39
The Night We Talked   63
The House is Full of Cars This Morning   68
Exile   75
Good Friday   94
The Widow's Widow   112
Mulberries   119
Stompie   123
A Gem Squash   127
This Balkan Woman   144
The Man of God   160
In Court   179

Author's Note

South Africa is the soil of my imagination. It appears in my work continually as the original world where things are as they must be. This world – sun, sky, stone, grass – has been, is, will be. If language allowed, I would not use a verb with a tense. The seeing of childhood does not know that anything changes or suffers history.

It feels comfortable and intimate to write to you in South Africa 'sun, sky, stone, grass'. I believe that the images you will bring to these words are the images I would invite. It feels comfortable to write without simultaneous translation, feeling that you hear the words I use without a foreign accent. Usually, even when my subject is the unitary vision of childhood, I must find my way through words I learned later than childhood. This morning as I walked in Cambridge, Massachusetts, among leaves falling and fallen at the early end of summer, a bitter smell in the transparent air between suburban gardens put me among Johannesburg plane trees at autumn and an afternoon after school. If I were telling an American about this instant of common sensation that fused my present and an afternoon when I was fifteen, I would identify the tree whose leaves smell bitter with the name I learned in this country, sycamore, translating.

When I grew up in South Africa I translated the other way, as children in a subordinate culture do. With language itself I lost connections with my own daily experience. I used words for what happens in England and Europe. I had learned them from books, and books rarely had South African words like khakibos, or blackjacks, or bluegums. The things I knew and did, so dense and rich, were things without their own names. When they were dressed in words from overseas, what I had known hid behind cardboard masks. Now that namelessness of South Africa feels stronger. When I came to the States, unexpectedly starved for the country I had left, I read voraciously about South Africa, and felt again and again that foreigners get it wrong. I believe that by now I also get it wrong. My main connection with South Africa now is through books, rare articles in newspapers, a few visits. I do less inner translating, though Americans still hear me with an accent. My written voice too remains South African, in rhythm, in accent, and most of all, in irony.

By irony I mean seeing simultaneously from two or more points of view, an adult vision unlike the unitary vision of childhood. Irony is endemic to wanderers. They see un-questioned certainties in one city with eyes that saw them as exotic in another. The practice of colonial translation taught me one kind of irony. 'May' might be spring or fall in any sentence, 'June' roses or frost. The year began with Janus facing two directions.

My South African irony goes deeper than language, into gesture. When I try to see what I mean, I think of the way I walked down a street in Johannesburg and my eyes met the eyes of other people. Immediately there was that wealth of exchange and intimate knowledge we have when we look into the eyes of another person. The whole life is there and floods out like light. People in cities learn not to look at each other that way. Everyone knows that when the subway stops or the light changes the person you are looking at will move on. You will never see each other again. You do not look into the eyes of strangers. But before I had learned urban reticence, I looked into people's eyes on the street. Sometimes the person I looked at, looking at me, was black, and part of the life streaming between us included knowing that we were set apart. The naked knowing of our seeing was forbidden. In South Africa blacks and whites learn to not look at each other, even when they are not strangers.

I suspect that when I first looked at black people as though they might be equals or friends, I looked as though I had learned to look when a black nanny held me or fed me. Somewhere I must have learned that the intimacy of unreserved knowing, of touch, or smell, has nothing to do with the way things are. The sensuous base of trust in another person who picks you up when you fall and feeds you when you are hungry can disappear because that person is a servant, a nothing. A servant is not a friend. A servant may be exchanged tomorrow for some advantage of price important to adults. A servant may go forever for the whim of a law that sends the intimate nanny away from the child's white world.

Perhaps I learned that sense of irony some other way, though I try to describe it as being at once close as a child to its mother and as distant as white from black. However I learned it, it structures the way I know everything. A field of namelessness separates what I know at skin level, at smell, at slouch and balance, from the official words I inherited. To fill that field I write, searching for words and shapes of story that fit and link. Other writers, not South African, have written to find out who they are and how they live. For me that field of namelessness close to myself, terra incognita, has a few landmarks I call South Africa.

I find another trait of my voice and imagery South African. I see the present itself from another point of view, as though over the present looms an apocalyptic sense that something must change, will change, in destruction and tears, but with some justice, some necessity. The apocalypse calls for biblical language to imply that it will be a judgment which will make clear the meaning of what is happening now. I used to think my apocalyptic imagery my private thing. Now I see it in many other South African writers. Some northern writers also have a sense of impending doom. They foresee universal destruction that will be simply absurd, as meaningless as it will be terrible. The underlying vision in South Africa is revolution, in the United States nuclear extinction.

Sharpeville was, for me, a foretaste of revolution. I left South Africa soon after, despairing that the change Sharpeville had seemed about to initiate would not come after all. Soweto opened the issues of Sharpeville again, but I have changed. I see now what it would take to change apartheid with greater sadness and less anger. I am less impatient for revolution, and less able to believe that it can lead to a just society. I have lost or grown out of the unitary vision of justice or injustice in which apartheid felt almost uniquely dreadful. I have learned that it is not unique. Soon after I left South Africa, the United States plunged into Vietnam. Again I was living in a society that behaved with intolerable injustice.

Interview

After a long absence, you're back on a visit to South Africa. Why did you decide to leave this country for the States?

I couldn't stand living in South Africa any more. I had thought of going to Britain but went to America to get married.

Do you think life in South Africa inhibited you as a writer?

Yes. In South Africa I wrote less and less and found it harder and harder to order my imagination or to develop any discipline. I had written as a schoolgirl and had a play staged before going to Wits. I knew I wanted to be a writer, but in South Africa I didn't write. I had a sense of universal oppression, uselessness, guilt, futility, rage … It sapped my will. I was unable to struggle against a weight of depression, living here.

Do you think South African writers have a particular duty to draw attention to the inequities of the system?

No. But telling the truth is bad for apartheid. A lot happens to try and silence people, to distort their vision of the world and keep them ignorant of the words that could set them free. The primary obligation for a writer is to tell the truth. But politics on the other hand requires simpler formulations. People who say you should write about the political structure, or about capitalism in the twentieth century, or about feminism, any pre-structured issue of this kind, know what you should be saying before you do. Let them say it for themselves. If you listen to their demands it will prevent you from saying what you have to say. I am an addict of Proust who argues in the most eloquent way I know that the obligations of the writer are to express what he knows as an individual.

Would you say that our obsession with politics blurs our free responses to literature and art?

This is probably so but it doesn't seem particularly South African to me. Very few people in our Western, English-speaking culture believe in art and literature.

Do you feel freer in America than you do here and if so can you say why?

It's a complex question. I feel freer partly because America's a bigger place and more choices become visible to one. Also, although the US is cancerous with hypocrisy in some ways, the basis on which hypocrisy grows is one which is essentially dedicated to liberty and this is manifest throughout the society in every little thing. Freedom becomes an effective possibility – even in trivial ways. I like it. People in the States protest with confidence in their right to do so against shoddiness, injustices. In South Africa I sense a kind of apathy, a resigned attitude which says – there is nothing we can do about it. In the Boston area where I live people know they are equal and free.

The events in your novel, The Family Reunion, *take place on the last day of the world. Why did you choose an apocalyptic mood?*

I continually ask, in story after story, what is the right life? A standard way of approaching this question is to look at life from the perspective of the last moment. Camus said 'Every day is the Day of Judgment'. It is also a way of bringing together many disparate feelings I had at the time. I was writing the novel at the time Nixon admitted that there had been an incursion into Cambodia and it was also the time of the Kent State killings. That time felt like the early days of Sharpeville here. In other words, apocalyptic. What I was writing about included members of my family – one of the people had died and so that came together in an apocalyptic image with things

I was feeling about America.

Would you define yourself as South African or American?

I carry an American passport now and I feel like an American in many ways but I'll never stop feeling that I am bound to South Africa. I shall feel this even more strongly when the country changes its name as I hope it will.

Do you miss this country?

At first I missed it very deeply. One of the first stories I published in America was called 'Exile'. This was a story about someone who couldn't bear to live outside South Africa but couldn't come back. During recent years I have realised that it *is* possible to come and go and I don't know whether this will remain possible for me but I hope it will. At first, when I was homesick, I felt closer to South African born friends – there are lots of South Africans in the Boston area where there are teaching hospitals now full of South African doctors. I hear South African accents in supermarkets and buses but I no longer have any particular impulse to approach them just because they come from here. Had I met them here I might not necessarily have liked them. My closest friends now are Americans.

How often do you return to South Africa on visits?

I didn't return for the first seven or eight years. Since then I've been back twice and now I've returned after an absence of four years.

Do you experience any difference on this visit?

Yes. Four years ago I had a firm conviction that the political situation was going to change. The coup in Portugal had occurred. Frelimo had come to power. There was talk of Angola becoming independent. I was quite hopeful. Not that I met people who were particularly in the know – one sees one's friends – but there was a sense in the air that things were going to change. This time I have the feeling that South Africa is full of people who don't know each other, don't know what the other person is thinking, don't trust one another. The country feels full of tiny antagonistic pieces right now and this is different from 1974. The effect, however, is similar to what I thought when I left in 1964 – that nothing hopeful is going to happen. I would like to be proved wrong. My impression is limited to the people I've talked with. Among those people are many who feel trapped here, unhappy to be here and unable to move out. I think this is a very hard country to live in – for blacks – yes, in all the obvious ways and for the obvious reasons. But for whites too, unhappily drinking their wine …

Why is the feeling of being trapped confined to whites?

Because they appear to have the choice. The feeling is also there for those blacks who appear to have the choice – those, for example, who come to the United States to study.

What about white prosperity – life in Johannesburg's Northern Suburbs for instance – this is often criticised as leading to idleness and boredom.

I've written a novel about a white man who made a bomb and put it in a station in a large centre. This is not a story about John Harris. My story was triggered by hearing about the bomb explosion before any names had been mentioned or any arrests made. As soon as I heard that newscast in the States I knew that this was what I wanted as axis of my South African novel. Well, in this novel I have a whole spectrum of things that people do in South Africa presenting themselves as choices to my protagonist. The inevitable image of the Northern Suburbs comes up – but I don't see it as an image of bored people. In fact my protagonist sees this as a valid choice – the choice of personal fulfilment and of responsibility to the family in the first place, personal friends, the life of daily contact. It is a valid choice but it is not one my protagonist can make.

Do you see it yourself as a valid choice?

I do. I think very few of us can do anything about the state of the world. A lot of people, women particularly, are cut off from power – often because there are young children and the lack of a sense of personal effectiveness and of worth. They hate themselves and they undermine themselves. Men willingly collaborate in this and see them as living empty, vapid, useless lives and mock them for it. I detest this – I think it is a cruel way to look at people in misery. Thoreau's insight – that most people live lives of quiet desperation – is, I think, particularly true of many women and in South Africa these women are sitting ducks for that kind of imperceptive cruelty.

Do white South African women have better chances than most others to develop their potential because they can so easily get domestic help?

Theoretically this should be so but in fact it seems not to be the case and this is because the consciousness of the women themselves is undermined by their sense of guilt and insignificance and also because of the lack of examples of what women can achieve; and also because of the masculine sexism that pervades this society. It is a rigidly hierarchical set-up – every man in his place, every woman below that. Of course there are South African women who have defied this expectation – Winnie Mandela, Nadine Gordimer, Helen Suzman – they are not unimpressive. But these women exist in this society as exceptions and thus they are not genuine examples. There is no sense of their connection to ordinary people, the sense of a route that lesser mortals could take. Instead there is a sense of mystery about these women – they are seen as giants, towering over the norm. I teach at Wellesley College in Boston which is a women's college where a whole process of assisting women to realise their power and use it in the world is articulated at a high level and actually implemented. For instance we have programmes for women, placement services and the bringing in of role models – successful women who come as guests, and guest lecturers.

Do you think South African universities should offer courses in South African literature?

Yes, I agree there should be such courses. Though I guess the danger is in the temptation to present material of interest as if it had a greater literary merit than it has.

Should South African literature be taught as one would teach European literature or should a different method be adopted?

Certainly not, if it was offered in a literature programme. In a political science course there would be another way of coming at it, but in a literary course the first concern must obviously be with literary qualities. My own feeling about teaching a course in South African literature would be to approach it comparatively, that is, not comparing it with a metropolitan culture but with other literatures with a similar semi-colonial approach to the metropolitan culture where works of outstanding quality have been produced to show that they *can* be produced in this kind of situation and to set a standard by which everything else should be seen in perspective to prevent exaggeration. For instance *One Hundred Years of Solitude* – by the Colombian, Gabriel Marquez, is an outstanding example. In the nineteenth century the Russians felt in the same relation to Europe – cut off from centres of civilisation, and yet they also set a standard. Although, of course, the nineteenth century sets standards in every way to fictional writing.

What do you think about the relation of South African literature to African literature as a whole?

South African literature is obviously related to African literature but also to European and other colonial literatures.

Do you still think of yourself as a South African writer?

Yes, my imagination is full of it – South African images, light, sun, space, ways of seeing people, ways of listening to them. South Africa is the bed of my early experience. Everything comes from South Africa. The kinds of things I was taught to read here. The reverence for the printed word which is so quaint and old-fashioned and still prevails here.

Why do you find this quaint?

The printed word has been the agent of imaginative power and freedom for hundreds of years but it is not going to remain so – especially in fiction. There will be other things. I think story-telling is such a permanent human activity that it goes on in every way in every culture. The novel and the short story are temporary Western forms that still have a good way to run but they are now sharing the human imagination with other agents like television – even travel.

How would you define a South African writer?

I don't like definitions. But I know one when I see one.

Spenser Street

The garden next door had a tree. It leaned over the lawn towards the veranda of the house and almost touched its wooden pillars. Its heart-shaped leaves cast a fluttering light and sometimes its leaves fell on the lawn. Their green was different from the small leaves of a vine trained along the veranda pillars, different from the glossy privet of the thick hedge and different from the dusty leaves of the wattle outside my bedroom window. When I stood in the space between our house and the brick wall of the house next door, I could imagine a tree on my side too.

The garden next door looked as though no one ever came into it but sometimes I saw the old woman who lived next door wandering there. She used to wear a purple robe over pink underwear and shouted at the gardener for not cutting the grass.

Our garden had a low wall leaving it open to the street like most gardens in our area. Its flowers straggled all over each other, nasturtiums, petunias, dahlias, geraniums and two roses. Near the gate, some violets perishing in the sun and glare produced five or six flowers a year. Weeds grew thick in the dark mouth of the space between my window and the brick wall of the garden next door. Only the weed wattle grew in the space itself. In the corner between my parents' bay window and our shiny red veranda grew a pink oleander but its poisonous leaves did not take a dapple like the leaves next door.

Down the road, an oak grew out of the concrete pavement. Its scrawny branches looked unkempt among the silvery telephone poles and tram stops and every year people lopped its branches clear of electric wires overhead. I once saw a horse standing next to that oak.

No tree grew in our backyard. The large part was paved with concrete, the smaller lay bare. Sometimes my brother and I planted peas and radishes in the bare earth. Mostly we left it for the sun to stare at. On VE day I planted a flag we'd been given at school, not knowing what else to do with it. I tried to think about the War and looked up into the sky to see whether it would ever end, but it just went on and on, blue.

My bedroom had once been a dressing room and on Saturday mornings I would sit in the niche between inbuilt wardrobes to read in the sunshine. If I stretched my hand carefully past the burglar-proofing I could touch the sinewy trunk of our tree. Sometimes I saw the woman next door, tottering a bit. She leaned on the wire gate opening to the street to look at passers-by. Passengers on the trams used to notice her, bright in the gap of her dark hedge. She lived alone. One of her sons was Up North with the army. Another had married a gentile, I think, and wasn't allowed to visit her.

She never changed out of the purple robe but she sometimes wore a red wig. She wasn't frightening, like a witch. She was too bright and did not seem much more strange than other grown-ups. There was nothing interesting about Mrs Goldberg. But to this day fairyland is to the right like her garden and has its green, enclosed silence and sunlit dapple.

One afternoon I went down the dark space outside my window to lie on the stones and look up at the leaves of our straggling wattle. I tried to imagine I was in England, in a forest or on a lawn under a tree. I wasn't successful. The ground was too hard and I worried whether people in the street could see me. It was too awkward trying to be like people in books. Most of my life seemed dull but in the world of books even things dull in the world I knew seemed to weigh more like cakes soaked in honey.

After Mrs Goldberg's son was killed Up North she used to shout even more at the gardener and shake her fists at him, so shrill the whole block could hear. 'Johannes! Johannes!' When he appeared words gushed from her, Yiddish, English, Zulu, Afrikaans, pell-mell. He hadn't cut the grass. She would show him how herself and kneeled down to tear up weeds with her trembling hands. Sometimes she tore the wig off her head and stamped on it. Sometimes she turned away from the stupid black kaffir, crying, and went into the house.

My mother invited her to visit on the eves of festivals but she felt strange, she apologised and didn't know what to say to people.

We moved from Spenser Street soon after the War. My mother didn't want to live in a house any more. She didn't feel houses were safe. Mrs Goldberg next door had been found hacked to death with an ordinary kitchen axe.

She'd been lying in her blood among the spattered walls, dust settling on the hardened pools, for more than a week. The gardener confessed as soon as he was arrested but he had been away visiting his family in Zululand and there was no case against him. His lawyers argued he hadn't understood the policeman who questioned him. His only European language was Mrs Goldberg's English-Yiddish-Afrikaans. The police ruled out robbery. The little money in the house had not been disturbed. After a few days, the murder disappeared from the newspapers.

My parents were shocked but then they forgot about it. So did I. When I passed through Spenser Street I hardly remembered I had lived in one of its shabby villas dwindling under the glaring sun. Someone had chopped down the wattle to stop its roots creeping into the foundations.

Lessons

When I tell how I learned about darkness, I feel that I carry a great stone on my shoulders, a rock as big as a giant seems to a child. I was a child then and all that happened happened to someone who did not guess the size of the world. There were few people and most of them were very large. The most large, the blackest, like a mountain and the clouds that hang over a mountain, was Mrs Casey. Only, when I say a mountain, it might seem far away on the horizon. I mean towering over me like a wave of the sea always about to fall over me and drown me. Already I taste the taste of salt and sour things, although I cannot speak their name.

Like her dead child. Mrs Casey was a woman who had lost her son, a widow who lay all night in a bed too wide for one person in her room with four walls and a locked door and waited for light to flush in the window. Only when she was sure that something can last and come back, when the birds began to sing with jocund noise, only at dawn could she unclench her body and sleep. In a few hours the maid, whose duty it was, woke her to a bitter cup of coffee. She began the day.

At that time I was not an adult. I had no idea of the inner life of other people or how it accumulates like lines on a map, some meaning rivers, some meaning coasts, the world becoming more known and filled in, even with terrible deserts like the Gobi and Sahara where travellers die of heat and cold and the thirst Mrs Casey knew. I understood nothing of the world at that time except the circle around me and over me as far as my eye could see. I was the centre.

I was a child and did not know how to read the inner life of other people.

I am a child sitting on the dark side of the world, in E row, where the windows give on to the stoep that runs along the classroom wall on one side of the tar playground where I am afraid to go out at break. Big break is worse than little break. I am afraid to be alone because to be alone is the worst thing that can happen. It shows that I am unpopular. Invisible stocks, no less wooden and unmovable for being inside me, fasten my arms, my head, my legs. I am a criminal and my body is a laughing stock: the village comes to look at me and jeer. If I try to pretend that I am not in the stocks and put myself at the edge of a group that has been laughing (I wonder whether they have been laughing at me) I know that they are thinking, 'Here she is, trying to push in again.'

Sometimes they say, 'Go away. We don't want to play with you.'

On the other side of the world the girls in A row sit where the sun shines through the windows and touches their golden hair. They are always clean and neat and get their sums right. In E row there are mostly girls from the orphanage near the school and other girls who are so bad they deserve to be orphans. All their books are dirty like their clothes and sometimes when Mrs Casey picks up a book she says, 'Ugh!' Sometimes she also says, 'Just look at this page!' and holds it up for the whole class to see. The girls in A row are astonished that anyone can be so bad. Then Mrs Casey takes a scurvy book full of blots and scratches and adds bright red weals and crosses and big circles. Wrong! Wrong! Nought! Nought! And then, because I get my sums wrong, she says, 'Give me your ruler,' and I give it to her because she is bigger than a human being.

Once there is a girl who is a new orphan with big bones. She is older than me, or she would never think of such a thing and when Mrs Casey tries to take her ruler from her she wrestles to keep it until Mrs Casey picks up the one on my desk and slaps her across the face with it and that stills her.

Then Mrs Casey says, 'Now hold out your hand.' So she holds it out. She hits and she hits until the girl cowers and the sounds coming from her almost like words are, 'Please miss, please miss.' There is other stuff coming out of her mouth too, dripping like a dog's.

Another time it is Fay, the girl who shares my desk, but all I can remember about it is the way Fay lies on the floor like a bundle of rags on the splinters. Mrs Casey is shocked that she fainted and sends Marlene to get water. It is lucky that Fay has no parents to tell the story to because although Miss Cheshire, the principal, knows about Mrs Casey and that she hits us, it is supposed to be against the law to hit girls. If Fay had a parent or someone to ask questions and take her to a doctor and show the welts ...

But if Fay had parents Mrs Casey would be less furious at her.

I know this although, as a child, I do not know how to say it: the protected are protected and the ones who are taken to the galleys are those who have lost everything already.

I am not an orphan. My parents wrangle in the room next door to my bedroom night after night like merchants haggling in foreign tongues. Sometimes my mother comes to the school to complain to Miss Cheshire, the principal, about Mrs Casey, but there must be something else she sees. Perhaps it is my mother's accent, perhaps it is the way she dresses. Perhaps Miss Cheshire can see something I cannot see. She knows that she can promise to do something. She knows that she can say anything and no one will punish her.

She tells Mrs Casey that my mother has come to complain. Then I beg my mother not to complain, not to come to the school.

I learn to smile. I learn to know what is happening when other slaves smile.

When I am older, I look at the eyes of blacks when they say,

Yes, Madam. Yes, Baas. It is not the custom in my country for whites to look into the eyes of blacks.

I learn not to tell my mother anything about what happens at school. People say that I have a very quiet voice and often ask me to repeat what I say on the telephone.

But although I have learned to shut up, I cannot conform my body to such mental indifference that anything can be done to it and I will not feel it, as I see in the blank faces of the orphanage girls, more and more as the years under Mrs Casey go on. At first I only bite my pencils though my mother says it will make my mouth ugly. Then I bite my nails and my hair and wet my bed at night and sometimes I wet the floor where Fay fainted. The orphanage girls don't say anything, though everyone can see the pool forming at the iron leg of my desk. When Mrs Casey finds out, she shouts, 'Baby! Pig!' I dream that she will eat me at night and after she has eaten me I will still be alive and she will be able to eat me again. With such gnawing and twisting of lips and such darkness and wetness going deep down into the mines and hell of things it could only be a dream, that is to say, a true image pouring out of my fear like the water that comes out of me when I am sitting at my desk and know that she is going to come and look at my sums in her green dress and say to me, 'Give me your ruler,' and I will put it obediently into her terrible pink hand and then she will punish me. She will punish me for her dead son and her dead husband, she will punish me for the itching wool that tormented her during the night in her empty bed; she will beat me for the chip on her coffee cup when the maid came to wake her. How can I know all that she is punishing me for? With such fury that now when I see movies with beasts leaping and snarling, their teeth showing, it doesn't bother me at all. It is only the people bigger than thunder, the voice all over the airport, the President of the United States saying, 'We are the strongest nation in the world,' that makes me feel Oh God, God save me, because there is no one else bigger than Mrs Casey.

Sometimes I know that God doesn't exist, or if he does, he is busy quarrelling with his wife when I weep like a child who can never get out of the nightmare.

The curious thing is that I was a child. I had not learned yet that there are people I must not love. At times I liked Mrs Casey and thought she knew everything. I was ready for heaven, able to believe the best of the worst. I was happy when she was in a good mood or had a fit of religiosity and remembered that Christ said, 'Suffer little children to come unto me.' Sometimes she tries to be nice to all of us, the whole class. She lets one girl, usually Marlene, sit on a desk in front of the class and read to us while we do our sewing. She takes us out afterwards and lets us run relay races.

Each captain chooses the girls she wants on her team so it is always bad like in the playground, but it isn't really as bad as the playground because no one can say, Go away. In a tone of voice that makes me really want to, right out of my body and my life. Though I am also a child, a young animal, I cannot really want to be not alive, though one of the orphanage girls does commit suicide when she is eleven, in the third year of Mrs Casey's class. So that we will never do it in her class, Mrs Casey tells us it was a horrible and cowardly thing to do.

When she taught us about the Bible, there were things she said with power: 'The Lord is my shepherd, I shall not want.'

Her favourite stories were not about the Good Shepherd or the ones Marlene read when we were sewing, but her own. The one she told most often and with curious details as though she had been there and seen it all, was about the woman in the department store who stole. The store detective saw her and stopped her at the door. He said, 'Excuse me, madam, will you come with me?' He took her to the offices on the fifth floor where there was a woman who searched through her bag and made her undress in a cubicle with a wooden bench. They found everything on her and they called the police.

Sometimes Mrs Casey makes the story merciful. The thief is a rich kleptomaniac who does not mean any harm. She says she is sorry and will pay for everything. Then they feel sorry for her and let her off.

Our whole class feels sorry for her too.

I didn't know which version to believe.

She also likes the story about the judge who condemned the murderer to be taken from the place where he was to the place where he would be and there to be hanged by the neck until he was dead. She says these words again and again, like someone who likes the sounds.

Like the judges who say it again and again.

Sometimes Mrs Casey says that it was not the murderer's fault. It was his father who should have been hanged.

Every year on the last day of school all the girls bring Mrs Casey presents and she is very happy. They bring tea towels and painted glasses and china cats and she takes them home.

Even the orphanage girls give her things. Fay gives her a stone. She has painted it to make it a paperweight and Mrs Casey does say, 'Thank you.' But the present she likes most is the gold brooch Marlene brings her.

Marlene is Mrs Casey's pet who sits in the sunny row, right in front and jumps up easily when she is called to clean the board or hand out new pencils. Her hair shines. When it is combed loose, I feel that the sun fingers each thread. Sometimes it is plaited in a thick braid, quiet as bread.

I know that I will never look like Marlene.

Every Easter there was a trade fair. They showed gold from the mines, diamonds, machines and the products of other industries. At some of the booths people gave us samples of toothpaste and cereal. Other countries also showed their wares and posters of what we might see if we went there. Between the pavilions people sold ice cream and handed out brochures. I stood at the chemical industries exhibit and looked at the tubes of glass and transparent liquid coloured like sapphire and ruby.

It was a hot day and when we came to an open space between pavilions, Mrs Casey let us all stop and eat our lunches. There was no shade and there were no benches. We sat on the ground and Mrs Casey sat on the kerb. She sat with her legs wide apart in a way I had been told never to sit because ladies keep their legs closed. I stared. I have never seen a white woman sit on the kerb like that with her feet in the gutter. Only they sit like that.

They do anything they want. They speak in their own language and no one understands them. My mother knows that they steal sugar and tea from the pantry and money from the house. She has to lock everything up and all the houses where white people live have windows covered with heavy wire mesh so that they can't break in and steal things. They never learn anything. They are like children.

Mrs Casey's back was round like a potato and her hair was falling out of the knot on top of her head. Although I was staring, I could not understand what I saw; she looked like a girl in E row.

Fay must have seen something too. She took an orange from the brown paper bag that held her lunch and went to Mrs Casey. She stood in front of her, 'Would you like my orange?'

Mrs Casey nodded and took it. But she did not say thank you.

Usually each class has a teacher for only one year, but my years with Mrs Casey are an exception. She remains my teacher for three years.

For a long time after I feel that if there is darkness, it will fall on me. I do not know why I have been singled out.

Or whether I have been singled out.

After a while in Mrs Casey's class, I used to vomit a lot. I had to raise my hand to ask for permission to go to the lavatory

10

to do it and sometimes she didn't see or thought I could just wait. She liked to do that when the girls waved and snapped their hands, wriggling, before she would say, 'Yes, what do you want?'

'Please miss, can I go to the bathroom?'

'May I go to the bathroom.'

'Yes, miss, please miss.'

'Say it correctly now: please, Mrs Casey ...'

Once she waited so long when I opened my mouth to speak, it all came out, plop, on to the floor and all the girls said, 'Ugh,' and Mrs Casey said, 'Go ask the cleaning boy for a rag and water. You can't expect anyone else to wipe up your mess.'

Then I became really sick and couldn't go to school. For months I lay on my parents' sunny bed and read a lot and slept and looked at the reflections the glass of water made on the ceiling. If I moved the glass, great membranes like butterfly wings made of light flew where I sent them. And sometimes my mother let me play with her diamond ring. When I twisted it, sparks of colour ran over the sheets.

Let me say one thing more so that I won't give the false impression that there was nothing else in that world or that there is nothing else now.

Days were enormously long. I couldn't think of an hour and a year was like the sky. I didn't cry much. I liked to play in the alley between my house and Mrs Pereira's. I used to pretend, because there was a little wattle tree growing there, that it was a lawn with oaks like those I read about in books about people in England.

Next door, in Mrs Pereira's house, there was a window opposite the window of the bathroom in my house. It probably belonged to a pantry or an empty bedroom because the light was seldom on at night. In the mild weather of my country, the window of our bathroom was usually open, although it had been glazed with bubble glass to screen the people inside from eyes outside. We knew that they were always looking at us.

One winter night when the air was sharp enough for the bathroom window to be closed, Mrs Pereira switched on the light and, as I looked from the bathroom door, I saw that the light from next door had divided and multiplied into thousands of flakes that sparkled like my mother's diamond ring. More than thousands – they were uncountable and moved with the slightest motion of my head, seeming to multiply and divide again. Every brilliant colour was in the seeds of glass and a white as bright as the naked thread of metal burning in Mrs Pereira's light. I thought of the burning metal of stars.

I knew that the stars are full of burning metal. My father told me. We were driving down to the sea for summer holidays. Our route lay through the desert Karoo between the gold mines and the Cape. I have travelled that way since. The road goes straight ahead for two hundred miles and if I travelled by train the heat was drowsy and deep like the first day of menstruation. If I travelled by car, I saw water gliding across the road like a snake. Although the desert seems perfectly dry, there are grey bushes that sheep can live off and plants that look like stones. When the rain falls, as it does every few years, the stones open and flower.

That time when I was a child travelling with my father, he took the Karoo at night to avoid the heat. I woke when he stopped at Beaufort West to fill the car and buy coffee for himself and cocoa for me. In that long main street where neon signs in red and green welcomed travellers, I heard him talking to a man at the service station in his own language. As though he was one of them. As though he was not white.

When we drove on, somewhere after the last straggle of houses, he stopped the car and we got out. 'Look.' He pointed up to the sky fogged like a milky glass. 'That's the Milky Way.' The fog was made of light. The stars that seemed to hang in front of it were part of it. Some of these stars were so bright that I could see they burned in colours.

My father told me that in the desert the air was so exceptionally clear that people came from all over the world to study the stars there, hoping to learn how the world began and what it is made of and how it will end; that each star is a sun so hot the rocks and metals in it are soft; in some stars, even hotter, they are still gas. He was speaking in a voice that asks questions like, Why? and after the first answer asks again, like a child, Why?

When I imagined the gas of stars, it was as a stream of gold. The huge sky was making me giddy, so I took my father's hand. Rays from the Southern Cross looked into my eyes.

On the night I saw the bathroom pane brilliant as the crowns of thirty kings, I called him to see it. Although to me it was a river of jewels pouring through the darkness, to him it seemed like nothing.

Like a grey stone before it has rained.

Once during my years under Mrs Casey, there was a day she took the whole class outside and said we should plant a garden. She gave us seeds to put in the earth and she took some into the classroom so that we could put them on saucers with cotton and water and see how they start to grow. I couldn't stop watching them, the way they swelled and cracked their skin, thrusting out their sharp thing that turned into a root. They wanted to go down into the earth and the other thing that came out went up. When I put them in the earth, they pushed up with a long neck, pulling the two seed halves with them and bursting them open with their leaves. The strength of the shoot pushing away the soil and breaking out and pushing up the seed halves – I had never seen anything like that. I didn't have words for it, but at that sight I felt that life is strong. Strong. Strong. The way those beans came out of the earth and grew so quickly with new leaves every day made me feel glad, as though they had to do with me. They developed bright red flowers and started to make long beans. Strong. By the time the school year ended they were growing in the centre of a world of forests and oceans, deer and a tree planted by living water; birds nest in its branches and beasts find shelter in its shade. It is like a just man who bears fruit for many seasons.

Light/Dark

There was always something mysterious about them and the way we lived with them. Something between us meant we couldn't really see them when we looked at them, they were hidden like a leg inside a stocking or the living face behind the faces children put on at Halloween. I find it hard to say what it was like.

Once when I was a child we had duck for Sunday dinner. I saw it before it was cooked, in a bowl on the step outside the kitchen door. Raw, yellow. Everything grown-ups and servants did had reasons. I didn't ask anyone why it was out there. Perhaps Beauty still had to singe the pin feathers off the way she did with chickens, or perhaps she had to clean out the intestines and lungs. She had to be very careful doing this because if the gall bladder breaks, it taints the whole bird with bitterness.

I was on my way to the backyard where there were things to do with stones and bits of stick. I loved the white quartz stones that half let light through like an egg and, in school, I read a story about painters who used colours pressed from flower petals. I went to the front yard and picked red and yellow cannas to make a sun on the whitewashed wall. Perhaps Beauty saw my sun, or Isaac the garden boy, or Beauty's husband Philemon who visited her on weekends.

I don't know why I turned round to look at the duck lying there in its white enamel dish. Ants were coming out of the hole where the neck had been chopped off. The whole cavity was creepy with them coming in and out in a ribbon like a glittering spill of black blood, beads of jet picked out on dressy dresses and splashed over the costumes of nightclub singers.

The ants poured into the basin like a pool. I ran inside to tell Beauty or my mother but they were talking to each other about the cake and didn't want me to make a fuss. I went outside again and looked. I was a city child and had never seen a corpse before.

There were guests at dinner and everything looked elegant – the herring on little glass plates, the radishes cut into flowers and the butter rolled into dewy balls. When Isaac brought the duck to the table it was golden brown, lacquered and shining like Russian tea in a glass with a silver holder. All round it on the platter were golden roast potatoes and ponds of brilliant green peas. I opened my mouth, but my mother stopped me before I could say anything.

So it became hidden, in that place we hide things we were taught as children not to talk about.

In high school I hated the big Rembrandt reproduction in a fancy frame outside the principal's office. Every morning we lined up to go to assembly there and waited for the other forms that filed in before us. It was always dark there where we had to wait and the prefect saw to it that we didn't talk while the forms filed in in the right order. I didn't know what I was learning there under the picture of Rembrandt's general wearing a gold helmet. Something in his surly, decaying face looked like a policeman. I connected it with all the things I hated, respect for authority, school spirit, neatness and ladylike manners. I didn't have words for the connection so it remained half hidden in that hiding place.

I wore my black gym and filed into assembly in my proper place and listened when the principal read from the Bible and school announcements and I sang a hymn and the Lord's Prayer before we all filed out in our black lines. My gym was often defiantly dirty but when the prefects stopped me and said I disgraced the school I felt ashamed.

The imagination's river running underground sometimes flows as if away from logic. I hated the Rembrandt because of the duck. I felt that yellow-brown portraits and oil landscapes stood for the manners of people who used catchwords like duty and honour. I couldn't look at a Claude or Lorraine or Constable and see what anyone found lovely there. But at university I found out about Rembrandt. A teacher showed us his picture of a carcass hanging from the butcher's hook.

My mother-in-law blamed me for taking her son away to a foreign country. She said, 'I'd never vote for the Nationalists, but no government's perfect.' She said, 'You have to close your eyes to some things.'

She had three sons. The youngest was born eight years after Eric. His father enlisted as soon as the war started and was away for six years. In the family photographs there is a studio portrait of him in uniform, the only picture of him alone. In all the others he is with his boys or part of a family picnic or wedding and in his own wedding pictures he is with Eric's mother in her white dress and veil.

In ten years I've heard her mention him once. She was asking Eric whether he remembered a little trick with a handkerchief that amuses children. Her voice sounded round and fresh.

I asked Eric whether his parents were happy together. He said, 'I don't know.' In his family no one talked about things like that. He thinks there was another woman those years away during the war.

It's not as though I saw things no one else saw. There were always weedy lots where you could see a piccanin or two with a soccer ball belly and a bud of green snot in one nostril playing with nothing to play with and no grown-up in sight. Everyone had servants coming and going in the backyard, making too much noise, everyone said, and getting arrested for something to do with a pass or smoking dagga. All our houses had iron netting over the windows or cast iron burglar-proofing made like curled decorations. There was always someone who wanted to come in and steal and murder. There were other things they would do but those were so terrible no one talked about them at all.

There were always friends with me on a Saturday afternoon when we came out of the bioscope still dreaming about Gary Cooper and the deformed things were there outside waiting for us, a few pennies and silver coins spread out in the bowl of a felt hat, shining like ringworm. They called out, 'Missus,' though we were still children, 'Penny, Missus.'

Children our own age danced on street corners to their own clapping or piping on a penny whistle. We gave them money. Even in winter they didn't wear shoes. Newsboys wore men's jackets and fumbled for change in the pockets at their thighs.

Everyone saw these things and heard the clink of milk bottles in the dawning street where the delivery boys were riding tricycles. Everyone gave when the school collected pennies for charity, the clinic in Alexandra, milk for the school feeding scheme, clothes for refugee children in Europe.

When I was fifteen Beauty was sick. My mother went to her room with medicines and her husband came to visit her every night. He ate supper with the garden boy. One evening, I went into the kitchen forgetting that Beauty wouldn't be there and saw him sitting upright in a straight chair against the wall. He was just sitting there in a dark brown suit and dark brown shoes and a grey felt hat. I didn't know what to say.

Afterwards, when I brought medicines to Beauty, I saw his white shirt glare in the light of her bare electric bulb. It was like a lighted parking lot at night when it's empty except for snow piled high at the corners. I've seen that effect in deserted platforms of midnight railways stations. Like in Rembrandt: light dark.

What my mother-in-law did want us to see was Barberton daisies growing wild near Swaziland. 'There's nothing like them in the whole world.' Other people also told about the mountain slopes covered with daisies, red, pink, yellow, orange. In New York I had seen them in flower shops.

At a party I met a gardener who said South Africa must be a beautiful country, 'so many garden flowers come from there'.

When Eric and I set off, that year's spring drought was worse than usual and newspaper photographs were showing pictures of desiccated cattle lying on cracked ground. Vultures must have feasted, but family newspapers draw the line at showing some things.

At the same time they showed pictures of a dune of oranges on a huge citrus plantation in the Transvaal. There was a glut and prices were too low to make it worthwhile to send any to market. After that there were letters saying the government should buy the oranges and give them to African children. People reading the English press in South Africa knew that black children were starving.

We didn't see that the drought was worse than usual until the car broke down in the middle of nowhere. We hitch-hiked to the nearest place with a name and garage and had the car towed. They said, three days, four days, they couldn't do anything without a new part.

There was one hotel, a car salesroom, a café with two pinball machines, three churches, a retailer's with men's wool socks in one window and a pyramid of toothpaste boxes in the other. On the counter inside a display of Kodak film featured a woman with windblown hair like Botticelli's Venus.

Eric remembered a school friend on a mission as near to Stoffberg as to any other place and Julian said he'd come to fetch us. We waited in the café and drank Cokes and watched high school boys killing time with the pinball machines.

On the way to the mission we passed through country as dry as the Karoo, but in the Karoo plants are adapted and after rain the desert becomes a fairyland. Here the loose soil would just pour away when it rained. It was flying about now in the wind, the sky was dirty with it and there were no clouds. At a cleft wide enough to be a river in summer Julian slowed at a flock of dirty tents where people had been moved out of their homeland. They wouldn't go peacefully and it had taken police. In this designated black area we couldn't see any water but there were some women down near rocks at the bottom with tin cans. We couldn't see much because as we were crossing the bridge children picked up stones and threw them at the car.

At the mission we passed a hospital and a school and a church and a monastery. We stayed the night and when we asked to see the hospital Julian put us off. But he did tell us the story. It must have been preying on his mind. There'd been an outbreak of measles and when children are starving and get measles they die or go blind or deaf and sometimes mad. The doctors were trying to prevent the epidemic from spreading and wouldn't let children leave the hospital and their mothers were holding vigil outside the hospital, sitting on the ground all day, all night, asking to have their children back. But the doctors said, no, they must keep the children or everyone would get measles. I find it hard to say what it was like, so many of them, wearing blankets, on the dead lawn, looking at us when we walked past into the hospital. Julian said, I shouldn't really talk about it.

My mother-in-law was disappointed we didn't see the Barberton daisies. She said all the flower gardens in Johannesburg were suffering from the drought and regulations against watering. My brother-in-law was not allowed to fill his new swimming pool and it was beginning to crack. 'But,' she said, 'you can't worry about everything.'

When we visited her four years later, we arranged to take her out to dinner for her birthday and, on the way, we bought flowers.

During the dinner, she started to tell us a story about her neighbour but in the middle she couldn't remember and stopped.

She was planning to leave the flat she'd moved to when her sons left South Africa. She didn't tell us what the doctor had said.

When we left her, we didn't talk about her and we didn't talk about what had happened before we saw her.

We had stopped at a street corner stacked with tiers of bloom in jam tins – mimosa, sweet peas, stocks – so cheap that for a few dollars we bought enough to carry like a child cradled in arms. Eric took out his camera to take a picture.

When the flower-seller saw the camera, she asked, 'Where do you come from, master?' She was wearing a chiffon veil and sequin dots of light winked on the long sleeves of her blouse.

'The United States.'

'America?' Like someone who didn't know anyone who had actually been there.

'New York.'

'Please baas, master, take me with you. Just me and my little boy, baas, my baby. I'll be your servant for seven years master you needn't give me any pay just food and a room to sleep please master. Only in seven years it's time for me to make the pilgrimage to Mecca.'

Twice Her Size

Every morning around ten o'clock her father stopped at home for a cup of tea. He took a loaf from the wooden trays at the back of the van and gave it to her mother and her mother cut a thick slice from it and spread it with butter and jam and gave it to the driver to eat with the tea she poured into an enamel mug for him. The driver sat on the back steps and gossiped with Cynthia's nanny while she did the ironing, or sat outside on the running board of the van and drank his tea and waited for Cynthia's father who drank his tea indoors. When her father was finished he would come out and tell the driver to get ready and call Cynthia from her play near his path and give her a penny. Then the driver drove him away and brought him back at one o'clock when all the bread deliveries were finished and he would have lunch and go to sleep.

Cynthia always took her penny to Mrs Haak's around the corner.

'Penny peas, please.' Mrs Haak put the coin in her apron pocket. Sheets of newspaper hung on a string nailed to the shelf where the vegetables lay. She tore off a sheet and curled it into a cone and, grasping a handful of unruly peas, dropped them into the cup, twisted the paper shut and gave Cynthia her purchase.

Hardly any other memories survived from that time. An evening when she seemed to be with her father on his delivery route (though as an adult she couldn't understand why he would have been delivering bread by night) and she sat alone in the dark cab as he went up the path to a door that opened. Light streamed out behind his figure. The woman at the door was wearing a red dressing gown and Cynthia could see her white petticoat underneath it make a triangle.

Once she was with her mother in a greengrocer's shop where a man offered her a banana but she didn't want to take it. Perhaps her mother had been flirting with the man. She sang a ditty, 'Oh, I like bananas because they have no bones.'

Most of her memories came later when they'd moved to the other side of the hill. She was seven and her brother Aaron was fourteen, a hero's height away from her in age. In everything. He spoke Russian. He had been born in the old country and their mother told the story of the fight he had there one day when he broke a tooth and his glasses, but the teeth were still milk teeth and the damage wasn't permanent.

He was tough now. When he got into fights he took his glasses off. She saw him turn with an unaccustomed face to meet a vague antagonist.

He said he'd always be twice as old as Cynthia.

He exhausted temporary passions. For a while he trapped pigeons and trained them to eat from his hand and fly back at his call. They circled the rooftops for half an hour every day at sunset. He built nests for them and invested in a pair of white fantails. He read about incubation. The next year he started a vegetable garden in the barren backyard and boasted of the quick radishes. He warned Cynthia that if she touched the peas he'd beat her. As often as not he shared the day's picking with her. They sat on the back stoep splitting the pods. In the winter he took up photography. He converted the room in the backyard next to the maid's room (he had used it for the pigeons before) into a darkroom.

He knew more than she could dream of, he could ask and answer riddles like a book and he had climbed Observatory Hill all alone a thousand times.

He had a girlfriend and a job. His distance from Cynthia widened. He worked as a travelling salesman for a company that specialised in fabrics and work-clothes. He drove into the country from store to country store. During the week he slept in the hotels of towns one street deep. His anecdotes grew smooth with use. On Friday afternoons he came back, he stopped at the house to pick her up and she came with him as he took his driver home to the native township and stopped at the office to drop off invoices and samples. He told her about the country he had visited, the citrus farms near Rustenburg where the orange blossoms smelled for miles and the mountains of the north where farms still seemed like outposts in wild territory. Each week he collected incidents for the odyssey at its end.

Once or twice he came back with a half-bushel sack of peas, that morning's harvest. They settled in a corner of the back stoep with a newspaper between them for the stripped shells. They gutted each pod with one draw of the thumb. Hand to mouth, it was a good way to live.

Rebecca came home and scolded them: they'd make themselves sick with so many peas; they wouldn't eat dinner. 'Ah, Ma,' Aaron teased her out of it and in lawless mood drove Cynthia into town. She cracked pods for him all the way. He tossed the husks out of the window. She did as he did and they left a trail, thicker where they stopped at red lights. She adored him.

He remembered the incident longer than she did. It came in that time of his life when he felt daring and uncompromised. He'd been in jail twice. Once, he was caught in a scuffle with ruffians and police who'd come to break up a protest meeting. Someone thwacked his head with a blunt instrument. He awoke in a hospital ward with mild concussion. He was under arrest. His name was listed on the front page of the morning newspaper. Isaac hustled it away and hid the paper from Rebecca until he heard, later that morning, that Aaron was remanded with a warning.

The second time Aaron was held on suspicion. He'd gone out to photograph the mine strike. He was lucky. Policemen fired on unarmed strikers. *New Age* bought his pictures and published them on the front page, seconded by incendiary headlines. But the police had nothing to charge him with and released him with vague threats. Later, as new laws were passed, they banned the paper and its successors under new names until, tired of banning the paper, they banned the editors and journalists instead. Aaron wasn't important enough for banning, but they didn't forget his name.

It was the time in Aaron's life when he hadn't yet learned that he would not be an artist. He still tried, changing the art every few months. A bout of theatre gave way to sculpture, then painting, composing, conducting, poetry, singing. His search was stern but when the muses undressed and it came to going to bed with them, he couldn't do it. He felt embarrassed and ashamed. Nothing he did was beautiful.

Instead it was Cynthia who went to the arts. She won a scholarship to the university. He despised her callow academic successes. She still felt cowed by his greater brilliance and reading. When she visited him at the apartment he had taken away from home, she laughed at his jokes and listened to his stories. She envied his mysterious adult life. On graduation she was awarded another scholarship. Isaac and Rebecca talked about it. If their daughter went to England they might never see her again. But they could not stand in her way. On the last day they took home a poppyseed bread, her favourite of those they baked in their small confectionery. Rebecca packed it with a roast chicken and some hard boiled eggs so that Cynthia would have something to eat on the plane.

In London she met artists and poets, men of name. She established a small, they didn't know how small, reputation for herself as a painter. Her graphics were surrealistic and sad. They sold fairly well, though at a modest price.

Aaron couldn't leave their home in South Africa. They wouldn't give him a passport, though they offered him the right to leave and never come back. He wouldn't take it. Not even later when it seemed the only thing and Isaac and Rebecca begged him (with tears in their eyes, they said and it was true) because South Africa wasn't a safe country any more. By that time Aaron had moved to Cape Town. He married. He climbed the mountain. He took his children to the beach. On Saturday afternoons he drove to the harbour and bought sackfuls of crayfish pieces. In the evening friends came over and they had a party, cracking the crayfish bits open like nuts, drinking Cape wine. He knew everyone in town. His anecdotes had grown richer and more ironic with the years. His friends were also painters, poets, men of name and the old political crowd from his *New Age* days. Additions had been made to that crowd during a decade of increasing ideology and passion – that was why South Africa was no longer a safe country for Aaron. Isaac and Rebecca knew that if he went on like this he'd be arrested one day.

But Aaron would not repudiate his friends. He took no direct part in politics. Instead he settled on the theatre. Other men's words did not humiliate him. The presence he had developed as a salesman carried well on stage. He took the lead in small productions of Brecht and Frisch.

Sometimes in discussions with his artist friends and intellectuals teaching at the university he felt that he had the advantage over them. He was in contact with real life.

His children thrived. His parents moved to Cape Town to be near him. He felt that he sheltered the family under his branches. Interesting visitors to Cape Town were brought to meet him at the immense casual parties that had grown out of those evenings of cracking crayfish bits and drinking wine. The fare was cheese and wine now, but the company drew the company and his parties acquired something of a reputation in their world. He bought a house, an old Cape Dutch dwelling whose simplicity was offset by noble proportions and fine gables. He planted vines and cultivated the fig tree in the garden. He felt that his life was good and would be better when he had the time to devote himself more to photography, resumed again with less ambition. He didn't call himself a travelling salesman now. He was a branch manager.

Cynthia moved from London to Boston, but she visited South Africa before taking herself off to even greater distance. She had grown into a stranger and an adult. They asked about her life, but she seemed reluctant, or perhaps they couldn't understand how it was there, overseas.

She visited her old friends too and Aaron threw a party for her friends and his friends, but they fell into factions, his and hers, often colleagues who knew each other professionally and wanted no more. She left before they could know her again and though Rebecca wept at the airport, she might not live to see her daughter again, there was something subdued in her tears, as though the loss she feared had come already.

This time Cynthia stayed away seven years. She wrote, but her letters didn't help them to comprehend her life of galleries and university appointments. They couldn't tell whether she was a failure or success, unhappy or at ease. One thing was clear. She wasn't married. From time to time Isaac pressed the urgency of marrying now, while she was still young, though by now she was nearly thirty; later it would be too late. Whatever her thoughts on the matter, she didn't share them with him.

Brother and sister did not write to each other. At New Years they sent greetings.

In the summer of her thirtieth year, winter in South Africa, Isaac's letters complained of a heavy cough he couldn't shake off. In late August she received a letter about how doctors at the clinic had taken tests and put him on to cobalt treatment. She called her internist to confirm her diagnosis of what Isaac's treatment must mean. She wrote to Aaron asking for more information. As she let herself in, coming from the mailbox, she heard the phone. Aaron's language was dry and medical and assumed that she also understood its jargon of metastases and lesions. Cynthia was speechless. Unlike Aaron, she lacked the habit of other people's words. She voiced no sympathy and asked only how long Isaac might live.

No one could predict with certainty, but perhaps three

weeks. 'You've got to come quickly. But not too soon. You've got to warn him first. Find some excuse for coming.'

'He doesn't know then?'

'No. Neither does Mom.'

'Wouldn't it be better?'

'Are you coming?'

After a cup of coffee, she rebelled against her brother's orders. The new semester was three weeks off. She called her chairman, explained that she would miss the first departmental meetings, but would be back in time to teach. She called a travel agent to ask what papers she would need. She called her internist to arrange for inoculations and a health certificate. She visited her bank to apply for a loan for the airfare. She went to be inoculated. She looked for her tax receipts and went to the IRS office to get a sailing permit. At the travel agent's office she insisted on the quickest route and connections. Offices closed for the weekend. She arranged for the cat to be fed, the newspapers discontinued, the mail held, the lights to be switched on and off, the gallery to be told when to expect her back. She called David. He offered to take her to the airport. The sweaters and warm dresses she packed felt intolerable in the August heat. They smelt of mothballs. She cabled Aaron to expect her.

Take-off was delayed. She sent David off, 'You can't wait all night.'

'I will go. I'm working on plans for the new high school. Cable me when you're coming back. I'll meet you.'

'Best of luck with the plans.'

'You'll cable?'

'I'll cable.'

'It'll be all right, Cynthia.' He closed her tight. He kissed her. He left.

Someone brought sandwiches to the departure lounge. She lent her winter coat to be a blanket for a child trying to sleep in an armchair. She sketched the postures of exhaustion in a notebook. Shortly after midnight they boarded.

Air travel frightened her. Death by water, death by fire. She watched the movie. When it ended she tried to read, but the light over her head flickered. She switched it off. Dawn was coming. By the time they landed in England it was deep day. She checked in her luggage for the second lap and they offered her a room at the airport motel. She knew that she would not sleep; she would be left staring at the plastic furniture. She refused. In London she looked at shop windows, bought some books, ate lunch in an Italian restaurant. She took the bus back to Heathrow.

In haste to book the quickest connection she had not noticed which airline offered it. Standing in line for a boarding card, she heard the Afrikaans voices, saw the faces that told her she was almost home; it would take only a few hours; already she was locked into the system of tacit support that went with being white. It didn't matter; she curbed her chafing.

She could not eat. There was no movie on the flight. She turned aside her neighbour's attempts at conversation and read a book. The title had caught her eye. *One Hundred Years of Solitude*. She knew how that would feel. One other passenger, sleepless like herself, stood all night and talked with the crew. At intervals she looked out. They flew over sea and desert, then jungle. In the morning the captain told them they were over Windhoek, South West Africa. They came in over the dry winter-remembered veld.

At the Johannesburg airport she called Aaron to give him the time of her arrival in Cape Town. 'Hello? What? Cynthia? Why the hell did you come! I told you not to come yet. I can't meet you at the airport. I'm busy. Go straight to my house. I'll tell Jenny you're coming.'

'You look terrible, Cynthia. Was it a bad flight? Have some tea. What about something to eat?'

'I couldn't sleep on the plane. I'd better do that first.'

'I'll ask Elsie to make the bed in Debby's room. Have some tea first though, won't you? You look terrible.'

Over tea, disarmed by hospitality, she said, 'Aaron should

learn some manners. He shouted at me for coming.'

'He's upset that you didn't warn your parents.'

'I've got a story for them if we're going to go on with this vile pretence.'

'I don't want to get involved. Talk to Aaron when he comes home tonight.'

Her confused sleep in Debby's room thinned in patches. She heard South African sounds – a hawker crying fruit in the sunny streets, someone hammering in the distance, the children coming home from school, servants in the kitchen. Debby woke her up in time for supper.

'How's school?'

'I'm in first year varsity.'

'Sorry, I did know that. They call varsity school in America. How do you like it?'

'It's okay.'

She'd expected Debby to be enthusiastic. She'd always been the brighter child and the most praised. Her skin had come out in acne. Blackheads grimed her nose. No wonder varsity was only okay. Debby had had no breasts when she left.

Aaron was waiting for her in the living room. 'Did you sleep well?'

'The kids've been pretty noisy,' Jenny apologised.

'It was good. I feel much better.'

'You look much better.'

'Have a drink,' Aaron offered. 'What do you take now? Sherry? Or have you gone American? I've got whiskey too.'

'Whiskey, thanks.' She might as well accept distance and change.

She didn't want him to slip into that tone he'd used on the phone of telling his younger sister what to do, outraged that she wouldn't listen.

It was raining outside. The house was cold. Cynthia tried to close the window near her chair, but the catch jammed. 'It doesn't move; it's rusty,' Jenny told her. 'Your brother's a fresh air maniac.'

'Don't you feel cold?'

'I go round shivering all winter.'

'Stop that chattering,' Aaron mocked, quick with witticisms as she remembered.

'I'll get adjusted in a few days. It was ninety-two degrees in Boston two days ago.'

'Shall we make a fire for you, Aunt Cynthia?' Joshua offered.

'I'd like that very much.'

After supper, when the children had gone to their own rooms to study, she sat down at the phone. Rebecca's voice hadn't changed. Isaac's was a hoarse whisper. She told them her story about coming to collect legal papers, something to do with visas. She didn't know whether they believed it.

'Brandy with your coffee?' Aaron did not ask after Isaac's state.

When she finished the coffee Cynthia said, 'Please excuse me. I'd like to go to sleep again.'

'Let me give you some towels.' Jenny came with her. 'Aaron's sorry about the way he shouted at you this morning.'

'He'll have to tell me himself. I'm fed up with him.'

The bathroom was icy. Another window that would not close. Cynthia fled to bed.

The waking hours submerged in sleep, like a dream between afternoon and night. Towards two in the morning she woke, hungry. In Boston it was suppertime. She switched on the light. Debby stirred and turned away. Cynthia read until she fell asleep again with the lights on.

'I hope it didn't bother you.' Debby's dressing in the morning had awakened her.

'That's all right. I hardly noticed, Aunt Cynthia.' But Jenny arranged for her bed to be moved to the small study where Aaron stored business papers, playscripts and old photographs. Cynthia was relieved to have privacy.

The maid opened the door to her parents' apartment. She

waited for Isaac to be brought back from the clinic. When the attendant released him he held one hand to the wall; didn't want anyone to support him down the short passage to his bedroom, but from door to bed he had to lean on them and take help to lie down and be covered.

'Excuse me,' he spent himself to make the whisper speech, 'I want to sleep. Can you leave the radio on?'

She left him alone until Rebecca came home from the bakery. 'You see your father. You see the way his clothes hang on him. I can't stand it. Stay for supper. Maybe he'll eat because you're here. Why won't he eat?'

Cynthia stayed.

Subsequent afternoons she left before supper. She couldn't afford taxis across the town every day; buses didn't run at night. Isaac's treatment ended. He didn't have to go to the clinic every day. She came earlier. He was too weak to concentrate on chess. They played rummy.

Aaron regretted the quarrel with Cynthia. She had caught him on the wrong foot. It was the busy season. Everything was in a rush. He had to go into the country on business. They should be reconciled.

He saw that the spring flowers were coming out. Tomorrow, if the weather held, it would be good to take Isaac out for a drive. The new life would give him hope.

When he came home, he found Cynthia and Jenny in the living room. Another fire filled the hearth. 'I've got something for you,' he told Cynthia. 'Wait, I'll get it from the car.'

He held the large bag behind his back. 'Guess.'

'I can't guess, Aaron. Tell me what it is.'

'No, you must guess.' They were back to fourteen and seven.

'I've never been good at this.'

'Come on, three guesses.' He had twice her power.

'Is it something to eat?'

'No questions.'

'Pottery?' He shook his head. 'A carving? Crayfish?'

'Close.' He showed her the package.

'You're brilliant, Aaron. Fantastic. How did you think of it?'

'Debby, get us some newspaper.' The old command was back.

They didn't wait; they were stripping peas and discarding pods into ashtrays before Debby could move. 'Hey wait, I want some too!' But they ignored her.

Jenny's plaint filled the space for Rebecca's. 'Your brother's crazy. We've got roast beef for dinner.' They smiled and ate as though they didn't hear her. 'You're both crazy,' Jenny resigned.

They sat on the floor with the newspaper between them. She wouldn't ask for more apology.

At dinner he opened a bottle of wine and praised its qualities to her. He smiled that she refused seconds.

The children had dates for the evening. They left early. Cynthia, Aaron and Jenny went back to the living room, the fire and brandy.

When Jenny took the coffee cups to the kitchen, he asked, 'How was Dad today?'

'About the same as yesterday. Pretty bad.'

'He looks shocking.' Jenny had come back.

Cynthia added a coal to the fire. 'I've been wondering how Mom's going to manage. Is she going to be able to run the bakery herself?'

'She's doing it now. I can never understand their financial arrangements.'

'Have they got any savings?'

'No. The bank gave them an overdraft.'

'Will Mom be able to pay it back?'

'I don't know. I've never understood why the bank gave it to them in the first place. I wouldn't trust their credit.'

'What about the medical expenses?'

'I've been paying them. Can you help?'

'I had to borrow money to come here. How much does it come to?'

'I don't know exact figures.'

'Have they got anything except the bakery? Didn't they buy some land once?'

'You're the most callous person I've ever met. You can't wait for Dad to die, can you?'

'I don't understand. I can't make him live or die. I'm here because we know he's going to die. I want to know what's going to happen to Mom.'

'Can't you wait until it's a real question?'

'Isn't it a real question now?'

'Can't you wait?'

'I'm leaving in ten days.'

'Ten days! Why the hell did you bother to come if that's all the time you can spare for your father when he's dying?'

'Don't be ridiculous, Aaron. I can't stop everything else in my life. I work for a living. I've got to start teaching in two weeks.'

'You can't do it. You can't do this to him. You must be made of stone.'

'You can't leave in ten days,' Jenny said, supporting Aaron.
'I must.'

'How can you be so cruel?'

'What do you want me to stay for? I can't stop him dying.'

'Shut up,' he shouted.

She set down the glass of brandy and stood. 'I'll go to bed.'

Cynthia was dressed in her winter nightgown when he knocked on the door. 'I'm sorry.' His thick embrace felt like darkness overwhelming her. 'I don't want him to die. I don't want him to die.'

'I don't want him to die either,' she mouthed at his woollen sleeve. 'Soon we'll be the only two left. The only ones left.' What about his wife and children? He's afraid for himself, she knew.

They followed a newspaper map to the best vistas of flowers.

The day was spotlessly clear. Aaron occasionally stopped to take slides. They couldn't go far. After an hour Aaron drove home so that Isaac could see the children, but he was too tired to remain in the same room with them. 'Can I lie down?' he asked. He slept on Aaron's bed until Rebecca had finished her tea. She needed to talk with her daughter-in-law, her grandchildren, the servants, people who weren't sick.

'Come with me when I take Dad home.' Cynthia went and on the drive back it was as if Aaron had fallen into the mood of yesterday's benevolent power. 'Let's stop and buy oysters. They're bringing the catch in from Oyster Bay now. Finest in the world. You like oysters, don't you?'

'Love 'em.'

The purchase was not enough. 'We're near Herman Prins's place. Want to stop? He's doing some good stuff these days. I've just bought a landscape. The one in the dining room.'

'Yes, I noticed it.'

'You'll be interested in his work.'

She didn't contradict him. He'd been the first to educate her savage taste.

In Herman Prins's studio romantic objects on tables and bookcases set an artistic tone. Cynthia looked at his work and commented with phrases she had learned to avoid hurting.

'What's your own work like?' Prins asked.

'You know it's no use describing; one's got to see. Do you ever come to the States?'

'I'm more interested in what's happening in Europe.'

'Well, if you change your mind, Aaron can give you my Boston address.'

Driving through the evening streets in a golden light they passed a large oak. Its branches hung over the street. A massy, crusted growth burgeoned round the old scar where a limb had been cut from the trunk.

'That's cancer.' Aaron stopped the car where they could see it.

'Why don't we tell him?'

35

'We're not going to.'

'I want to tell him.'

'You're not going to. You're leaving in nine days.'

'He's my father too.'

'You're leaving. You've got no right to tell him.'

She conceded by default. Isaac had enough information to be able to know, if he wanted to.

The cobalt treatment had produced a remission. He attributed it to his happiness at seeing her. 'It makes me feel better to see you,' he coughed. She held his hand. Rebecca wept.

'Don't cry, Mom. Let me be with Dad.' Rebecca left. He held the hand she held him by. He wept.

He lived out the spring flowers and the summer. Aaron took him for more drives among the mountains and sea vistas. It seemed that he would recover, Rebecca cheered up. At the end of summer the cough grew worse. A few times in the lines he added to Rebecca's letters he spelled Cynthia's name wrong. Once he called her Dora, a name they'd thought of instead of Cynthia. 'It's the heavy medication,' her internist told her, 'or it might mean metastases to the brain.'

Rebecca told Aaron he was too heavy for her to lift when he needed to go to the toilet. She thought that one night while she was supporting him he would die. He was almost dead weight now. He could crush her or drag her into a dangerous fall when he crashed.

Hospitals refused him, but they found an old age home. There were no telephones at the beds. Cynthia had been calling from Boston. She could not speak to him any more. They read him her letters.

Aaron called her in Boston. 'You've got to come.'

'I can't. I'm broke. I'm in debt from the last trip.'

'He's dying.'

'That's why I came last year, Aaron.'

'You'll never see him alive again.'

'I know that.'

'He doesn't know where you are. He wants to see you.'

'I can't come.'

It was as if she couldn't breathe.

She phoned Rebecca. 'I can't come, Mom. You understand, don't you?'

'I understand. You must live your own life. There's nothing you can do. No one can do anything. I went to the doctor. I said, doctor, these days you can perform miracles. Give him a transplant. I don't need two lungs. He said it's impossible; even if we could do it, it'd be too late.'

'I'm sorry, Mom.'

'I know you're sorry. What can you do?'

'Will you tell Dad that the reason I came last year was to see him.'

'I told him.'

'Tell him again, Mom.'

Aaron felt his father's death falling on him alone. He called her.

'I can't come.'

'He can't understand why you aren't here.'

'I can't come.'

In extremis, he resorted to another's words again. 'He thinks you're dead. His daughter would come if she's alive.'

She heard it as a malediction. 'I can't come.'

She phoned her mother again.

'I told him, Cynthia, but he doesn't understand. He doesn't remember things. He doesn't even recognise me when I come to see him. I go every day. It's two buses when Aaron can't take me and when I get there he doesn't recognise me.' Her mother had no space for anyone else's pain. 'Yesterday he smiled at the nurse, but he didn't know me.'

'It's his brain, Mom. He can't remember.'

'So why should he remember you? You're right not to come.' Her voice sounded spiteful. 'Maybe he wouldn't know you either.'

In the spring of her thirty-second year, driving to work, she was stuck behind a truck. They stopped at a light. The grassy verge was sprigged with dandelions. She could see through the rear window into the truck. It was carrying loaves of bread. During the first confusion after Isaac's death, feeling herself cured (he thinks you're dead), she had forgotten the daily gift when he had given her pennies that she'd taken to Mrs Haak's shop to buy peas. Aaron had had no share. He must have been at school when Isaac came home for tea. He didn't know everything. Although she'd heard him using their father's words to curse her, she was still alive. He couldn't be twice her size any more. She was alive. The light changed. She moved into first gear. The truck turned. She went straight.

The Sisters' House

The wedding brunch would recapitulate good times in the house, summer holidays with the Johannesburg cousins, lunches of mussels pulled off the rocks and fish with bright eyes that Pauline's father had caught. There would be pleasant preparing in the kitchen again like the hours with her mother and aunts discussing how to cook and serve. They would buy yellow and red tomatoes, heaps of shining peppers and lacy herbs at the Hemel en Aarde farmstall. Everyone would exclaim again – look at this, smell this, so fresh.

Again they would praise the earth and its fruits, each thing perfectly itself. Praise used to fill their hours with resonance to other hours in different times and places, France, Italy, Russia.

The sisters had bought the house at Restless River to keep the family together. They used to send the children to sun and gossip on the beaches and the cousins rubbed lotion on to each others' limbs and backs and collected shells to put on the table in the living room. Pauline, the oldest cousin, proposed excursions to the marsh and the little Greek chapel at the beach and cajoled a grown-up to drive them to the market where they could buy fresh pear juice. At night the grown-ups lingered in the long room telling stories, while the cousins sat on each other's beds, talking about teachers and sex. They breathed each other like puppies from the same litter.

Everyone except Pauline's sister who slept in a room of her own. She still wet her bed and smelled.

They envied their parents' luck to have lived in interesting times and wanted to do something – write books, paint pictures, make films. Pauline's father, Leon, had once been an activist and knew leaders now in exile.

Years later, the cousins evoked those summers, 'Remember

Leon's story about the farmer in the Long Kloof.' 'And the day he took us snoek fishing.'

When the family wandered round the market, they knew themselves a tribe apart, distinct from the politicians and millionaires with houses in the harbour town. They belonged among artists and writers and people with taste. Their parents' friends flowed easily in and out of the sisters' house, welcomed with local wine and olives from trees Leon had planted. The cousins would walk down to the public picnic table overlooking the bay and the mountains. They would all wait on the patio while Leon broiled his fish. There were always stories.

They seemed to be living in one of the books about Provence that Pauline's mother read and sighed over – Leon had been refused a passport years ago – or a Russian novel where the dacha is filled with passion and intelligence. Everyone seemed to share the idea. The life they were leading was unconventional, rich in friendships, steeped in culture.

On the road home to Cape Town, they passed the familiar hardware store whose sign promised, 'Everything and still more.'

It would be like that again.

Bram won her parents' approval the first time Pauline brought him home to dinner. In the spacious dining room, he touched her mother's yellowwood table with his fingertips, 'What a beautiful piece. You can't get a table like this today, Janet.'

'How old do you think it is?' her mother deferred to him.

'They haven't cut big trees like this since the 1930s and they stopped making lathes with this curve around 1910. I'd say it's even older. 1860s?'

He compared her mother's ossobuco to a stufato he had eaten in Milan. 'I go there every year to keep up with design trends.'

Janet sighed.

He added, 'I keep in touch with the classics. My high school teacher used to say the Romans would recognise us as brothers.'

He won Leon by talking knowledgeably about wine and local lore, 'That area round Restless River where you've got a holiday house has got quite an artists' community.'

Clearing up, Pauline asked, 'What do you think, Mommy?'

'He's got taste.' Janet opened the gold foil of a slab of chocolate and held the dark end to her daughter. 'He's older than I expected. Is he getting divorced because of you, Pauline?'

'There's no life left in the marriage.'

'That's what they always say.' Janet put wine glasses in the sink and filled it with hot water. 'Has he got children?'

'Two girls and two boys.'

'Are you breaking up a family, Pauline?' She squirted detergent into the sink and handed Pauline a cloth.

Where was the tolerance she showed at Restless River? 'He's leaving his wife because there's nothing left between them.' The conversation felt unlucky, like laying eyes on a carrion bird.

'That's nonsense,' handing a rinsed glass to Pauline. 'He thinks you'll make him young again. That won't work.'

Janet wiped her hands on a dishcloth, broke another piece of chocolate off the slab and offered Pauline the last row. 'You can have anyone, darling. Why do you want a man old enough to be your father?'

One of the cousins in California called, 'I wish I could come. You always dreamed up fun things to do, but we start shooting next week.'

Her aunt in Brooklyn called, 'I'm just reading about Provence. They make a wonderful confection for weddings. Almonds. I'll send you some.'

Touched, Pauline fell into wistfulness like her mother's, 'I wish you were here with Mommy.'

Her aunt sighed the way her mother sighed. 'Remember the Lebanese grocer – just where you took the F-train? He'll have almonds.' When Pauline's first marriage was breaking up

41

in New York, the aunt had invited her to live with them while everyone worked for reconciliation.

The other aunt, now in Australia, called, 'We can't come for the wedding, but we'll be in Cape Town in December.'

The family had scattered through three continents. They used to be so close.

Ruth could not come. The month after Pauline posted the invitations, she was committed and had to drop out of nursing school.

Pauline's first fear had been that Bram would reject her because of the blot, but he said, 'Poor child. Mental pain's the worst.'

Pauline went to visit Ruth in the hospital. She seemed the same as usual, looking at Pauline from dark blue eyes that brimmed with compassion. After a while, Pauline noticed that she was asking the same questions again and again and stopped talking about the wedding. She laid her hand on Ruth's and Ruth looked up at her, but soon drifted off.

'They're trying a new drug,' Pauline told Bram. 'They think it's helping.'

Bram did not meet her eyes but looked out over the moonlit sea, 'What happened to her, Pauline?'

'I don't know.'

David called from Australia. After graduation, all his deferments used up, he had said, 'I'm not going to fight for apartheid.'

Leon had warned, 'You'll never be able to come back.' For years now, their conversations had turned into shouting matches.

'Don't worry, I can stand on my own two feet. I won't have to come back.'

Pauline was about to retort, but her mother intervened, 'Help me make coffee.' She closed the door behind father and son. She used to try to make peace between them but neither seemed to hear her. Now, she retreated and the house filled with shouts spilling out to the servants' rooms and beyond.

'He's leaving to get away from Daddy,' Pauline said.

Mother and daughter cleared the plates, put them in the sink and filled it with water. The maid would wash them next morning. They drank coffee at the kitchen table and finished a slab of chocolate.

Falling asleep, she recalled a weekend before she left for America. Busy with university projects, David did not come often to Restless River, but that Saturday he came and drove to the fish harbour with a neighbour. When he showed Janet the kabeljou, she said, 'Look at the gills. They must've caught it this morning.'

'That's what they told us.'

'We'll have it with purple peppers.'

He was reading in the long living room at the lamp table, where they used to put shells, when Pauline joined him. He said, 'We drove miles out of the way to avoid Fairview.'

'Well, it smells awful.'

'You're missing the point, Pauline. We don't want to admit it's there. It's an accusation against our way of life.' He stood and paced between her and the wall of windows, 'That's how good Germans never saw concentration camps.'

'We haven't got concentration camps.'

He stopped in front of her and looked down, 'Don't be blind, Pauline. What do you think it's like to live in those shacks? Let me take you to Fairview tomorrow.'

'Don't be ridiculous.'

Perhaps he really did want to get away from apartheid.

In New York everyone had asked about her accent and then about apartheid.

She had hated New York, assaulted by the noise, people talking to themselves, urine in the lobby. No longer interested, her husband said, 'Don't whine. If you don't like it here, go back to Cape Town.'

She did. While she wept, Leon stroked her hair. 'There I

43

was, hustling that lousy waitressing job to support him and he was screwing women in his class.' Janet shared chocolate with her. She found it sweet to rage and be soothed, the loved child again.

Next morning Leon took her up Table Mountain at an hour New Yorkers thought not fit for waking. Birds were singing and the sun was rising.

Their first weekend at Restless River, the house rearranged itself around her like a comforting blanket. Neighbours saw the car and their dog and came by, Leon offered wine and soon everyone was sitting in the long room. Leon launched into one of his stories and they all laughed and asked for more. In the kitchen with Janet everything was the way it used to be.

'I haven't seen these before,' Pauline picked up a bowl with a blue spiral.

'There's a new potter at the market. We'll go tomorrow.'

They shopped and nibbled at their favourite stalls and stopped for coffee at a new place. They watched conservative politicians and Afrikaner millionaires and tourists come to look at whales. 'In New York people don't think there's anything here except apartheid, but people sleep in doorways there, even when it's snowing.'

At the silversmith's they caught up with gossip and came home carrying bags and parcels. Leon was out fishing and Janet wanted to read so Pauline took the dog walking on the beach.

At dinner conversation turned to the concert season in Cape Town. It was not exciting like New York, but it was comforting. She smiled and teased every man at the table. She was a woman again.

When their guests asked about New York, she burnished an anecdote about her waitress job, 'My first order was BLT on Jewish, one regular and OJ. All I could understand was "on" and "one".' Everyone laughed and she felt who she used to be.

The sculptor asked, 'Is California really like the Cape?'

Others answered, 'Not a patch on what we've got here.' 'They say it's as beautiful as the Riviera.' 'The Mediterranean's full of turds.'

A poet said, 'America's a savage country. No culture.' Smiling at her. Leaving, he looked at her, 'It's a good life here.'

It seemed an invitation, and she opened the kitchen door. He must have heard her, but did not look back.

One night in Brooklyn, without knowing why, she had found occasion, out of sight on the landing, to kiss her aunt's husband on the lips. He pulled back and, after that, would not look her in the face.

Next day new guests came to share the snoek Leon had caught. They sat on the patio, drinking wine. Janet closed her eyes and raised her face to the sky. 'I'm going to paint you like that,' a neighbour promised.

By Monday morning Pauline was ready to look for a job. In two weeks she was Bram's assistant.

David called from Australia. 'I'm getting married myself next month.'

'That's wonderful.' They talked about the Australian bride. 'Are we invited?'

'Of course.'

'And Mommy and Daddy ... No, David, you have to invite them.'

Afterwards, she told Bram. 'I never expected David to hold a grudge.'

Pauline and Bram went to Restless River, snorkelled, climbed or read in the long room with windows on three sides. If Janet and Leon were there, the women resumed their conversation of appreciation or nostalgia for a place where people with taste lived as life should be. The men caught fish or bought them with skilful banter and trained masculine eyes. Mother and daughter missed their distant family. Only one child left in the sisters' house.

Leon and Bram liked each other and talked to each other in Afrikaans. It became a kind of secret language between them. For Bram, Afrikaans was his mother tongue. For Leon, born in Lithuania, it had become a tongue closer than English. Yiddish was his first mother tongue, but no one he knew talked Yiddish. He talked Afrikaans with his customers in general stores among the orchards and wheat lands. He relished the look and smell of the land and the idiosyncrasies of the Afrikaners who lived on it. Driving to the house on Friday afternoons, he stopped at farms where he bargained for the best potatoes or cucumbers, strawberries, peaches – he knew every nuance of the harvest and who had the best of what. The produce he bought was a paean. Binding himself to Bram's world, he excluded the women, who spoke English. He wore a short beard like Bram's and sometimes addressed Bram as 'broer'.

Ruth was discharged, went back to nursing and met an Englishman who supported apartheid. Janet looked at his clothes and said, 'He's got no taste,' but Ruth married him and they left for England. Her letters showed more affection than Pauline had expected.

Pauline bore a son, Elias – Eli for short. Soon after, Leon stopped at a country auction and saw a Bible with Bram's family tree in the flyleaf, an Elias in the third generation. He bought the heavy volume and handed it to Bram, 'Give it to him when he's older. The same family names on both sides.'

'Same Testament,' Bram said.

'We're not that far apart,' Leon said. 'You Afrikaners also see yourselves as the Chosen People.'

Bram closed the book on his lap, looked down the length of the room, took a thoughtful sip of wine and said, 'I don't.' Pauline heard him rejecting the myth of a God who chooses and the myth of Afrikaner destiny.

In the heat of the day, he and Pauline lay down in their room. Looking up from his book, Bram said, 'What did he mean?'

'He's lonely for family. Mommy talks about family all the time. She's got sisters and cousins and everything, but he's got nothing. He wants to belong, though this is his second country.'

'He'll never be a true Afrikaner.'

After that claim on a distance his father-in-law could never bridge, Bram held aloof. One weekend, edgy about a proposal for a new client, he listened to Leon making pronouncements with his usual air of seeing through pretence, 'Economists try to make it sound complicated, but there's nothing to it but supply and demand,' and said, 'Your father thinks he's the Pope.'

Prompted, she noticed Leon's dogmatic tone on wine, food, art and European history since 1850. Beyond these topics, Bram pointed out, Leon took no interest in subjects other people raised.

Walking on the beach after an evening with the usual guests, Bram said, 'We never talk about our work. We've got opinions about anything except our own business.'

Defending her parents, Pauline said, 'British education. Trade's vulgar.'

'It's not the British. It's self-deception. Your mother doesn't want to see where she is, your father doesn't want to see who he is.'

She stopped on the heavy sand, looked at the restless lines of froth making a low sound like Bram's sleeping breath and tried to see her parents as he saw them. 'Perhaps they don't want to see Daddy as a smous.'

'A Jewish pedlar ... What's wrong with that?'

'Do I have to explain?'

He turned her and held both shoulders. 'Tell me.' A wave whispered towards their feet and drew away.

'A wandering Jew. An outsider forever, with no place of his own.' A tear rolled down her cheek.

'You Jews are strange.' He kissed the tear. 'Pauline, you have a place of your own. Here.'

At first Janet's doctors were reassuring, but Leon sounded frightened and glad to come to dinner. He brought wine and a jar of his own olives. Pouring the wine, 'I'd like to know what you think of this pinotage, Bram,' he swirled the liquid in his own glass and bent forward to sniff it. Taking an olive, he savoured the vineyard owner's personal attention. 'He took out this reserved bottle and let me buy the last case.'

Pauline left to garnish the paella.

Leon reached for the last olive, 'I'll make these with garlic next year ...'

When she brought out the colourful platter, he said, 'Real saffron. That must've cost you an arm and a leg.' Pauline felt ashamed of the tasteless remark, but Bram did not seem to notice.

Leon opened another bottle and asked Bram, 'What do you think of the nose? Fruity?'

Clearing up, she accepted a glass from Bram, 'Mommy always asks about our trips. I don't understand him.'

'He isn't interested in anyone else.'

She set the dishwasher going and took her wine to the couch. 'I'm tired of talking about wine and food.'

He put an arm round her shoulder, 'It's a bit much when his wife's life's in danger.'

'Danger? They said tests.' She set her glass on the table and started to weep.

Eli woke at the sound of her sobs and came out of his room.

'Go to bed, Eli,' his father said sternly. The boy looked at them, assessing whether to obey. 'And let me hear you close your door.'

Eli left, slamming his door to show how he hated it when adults kept him out of things.

Bram said, 'Please don't expose the child to your hysteria.'

'What did they say? I beg you, answer me?'

'They haven't told me anything, woman. She's in hospital.'

Pauline allowed a quiet paroxysm to overwhelm her. Bram watched, but would not indulge her.

'How bad can it be, Bram?'

He took her hands, 'It'll be all right. It'll be all right. We love you. Eli loves you. I love you. It'll be all right.'

It was worse than anyone expected, already in the lymph and starting on the brain.

Pauline visited every day. Coming through the back door, she greeted the maid quietly, put bags of groceries on the kitchen table and tiptoed to her parents' bedroom. If Janet wasn't sleeping, they would talk while Pauline made her mother comfortable and gave her the new box of chocolate. If Janet was sleeping, she left the chocolate on her bedside table and went to the kitchen. Bram and Eli and Leon would come later.

Ruth called twice a week and visited with her husband for ten days. 'He can't take more time from work,' she said mournfully, looking at Pauline with dark eyes.

They sat with Janet while she was awake and went into the living room when she slept, taking the armchairs reserved for adults. Ruth had a daughter now and they compared experiences as mothers. Friends for the first time. On their fourth day, Pauline said, 'We used to be so mean to you.'

Tears rose to Ruth's eyes. It was true then. Ruth's recognition felt like a cut.

'It's a long time ago,' Ruth said, but her eyes refuted her. 'Let's leave the past behind.' She came to Pauline and gave a clumsy embrace. She did not smell of urine now. 'You're my sister, Pauline.'

'Let's go to Restless River before you leave. There'll be whales.'

'There's no time.' She had never loved the sisters' house.

'Let's not drift apart.'

Tears slid down Ruth's cheeks. 'I'm on new medication, happier than I've ever been.'

When Pauline told Bram, he said, 'Your parents never talk about Ruth.'

'I never used to notice.'

'What did they think was happening to her?'

'I don't know.'

Heavy hearted. What else was there she did not know?

David called from Australia. 'Will they arrest me if I come?'

'There's too much going on. Riots all over. They've got their hands full.'

'Are you safe?'

'Just scared … Remember when we wished we lived in exciting times.'

'I'll come when my divorce comes through.'

When he arrived, Janet was far gone. Holding his hand, she looked at him. 'So short,' she said, 'so short.'

Afterwards Pauline said, 'Let's go to Restless River.'

They spent the morning exploring rock pools and ate at a café overlooking the harbour.

Driving back to Cape Town, she asked, 'What's going on with you and Daddy? You're still not talking to him.'

'I despise him. Do you know he's sleeping around?'

'I don't believe it.'

'Ask Bram.'

'He's never said anything.'

'All those trips. He's been doing it for years. You think he'd ever deny himself?'

'Does Mommy know?'

'He doesn't even bother to hide it. He'd call it hypocrisy.'

When Leon came home and settled in his armchair, a glass of wine in easy reach, father and son started to talk. Bram stood. 'Eli,' he took his son firmly by the shoulder. Eli resisted, but Bram pushed his son out of the room and closed the door.

Soon David was shouting, 'Don't you have any decency, you swine?'

'It's my life and you've got no right to judge it.'

'Can't you shut up, for Mommy's sake!' Pauline pleaded.

But they seemed doomed to where they could not stop. Fury poured from the room into the street.

'Get out of my house,' Leon shouted.

David ran out, Pauline after him, 'David, David.' Servants and neighbours knew the son was back. 'Please, for Mommy's sake.'

Driving home, she felt fear and darkness. Where would this fury end? When Bram opened the door, she clung to him.

'Come.' He poured wine. Eli was safe, asleep behind a closed door. Bram shielded her with his arm. The sea glistened. All the way to the south pole. Forever. The black bird on her heart clawed tight.

What was she bringing from her family to Eli? To Bram?

At the funeral, father and son sat apart, not looking at each other. Friends found Leon in the living room dispensing wine and David at his mother's yellowwood dining table. Pauline shuttled from one room to the other, distributing gifts of cake and chocolate.

Before dinner, Leon said fiercely, 'She was a great woman,' then, in a meek voice, 'I can't go through her clothes and things.'

'I'll do it, Daddy.' It was sweet to show him tenderness.

'Did I ever tell you how I proposed? I was camping in the Helderberg with my closest friends. We had a session talking about being bald and forty and then we phoned our girlfriends. When Janet answered I talked about camping and said, "By the way, I phoned to tell you I'm getting married." "Who to?" "To you, you bloody fool." '

'She was a fool to accept a proposal like that,' Bram said.

At the door, Leon turned to her. Holding him was so sweet

it felt forbidden.

Leon came again. These days he spoke gently to her.

It was comforting to go through her mother's clothes and jewellery, books and mementoes. She took the engagement ring and some cookbooks.

Soon after, Leon adopted a new habit. When a bottle of wine was done, he would lay it on its side for ten minutes. Then he would pour himself the small drink gathered out of the last drops. 'He's tight-fisted,' Bram said.

She looked at him in the bathroom mirror. 'That's ridiculous. His house is always full of people drinking his wine and eating his food.' She started to rub lotion into her skin, smiling and teasing, 'You're succumbing to an Afrikaner stereotype about Jews.'

'Look what he does with leftovers.' He took the vial from her hand, poured a coin into his palm and rubbed it into her back.

In Leon's refrigerator mysterious fragments swathed in plastic supermarket bags crowded the shelves, leftovers he would eat when Pauline did not come to cook. At her house, he asked for the bones and scraps. 'I'll make soup for my dog.'

She excused him, 'He was a Depression child. French cooks also save everything.'

'They're also misers,' Bram put her vial on the counter and rubbed the small of her back. Her nipples rose, but a black bird hopped on her heart. 'When has he given Eli presents?'

'We spoil him.'

'That's what grandparents are supposed to do.' His hands had reached her buttocks and lingered. 'Does he ever spend time with Eli? Teach him fishing? He's selfish.'

His eyes in the mirror were ardent, but she held off, 'I've always thought he's generous.'

'Think about how he proposed.'

She put her hands over her eyes, 'You want to put me against my father.'

He turned her from the mirror. She wept, he stroked her hair; she reached round his neck and let him carry her to bed.

Bram confirmed David's story. 'It won't take him long to find another woman now.'

But she was not prepared for him to choose Maria, her high school friend.

Leon brought her to dinner one night, 'I bumped into her in town.' It seemed natural enough. Maria still spoke to Pauline in English, but slipped into her family's tongue to make semi-private remarks to Leon. When she praised the food, her word was 'Lekker!'

Pauline could not read Bram's expression.

Talking to Leon in half-screening Afrikaans, Maria mentioned setting the alarm for next morning. Bram's eyes met Pauline's. He lowered his eyes. Meaning, we'll discuss this later.

When Leon kissed Eli goodnight, Maria kissed him too. Fury slashed through Pauline. Leon and Maria left together.

Alone with Bram, looking out over the black sea, Pauline wept, 'I can't believe it. She started to menstruate the same week as me. When I think of her, using the back door like family ...'

'You'd be upset no matter who.'

'No, Bram. She's like my sister. You know this is worse. In Mommy's bed!' Didn't he know any limits? Hadn't she always known that he did not? Even when she was little, holding her on his lap?

How had her mother put up with his lawless appetites?

Bram bent to kiss her, hungry. Their own appetites had been lawless too. She abandoned herself as though they would not have much time before the curse that must come.

It came through the sisters' house.

For the first year after Janet's death, Pauline and Bram came to Restless River as of old and Eli put urchin shells on the table under the fading posters in the long room. But when Leon brought Maria, the two women could barely be civil. If he put his arm round Maria, Pauline walked out of the room.

'Why must he rub my nose in it?' she asked Bram.

He held out a box the size of a slab of chocolate.

'Oh, Bram, you knew I wanted it.' He fastened the necklace and kissed her neck. Since Janet's funeral he had given her a Mercedes, diamond earrings and, every few days, chocolate.

She was happy but his hunger tasted of fear. He worked out at the health club twice a week, would not touch the chocolate himself and took no more than one glass of Leon's wine.

Pauline turned to her aunts to talk. The sisters, once so pleased with their holiday house, were dismayed to hear it held a traitor.

The aunt in Australia said, 'Aren't there any limits?'

To the aunt in Brooklyn Pauline said, 'Maria's such a slut and Daddy's such a swine they could have been doing it when Mommy was dying. She was always in the house. It makes me sick to think of it.'

'Don't talk about your father like that, Pauline. You don't always know the limits of decency yourself.' Pauline had forgotten the kiss on the landing and felt ready to scream until her aunt added, 'But he does seem to deserve it.'

That October, when they were all at Restless River, Leon told her he would sell his Cape Town house and retire to Restless River. 'Property values are slipping, I'll sell as soon as I can.' Now that the old order was over, whites were leaving more quickly than before. 'Maria wants to open a boutique near the market.' The old elite still lived as though there had been no change.

The area had lost some of its charm. Most of their old friends had died or emigrated. But the first artists and writers had drawn younger ones and Leon had always known how to attract interesting people.

They were preparing a fish stew and Maria was out

shopping when Pauline talked of coming for the Christmas break. Leon said, 'There won't be room. The place'll be full of furniture from the Cape Town house.'

'No room for us? Why don't you store the furniture?'

'Janet's antiques? They'll be ruined.'

She looked out at an olive tree. It had lost a branch and the broken limb and brown leaves lay on the ground untended. 'It's a family house. Mommy's money paid for it.'

'You don't know anything about it. You and your aunts have developed a story and won't listen to facts.'

'How can you do this to me?'

'If you want a holiday house, buy one.'

'We haven't got the money.'

'Bullshit. You've got enough for a Mercedes and a trip to Europe every year.'

Whatever it took, whatever Bram's dismay, 'All right,' her voice a reckless threat, 'we'll buy it from you.'

'Fair market value.'

'You'll make me pay for Mommy's house like a stranger?' Savouring pain like chocolate.

'It's my retirement. Where'm I supposed to live? I never expected a child of mine to argue with me about money. What sort of woman have you become?'

Now she felt calm as stone, 'You've got enough money to live on.'

'You want to kick me out of my own house. You think I'm an old man now, you can throw me on the scrap heap.'

They heard the glass door slide open as Bram and Eli came back from the beach. She went to collect their towels and trophies. Bram had parked near the broken olive tree.

Next day, preparing a salad with purple peppers, her mother's favourite, she asked, 'What'll you do with the copper-clad pots Mommy inherited from Minke?'

'Keep them, of course.'

'She wanted me to have them.'

'She never told me that.'

'Let me have them, Daddy, please.'

'You've turned into an avaricious, grasping woman.'

She gasped, 'Maria's poisoning your mind. She hates me.'

'Get used to Maria. The phase of my life with your mother is over. I'm being realistic and getting on with the next thing.'

'Maria's a slut. She'd sleep with anyone who'd take the trouble to want her, man or woman.'

He laughed. 'We've known each other a long time and we suit each other.'

'You couldn't even wait till Mommy died to betray her.'

'Janet betrayed me. She promised she'd give up smoking and didn't.'

'Is that your excuse?'

When Bram and Eli came back from the beach, she had packed.

She called Brooklyn. Her aunt said, 'He slammed the phone down when I mentioned the house.'

'You did buy it with Mommy, didn't you?'

'With Minke's bequest.'

'That's what Mommy told me. Can't you claim your part?'

'It's not in a legal document.'

She carried the phone to the porch. It was evening now in Australia. She called that aunt. 'There's nothing we can do. In any case, you can't hold on to your childhood, Pauline. It wasn't as perfect as you remember.' Out there on the sea was a boat, human life. Beyond it, a frozen continent.

She went inside, poured herself a glass of wine and called David. He said, 'That's just like him. You remember when we wanted to say something was really bad, we used to say, "That's just like Daddy!" '

'I used to think we were a close family. Weren't we happy?'

'What about Ruth?'

'We teased her and left her out of things because she wet her bed.'

'Is that all?'

'What else is there?'

'I'm in therapy now, remembering a lot. You were getting all the favours. Did Ruth ever do anything right? Did anyone ever love her?' Craving drowned Pauline. Bitter chocolate. Now. 'We were really mean to her, but no one stopped us.' She opened her underwear drawer, feeling for the slab stashed for emergencies. 'Remember how he proposed?'

'It was a joke.'

'You think Mommy found it funny? He'd had a passionate affair six months before.'

'She loved his sense of humour.' She tore the foil off with her teeth, bit into the slab and let it stanch her need. Now she could be calm. 'What are you saying, David?'

'That they were cruel to Ruth.'

'You make them sound sick.'

He remained silent.

She bit into the dark solace. 'People love him. Our house was always full of people. He still has friends over every weekend.'

'Do we look like the children of a happy family?'

She saw herself through his eyes. Divorced. In retreat from America. Married to a man old enough to be her father. What else?

If her father was not who she'd thought, her mother a compliant victim, her past not real, who was she?

Before calling Ruth she gave Bram and Eli dinner. Eli spilled his milk and words she had heard years ago sprang to life, all aimed at Ruth. 'Oaf', 'Klutz', 'Can't you do anything right!' 'How many times do I have to tell you?' 'I don't know what to do with you.' When anything went wrong, when she and Ruth were naughty, when she broke the blue vase and her mother blamed Ruth, 'You'll drive me mad.'

She had been the loved child, Ruth the cursed.

She took the phone to the porch and looked out at the dark sea between England and Cape Town. Phosphorescence flecked the waters.

'What did we do to you when we were growing up?'

'It wasn't your fault, Pauline. You just did what Mommy and Daddy did.' Ruth and David must have talked about her, the unfairly favoured. What else had they said?

'I love you,' Ruth said thousands of miles away.

'You don't need the house,' Bram said.

'It's my connection with my mother. She wanted Eli to have it.'

'You're still grieving for her, aren't you?'

'You don't think I should?'

'You're a mother yourself now. Eli needs you to look forward.'

But she could not look there where the curse waited.

For Eli's birthday she arranged sleepovers for five of his friends with a picnic and ice cream and cake and then TV at home. It was almost like the old times at Restless River. Next day, each unwilling to enter the other's house, they met Leon and Maria at a Thai restaurant in Kloof Nek and split the bill.

Leon joked with the waiter. Later he told about how, thirty years ago, living in this part of Cape Town, he gave a party and so many people came the floor buckled. He demonstrated with a sweeping curve of his arm. Everyone laughed. 'We pushed them out and had the party in the street.' Bram added a story of his own. She saw that in Leon's presence people laughed and came alive. He loves being alive. He's not a monster.

But she ached. For the Christmas break they rented a cottage near the harbour and Bram took Eli up the mountains as though this year was no different from years before.

Word of the quarrel went out to friends, employees and the community of Restless River. When Pauline bumped into friends at the market, most talked as though nothing had happened. The poet put a hand on her arm. Tremor and bone. 'Our lives are grass that springs up in the morning and is cut down at night.'

'Getting senile,' she told Bram.

'Quoting the Bible.'

Bram's eyebrows were also thick now, his beard turning white.

Out the window of the rented house a wine sea reached from mountains to horizon. Nothing human lasts. Only the icy waters and whales sporting in it would survive. Perhaps not even the whales. They might be gone when Eli was grown. The world is fragile as glass.

She turned her back on the sea, towards the sunny room, and put her hands on Bram's shoulders, 'Will you always love me?'

He nibbled an ear, 'As long as I live.'

Leon bought a house in a cheap suburb of Cape Town. 'I need a base when I've got business in town. It's never going to be my home.' He stored Janet's furniture in its rooms.

One Sunday, strangely out of breath, he needed help packing his samples and called Pauline. She drove through treeless streets. When he let her in, she glanced into the dark living room, curtains drawn, floor impassable with boxes and black plastic bags. Corpses. Their past life.

'What do you need, Daddy?'

At the toilet, an hour later, she read a sign he had not taken off the door, 'The Wee Room'. She used to think he wanted to live where everything showed taste. Were the rituals of praise that filled the house at Restless River only her mother's and aunts'?

What sort of marriage had it really been?

Had they really cursed their own child?

Ruth had grown up in front of her eyes. Why had she never seen?

Leon called, 'Just don't get hysterical, I beg. People with cancer live for years.'

The doctor said, 'Months, not years.' A carrion bird pecked

at her heart.

When Pauline spoke with Leon again, he said, 'There's nothing wrong with me. But I've made a will. I'm being perfectly rational.'

She called Maria, 'He's going on with his life. It's the best thing he can do.'

Ruth said nothing about coming to Cape Town.

David said, 'Soon,' but meant later. She told him, 'They're going to remodel the house at Restless River. Maria wants a better kitchen and a bedroom with a view of the sea.'

'He's going to give her the house, Pauline.'

She could not stop talking about the house. Bitterness filled her mouth. She called New York, Australia, California, England. Couldn't anyone help?

The contractors wanted Leon and Maria out of the way when they knocked down walls and demolished the kitchen. He would rent the poet's house, still vacant and unsold five months after the funeral.

She said, 'Your voice sounds tired.'

'There's a lot to do.'

'I'll come and help.'

Bram said, 'You're torturing yourself.'

'He needs me.'

'I'll keep Eli here. It's too much for him.'

It was too much for Bram too, but she dared not stop.

'He's so obstinate. There's no phone in the house and he won't let me buy him one.'

'Just buy it.'

'He won't use it. He'll never admit he was wrong.' A sob swelled, 'We won't be able to reach him. As if he's dead.'

She packed the phone, soap, towels, lunch and chocolate. Parking at the broken olive tree, brown limb untouched, she saw Maria in the long room sealing a cardboard box. When Pauline slid the door open, Maria greeted her cheerfully, 'I'm almost gone. I have to open the boutique.' As though no river of enmity ran between them.

'Where's Daddy?'

'He'll be back in a minute.'

Pauline walked through the ruins. The room that had once been hers was full of plastic bags like the living room in Cape Town. Other rooms were impassable with ladders and bags of cement and builders' gear. The table where the sisters had cooked still stood in the kitchen, loaded with boxes. These broken walls were not the place she had known.

She heard Leon's van and carried out a carton of plasticware. He was standing at the back of his van, gasping, his flesh grey and meagre. Sunlight showed its erosion with minute precision. He did not meet her eyes. 'Come sit, Daddy. I brought some juice for you.'

'Later,' he said and tried to lift the carton. Skull under skin. She had found the box light.

'Okay.' She turned towards the house to hide the spurt of tears, walked into the long room and found another box of kitchen stuff.

He leaned against the van, conserving himself. This shrunken man, her father, had forced himself from his home and his children, from himself. He would die without a home.

'That's enough,' he said, though the back of the van was half empty.

'You drive. I'll walk over.'

She crossed a field of coarse grass. Calm tears streamed from her eyes and she did not brush them away. She wept as though no one was watching. Sunlight blinded her and her heart felt blinded too, pure and free of rage.

Before she came in sight of his van, she stopped and wiped her face.

Some change had come over him too. He sat at the wheel, not moving to get out. She came nearer. 'Miriam?'

She drew near as though that had always been her name and asked, 'Have you got keys?'

He fumbled in his pockets. She led him on her arm, the way she had led her mother in her last days. The door opened to a room with a couch. 'Come,' she guided him to it. He looked up at her, his eyes green and bloodshot and puzzled.

'Water, Miriam.'

She saw the kitchen and found a cup. Taking it from her hand, he asked, 'Isn't there a glass?' with the irritable note she knew.

'I'll look.'

'Nein. Zitz, Miriam.' She sat. He looked at her, still puzzled. Was he trying to find her in Lithuania, before she was born? He fell asleep.

Near evening, Maria called, 'I'm leaving the boutique now. Why don't you go home? It's a long drive in the dark.'

She parked and Bram opened the door. Eli was watching from inside. She read his face and said, 'Daddy's dead.'

Bram held her. 'He had enough morphine.'

'She gave it to him. I know she did. Before he could change his will.'

'Let it rest, Pauline.'

'She wants the house.'

'Enough, darling.'

She clung to the shelter of her husband's body, Eli pressing himself between them, and wept as she had wept in the field, alone.

The Night We Talked

Yesterday Gus and I talked about God. We have been friends more than twenty years, one of his sisters is a minister, he knows I go to the AME church every week and sing in the choir, but we've never touched that before.

Our friendship goes back to a party that started at a movie followed by an hour at our host's eating, drinking and despising the movie. Bonded in dislike, we liked each other. The following week we met for a drink at a warm place I'd never been with my husband. I was hoping for a new life with new possibilities. In the hum of other conversations and laughter where it feels easy to confide anything, we talked about books and concerts and at some stage I realised, he's gay. But by that time we were laughing at local politicians and had agreed to see another movie together.

Some movies later, I told him, 'I'm thinking about business school,' I'd never be able to clothe two teenagers on my clerical salary, 'though the maths exam could kill me.'

'I'll coach you, if you like.' He is an economist and maths is as natural to him as singing to me.

Three mornings a week, I brought bagels after his hour of psychoanalysis and he gave me coffee and walked me through equations without making me feel a fool. I don't know exactly what trouble sent him looking for help or able to give it. Growing up gay in Tennessee, maybe.

I was making new friends after the divorce. He was coming out. We did not discuss these matters, though each got glimpses. It was a nightmare time for me, full of nasty surprises, like the friends who dropped me. 'I guess they were friends of convenience.'

'Like mine in Tennessee. Getting away to Dartmouth saved

my life.'

He never said people called him names or spat or beat him up.

Once, he described a high from a heart drug that expands the blood vessels, 'It makes sex unbelievable.'

'I hope you don't kill yourself,' I said, feeling stupidly out of it, a mother. We never talked about sex again. We never talked about race. We still haven't, but that doesn't seem to matter now. We understand enough.

Mostly we talked about general topics and sometimes didn't agree. He's an economist and talks as though people behave rationally. I find that absurd. I'm black. I've been married. And divorced. No rationality there. So why believe people are rational about money? Gus had other reasons to doubt human rationality. He'd been in analysis three years. What is psychoanalysis about if not irrationality?

Our disagreements were also absurd, about things like whether a meteor caused the extinction of the dinosaurs. 'Ridiculous!' Gus flared up when I told him about the hypothesis.

'No need to get mad about it. I'm just telling you what I saw on Nova.'

But he remained mad. Maybe growing up gay in Tennessee leaves explosives around for life. Maybe he was still raging with grief about Larry, though that loss was two years old. Part of it was outrage. Gus is white and did not expect a healthy, young, prosperous American male to die of appendicitis because he was Jamaican.

He threw himself into fund-raising for a choral group. I graduated and got a job. When Gus came to dinner and the boys were there, he'd joke with them. There'd be lots of high-fives and they'd translate lingo for him. When they disappeared, he'd grin, 'I just love your kids.'

'They tell you more about what's going on than they tell me.'

'You're their mother.'

They couldn't tell me without losing status among their

peers.

Gus told me where I could find money to send them to college.

He didn't like his job at the time and found another. He met Nick and introduced us but Nick doesn't feel comfortable with straight women or blacks, so Gus and I saw less of each other.

One Sunday when Nick was away, Gus's choral group put on *The Magic Flute*. 'I'd love to come. I've been missing you.'

We laughed at the children in their animal costumes and at Papageno and Papagena united at last and foreseeing children. After the performance we brought Chinese food home to eat with the boys.

When they went off to a friend's house, Gus talked about his colleagues. 'They notice I don't bring women to parties and don't talk about dating.' He was sitting forward in his chair, his face in shadow from the reading light behind him. 'They might not choose me for projects because of their clients' feelings.'

I know too much about that kind of thing and wanted to make it better, like a mother, 'Is that happening?'

'I don't know.' He put his head in his hands for a moment. That's how they do hatred in places like his firm. Not open slurs or invective. Not dragging you along a road till you die. Not beating you up and tying you to a fence. Just cutting off lifelines. Gus knew that. He probably learned it at Dartmouth. He pulled himself upright, 'I don't want to hide, lie or feel ashamed.'

'If they're bigots, Gus, go somewhere else. It'll be their loss.'

After a few months, he did.

That was the only time he let me see what we share. He's proud and dresses well. When he gets mad, his face puffs up and he looks like a southern sheriff, but when he is calm, he looks like a lover of opera.

That conversation sent me back to my silences about faith. I used to think, this is no one else's business, but faith always comes up, often as soon as I meet someone, whatever the matter in hand. As if it's an insect bite they must scratch at, some ask, 'Do you really believe ... ?' what they baulk at.

Sometimes I wonder if anything is more taboo than faith. Before that conversation with Gus, I used to keep silent, in my closet. Since then, I speak up and deflect argument.

I never challenged Gus on his work, though it troubled me that one of his clients must be a notorious polluter. It is hard to find clean work. I would have taken a defence job if I had to, though other mothers' children die by our devices. Maybe Gus thought his client right, justified by economics.

Work took him travelling and we saw less of each other. We could pick up like old friends. I could always turn to him though he believed economic theories that it is wrong to help people. It doesn't square with his behaviour or, I hope, with what he teaches his nieces and nephews. He has become a doting uncle and children's books take whole shelves in his flat and country house. He laughs talking about them and I suspect they're defusing the Tennessee pain.

Nick is teaching in Utah now and Gus and I eat dinner together once in a while. Last night we had wine in his flat and he showed me a gift from Nick, a lavish astronomy book with computer pictures. Gus hopes for life out there.

I resent the millions spent on space exploration instead of schools and asked, 'What difference would it make to you?'

'Wouldn't it be wonderful if there's something in the universe that gives rise to life?'

'There is. We're here.'

That wasn't what he wanted. I heard his wish for life as a hunger, not for people like those on our own Earth and its wondrous creatures, but for life beyond the life we know, for awe and praise, for company and meaning.

A few sentences later Gus cited a philosopher he had been reading, 'He says the whole is other than the parts and the human person more than our component chemicals.' Gus paid attention because this philosopher commands respect in academic journals, 'I've never read anything before that makes the idea of God sound reasonable.'

Reasonable? Like economics? Absurd to ask of faith, as

absurd as racism. Absurd as being in love with someone full of paradoxes and surprises. Like God, who was also spat on and pinioned where he would die.

Gus had been carrying the philosopher's words for months. 'It makes sense to me,' I said. 'I'm not only my parts and neither are you.'

I wondered whether we would start arguing, but he was listening as if he had been longing to talk about God, so I said, 'The most important thing is what makes you, you and me, me. That's what takes me to church.' I stopped, wary. He was taking a risk with this taboo and intimate topic. I felt at risk too and wondered if it's as hard to talk to a Martian as to another person.

He said, 'When I mention God to my minister sister, she changes the subject.' He must be lonely in his longing.

I changed the subject from his sister. 'I've a hunch, Gus, you've been looking for life in the universe a long time.' Thinking of his psychoanalysis and that drug that expands the heart.

He did not answer and that was as much as I dared, though our years of oblique confessing said he was brimming with more than he would tell.

Then we went to a Chinese restaurant. He knows I'm still in debt from the MBA and now the boys have got their own debts to pay.

We talked about a fund-raising project Gus is dreaming up for Dartmouth and tossed donated millions and big names about like confetti as though we were celebrating something. Near the end, we almost bumped into an argument about genetically altered food, but skirted it.

When we cracked our fortune cookies, his read, 'The heart is wiser than the brain.'

Mine read, 'You will soon inherit a large fortune.' I shook my head. 'I'm glad it's large. What would I do with a small fortune?'

He's never dropped his Tennessee courtesy and held my coat.

The House is Full of Cars
This Morning

Tuesday 8

I bought a cyclamen this morning at the supermarket. I've never been able to afford one before, but something must have happened to the demand, this was half the usual price, only $3.75. Last time I thought of buying a pot they were going for $7.00 or $6.95 – it's the same thing. Perhaps it's inflation, or the mild winter, that brings down the price of flowers. Or maybe they produced too many this year, they miscalculated something about our feelings. Or maybe it's a new strategy. They'll sell more and make more profits that way instead of by a big margin. I shouldn't really care now that I've got my cyclamen, but I wonder. Other things in the supermarket are so scary. I stopped buying hot dogs or processed meats for the children years ago, but even the others are full of hormones and antibiotics and nitrates and nitrites – there's no way out. Yesterday I heard someone say on a talk programme that even if you grow your own fruit and vegetables, they get polluted. The cities spray by plane to protect the street trees, then there's lead from the automobiles and I don't know what else. That's what frightens me. There's no way to find out what's in what, and there's no way out.

But my cyclamen's beautiful. It's got round leaves that draw in toward the stem, like a heart, but the other end, where they point, is rounded, not sharp to stab like the Queen of Spades. She's death they say. The flowers are round too, face down, growing from a little cap like Emily's elf-cap in the school play. My cyclamens are white, but just under the cap there's a ring of pink, nearly red. It flushes out into the petals. I think it must be a new variety. I remember a greater reflex in the petals of the other cyclamens I used to look at before Christmas every year, and in February, when I need flowers. The winter's so long here. Sometimes I think of going south, but there's no one to look after the kids now that Jim's mother's died, and there's never any money for vacations. Even camping this summer came out of the grocery allowance.

Maybe the petals will reflex more when the flowers are more mature. I bought a pot with young buds, six, so that I know they won't die in a day or two. I looked under the leaves too, and saw some more buds coming up there, but I don't know if I'll be able to make the pot last that long. They must be difficult flowers, I think, if they're so expensive.

Thursday 10
They seem to be doing fine, so far. I've got them in a good spot in the living room bay. They get some afternoon sun there. They don't need too much light. That's good, because in winter we don't get it. The shadows are too long, and the house next door blocks out our light. In the summer there's no problem, it's the other way round, like those trick coins – heads I win, tails you lose. My Uncle Ted had one. He used to call it his lucky coin. Of course it would be, with two heads. I wonder how that happens, if it's forged, or a mistake in the mint. I asked Jim, but he got irritated at me. He doesn't like to think that there could be hanky-panky in the government. He's patriotic.

Friday 11
The leaves have a lighter marking. At first I thought it could be water spots, but when I looked more carefully I saw that there's a faint line a third of the way in, where the spots stop. The margins of the leaves have a little scallop, and the scallops have a rhythm of their own, they come to peaks every three or four little bends like a fancy edging. Two more buds have opened, and some of the ones I saw under the leaves are coming out now. I looked and saw more buds, so many I can't believe it, it's too much like a promise they'll just go on and on

producing flowers, as if blooming could go on forever. I can't believe it. Life isn't like that. Though I suppose it might be in forests or in nature. I wonder where cyclamens come from, and whether there are parts of the world where they spring up every year, season after season. Perhaps I'll be able to look it up while the children watch the movie show at the library next week, if I can persuade Emily to feel safe without me. I wonder why she's such a frightened child. Even so, with flowers it's not the same individual, just a new generation – the stock goes on forever, from Adam into my children. Not Adam, of course – *Pithecanthropus erectus,* or someone with a name like that, though I suppose his wife had another name for him. I wonder if they had wives in those days, or if it was more like the cartoons, a man grabbing his woman. They don't show the children how he rapes her, they just lay the scene. They'll get the message.

Monday 14
Weekends feel so hectic. By Monday mornings I have to spend an hour after everyone's out of the house again and I've been quiet, clearing the breakfast things and doing the beds and getting the laundry going before I know who I am again. Tom wants to play with cars all the time. He likes to crash them. Cars and war, that's all he's interested in. I hate watching the news on TV when he can see it there again. The real world, TV, where grown-ups live, is all cars and war. I tried to tell him that grown-ups have to know about the world they live in so they can know what's happening and decide what to do. It's a lie. The war's been going on so long. Jim walked out of the room when I said Nixon doesn't really want peace. Anyhow, the house is full of cars this morning. I keep stepping into them like roaches underfoot. I try to get the children to pick up after themselves, but the things they don't see are always left. There's litter in every room. In the bathroom when I go to take a shower at night I find plastic figures lying under the sink and behind the shower curtain.

Monday 21

I knew we couldn't have a winter without these storms that dump snow all over everything like loads of wet washing. It's pretty for a minute in the morning, and then it's filth, you can see what goes into your lungs lying black on the snow. I heard that Massachusetts has one of the highest cancer rates in the country.

I've been feeling as if I'm going to die soon. I saw my first grey hair today. It's been late coming. Lots of my friends have had grey hair for years, and they're not old. I saw it as I was washing the sink in the bathroom – the children leave it full of soap spatters. I'll have to teach them not to. I looked in the mirror again, and then to make sure, I pulled it out. It was a long hair. I wonder how long it's been there, and how many others I don't see.

It'd be young to die now. I don't think I'm sick. I should go for a check-up but I don't know where the money'll come from. Still, I'm on the pill, I should go for a check-up.

But the way I imagine it is in a crash. I'll be in the car or crossing the street. It's almost happened. When I'm tired and absent-minded I don't notice cars coming towards me. There was that man who swore at me because I started crossing the street carrying Emily without seeing him. That's how I dream of him coming at me again, swearing too late. I dream I can hear myself screaming. I wonder whether we kill more that way or in the war.

Friday 25

The first flower is starting to die. Its petals are going brown. I wondered how it would be.

Tuesday 29

Loretta phoned today. We had a long chat. She wants me to go back to school in the fall. I said we don't have enough money. But I'd like to. I want to get out of the house. As if it's my last chance. As if I'm not really old. It's only one grey hair. Women begin again these days, when their children are in school. I needn't be the only older person in the class, ignored for having no experience of their world, no possibility of entering into it. I'm not sure I do want to go to school, but I said I did, and she said that she'll see that I get the forms and applications for a scholarship. Do I want it? Yes. I want to get out of the house.

But there won't be enough money. It'd take babysitting too. I won't be able to do it. I painted the passage again yesterday, but the drawings the children made with magic marker still show through the paint – it's the fifth coat. They said the colours were washable. I wonder if that's the way they're non-toxic too. You can't tell. I saw a programme about children's toys before Christmas. They were all killers. Plastic splinters, sharp metal corners and parts inside dolls, cars that break and leave rough edges, poison in beads and paint, darts whose caps come off, flammable dolls' clothes – babies' clothes too. Afterwards I took away Emily's ballerina doll because it's made of the brittle plastic that cuts and leaves such bad splinters, and she was mad at me. She stamped her foot and shouted and said she'd murder me. She's not afraid at home. I suppose children just have to talk like that.

Monday 6
Jim and I had a terrible fight last night. He says I'm a slob. The house is a wreck. His clothes aren't mended. He complained that most of his clothes are dry-cleaned, was it too much to ask me to look after the rest. After all I don't work. This kind of thing is my work. I suppose it is. Not much better than his papers and reports. It doesn't feel right. Sometimes I think about going to Africa, or somewhere where we could do real work, teaching or health care, something that would make sense. I'd feel better about the children too if we weren't living as though there's no sense in life. Maybe there isn't. Everyone dies. Like the cyclamen. I knew it would die. They always do. Now the leaves are turning yellow and the flowers are dying.

None of the new buds are opening. The stems just grow longer and longer, gangling over the flowers that have opened. I wonder what's wrong.

Wednesday 8
Jim and I had another bad night. I told him that I'd been thinking about going to Africa or somewhere, but he said that it was all nonsense. He didn't even listen to what I said, he said he knew it before I said it. Afterwards when he touched me I couldn't respond. He says I'm a frigid woman, I make him impotent. I wonder if I'm frigid.

Friday 10
It's Tom's birthday next week and I haven't done anything about a party yet. There's no money for it, but I suppose I can squeeze some out of the groceries. He wants a machine gun, but I said I couldn't get it for him. Maybe I'll skip a party and take the children to a movie instead. No, a party would be best. Tom saw a wildlife movie at Jim's sister's house. They watch all that vile TV stuff there, and I don't like to take them there, but it was Sunday and Jim said we had to visit his family once in a while. Tom told me about the movie afterwards. There was a lion that hunted a buck and tore it open to eat it. Tom liked it.

Monday 13
Another snowstorm on the weekend. The children get so impossible when they're cooped up all day. Jim wanted to go to Marge's again. I said the storm was too bad and we'd just been last week. Afterwards I was so exhausted I just sat down in the living room and rocked and read. Jim was black about it. The kitchen was in a mess because I'd been making cookies with the children in the afternoon and hadn't cleaned up. But it was good to rock. I haven't done it for years, not since Emily was a baby. I didn't do it long. Tom was playing with toy soldiers and he kept putting them under the runners of the rocker. He wanted me to crush them when I rocked. I wouldn't

do it. I won't do it. Emily's dolls were fighting. They were hungry and there weren't any more cookies for them. They wouldn't eat bread and jam. I told her they couldn't be that hungry then, but she stamped her foot and threw a tantrum. I think she's jealous of Tom's party tomorrow.

Thursday 16

Jim bought that machine gun for Tom and didn't even tell me about it. Tom brought it into the bedroom yesterday morning so excited. He'd found it next to his bed, all wrapped up in birthday wrapping. I couldn't take it away. Tom kept pointing it at me and shooting. It makes a horrible rattling noise, just like the real thing. I didn't even talk to Jim. I'm going to leave him. He doesn't know why I've been so quiet. He thinks I'm just tired because of the party. It's enough. It's been rotten right through. I should have divorced him before we had children. I've phoned Loretta. I can take the children over there this afternoon, she's got room for us. I've been packing all morning and drinking gallons of milk as though I've got an ulcer I can quench that way.

I'm going to throw out that cyclamen. It looks disgusting, gangling and dying. But I'll have to take that gun. Tom'll hate me if I don't.

Exile

Stephen Katela dozed at the back of the car. Occasionally he opened his eyes to look at the two dark heads in front of him, the kind white couple who were taking him to their home. Yesterday he had been at another college and had given a talk on African music and another kind white couple had taken him home as their guest and he had talked about South Africa. He closed his eyes. A theme kept palpitating under the surface of his attention, its outline blurred like a cat in a bag, like his own young body when he crept down to the bottom of his mother's bed and thought that no one could see him because it was dark under the blanket. His brother played with him there, a touch and move game in the shapeless dark, a hide-and-seek without rules, until they started to wrestle and wriggled so fast they rolled off the bed on to the humourless floor. Then their mother scolded them while she fed another baby mieliepap with one hand and attended to the tea and remaining mieliepap on the stove with the other. Stephen and his brother went out to play until she called them in to breakfast. They ignored her injunctions to take soap and wash under the tap in the yard. Winter was too cold for washing. She would come out when the baby was fed and give them a slap and another scolding, would oversee their mutual lathering and squirming at the tap and when the relics of their brief exploration had been washed off them – cinders of a brazier in which they had poked for coal, gritty smears if they had been examining the rubbish in the street – she would fold them into the bosomy warmth of the room. The reminiscent smell of early morning fires, the grey blue haze of the township, bit like an acrid, toxic gas into the tissue of Stephen's memory. He opened his eyes again to fill them with the two silhouettes in front of him, the white couple driving home through a heavy mist that the headlights held pale and solid, close to the car.

The road twisted and heaved. They had come off the smooth turnpike, homogeneous from Virginia to Maine, that made Stephen feel that this whole lecture tour was a hallucination in which distance had no more dimension than in a dream. Episodes that repeated the same obsessional pattern followed each other arbitrarily in settings that differed only like the scenery of an impoverished theatrical company. Every road was the same road. The arrangement played with slightly differing signs and overpasses, discreet banks of grass and trees that only gradually and reluctantly admitted the grey agglomeration of cities whose suburbs had long been suppressed by the same green uniform as the countryside. At last, off the highway, an idiosyncratic thrust from the land moulded the road into a pliant index of fields and streams, pulled straight over flats, packed more densely in steep valleys and rises. The mist was so thick he could hardly see the vegetation. From the dancing swell of the road he could imagine himself back on the stretch between Mooi River and Pietermaritzburg where frequent mists nourished the land and cattle condensed the airy whiteness into substances richly edible – for those who could afford to buy them. But every now and then a leafy intrusion over the road caught his eye, the uneven bars of a wooden fence, or irregular stone globules of a wall, and Stephen was reminded by these foreign shapes and colours that he was not on that Natal road, he was somewhere in New England, going to spend the night in a strange house among strangers. These sights, like foreign substances grafted among the tissues of what he had seen, lived and compounded into organic constituents of his own self, set up a resistance. Each reminder that he was not home accelerated an irritation, a process of rejection. His body, his perception, the accumulated chemicals of his own being barred these alien elements and tried to seal their pernicious proximity off from himself, to cast them off like a foreign skin or organ, to expel all toxic strangeness.

He shut his eyes. He tried to lull himself. Let him not think that if he did not learn how to assimilate America there would be nothing left for him to see, no place where he could retain that dwindling self he felt to be his own. He thought of his brother and the dusty soccer field where they used to play when their mother went off with the baby and a bundle of washing wrapped in a sheet, to the white city where she worked until night came. How did that theme shape?

His host was also a composer. Stephen had heard a quartet by him. It had been played at one of the colleges where Stephen had contributed to a symposium on modern music. There had been lectures and workshops during the day. In the evening there was a concert and Ken Radley's String Quartet, cited as an example of some of the finest composition in the United States, was played to instruct an audience that might find such compositions hard to come by. To Stephen the quartet seemed unintelligible, thin and boring, but he blamed his response on his own ignorance. Ken's quartet was one of the many signs, like billboards on the road, that said to Stephen, 'We don't speak to you. We are not written in your language. You have nothing to say to us.'

The car slowed, turned up a driveway and they had arrived. 'We're here,' Janet announced smiling. This was her home. Stephen smiled to her. They were so kind. Ken opened the door and light flared out of the amber hall over damp steps. Inside there was more light. 'Why don't we wash and have a drink while Janet's preparing supper?' Ken suggested. 'I'll show you your room,' and he took Stephen's suitcase, which he had already fetched from the car. Stephen wondered whether it was right to let Ken carry his suitcase; or did he feel uncomfortable because Ken was white? 'I'll take it.' He reached for the handle. Ken let him take it and picked up another suitcase. He led the way up carpeted stairs, pointed out the bathroom and gestured inside the doorway of a room at the end of the passage, 'This is yours. See you downstairs.' With a quick smile he indicated his confidence that Stephen could manage from this point. He could, in a manner of speaking. He had done it before. He took the smaller of two towels neatly waiting for him at the foot of the bed and the cake of soap, still wrapped, and went to the bathroom. It retained the old-fashioned tub of an old house, but a combed sheepskin on the floor and a shelf over the tub for an ashtray, two detective stories and a small vase of brightly dyed star flowers indicated that it was not a place where Ken and Janet expected austere behaviour.

When he came back to the room they had given him Stephen noted the artefacts of someone else's life. A childhood unimaginably unlike his own surrounded him. Behind the bed hung a drawing of the beach. The sea was a properly undulating blue on whose conventional waves there sailed the black outline of a yacht, innocent of the relatively immense fish whose profile stood mute, motionless and symbolic between it and the yellow and purple sand, where a green scribble suggested grass. In a low bookcase under the window, children's books about shells and birds, adventure stories, Webster's illustrated dictionary, a microscope under a plastic cover, indicated another layer of the American boy's life. The most recent stratum was evidenced near the dressing table where a poster of Humphrey Bogart ignored college pennants and the image of the alien in the mirror.

Stephen sat on the bed. He felt his knees under his palms. He insisted on his own undeniable life, on his own childhood in and out of the dusty location and the dusty mission school, on his skill to be as slick as a tsotsi who wore tight trousers and carried knives. He had been as mocking as a mosquito when he played the penny whistle on street corners, when he demanded a penny, a tickey, a sixpence, baas. He went downstairs for a drink.

Janet was busy in the kitchen separated from the dining area and lounge by a wooden counter. He noticed that she was wearing a string of those grey seeds that white women didn't think smart in South Africa. Here they were favoured by the wives of college professors like Janet and girl students from good homes.

It was fine to sit in the same room as a busy woman preparing food. 'Haven't you got some vegetables to peel?' he offered. In America it was all right to help like a piccanin.

'It's all done, frozen and sliced,' she laughed, 'very American.' She untied her apron and hung it over a rail. 'Come and have a drink.'

How casually legal it seemed to her to offer him a drink. How legal and unremarkable to be alone with a black man. In South Africa when white women offered him drinks, he was wary. Even at mixed parties he felt his safety as sharp as a blade's edge. With Carol Barton he would drink; after dinner, meat and wine, she offered him brandy and liqueur. After slow talk and darkness he would wake to hear his heart slamming, police banging on the door and his brother crying, sick. When the police arrested David Msimang with a white woman and found out that he was a musician, they broke his eardrums, just for fun. After that, Stephen would not visit Carol alone any more and on the phone she said, 'For goodness sake, don't explain. There's nothing to explain. If you don't want to come, don't come. You don't owe me anything. I'm not your white madam.' She never allowed him to tell her about David Msimang.

In New York he went to some mixed parties given by Andrew Mohone. South Africans who had left with the cast of *King Kong*, after Sharpeville, after Mandela, after Sobukwe, after waves of arrests under the sabotage laws, after Vorster, on scholarships, on exit permits, on passports and family money, met each other at mixed parties and felt that the old risk and thrill could be recaptured. They repeated the gestures of defiance that here did not defy and knew again that they were singly brave and free. Some of the whites at Andrew's parties were Americans – young reporters, instructors at Columbia and the Free School, churchmen with missionary acquaintances – a miscellaneous lot who, like the South Africans themselves, of different generations and concerns, seemed to have little in common but a geographically named node of feeling. By two o'clock in the morning the parties had usually divided into Siamese twin parties, one black, one white. In South Africa the mixture would have lasted all night. Mixed parties here missed the police.

Once or twice black separatists came instead of whites. They made remarks to Stephen like, 'I can see you come from Africa. Your face is so proud.' They had never heard his music. The mixed parties were easier. At first, the old South Africans asked him for news and gossip. 'Do you know Diana Zindberg? ... What's she doing now?'

'Didn't she marry an Englishman? I think she married an Oxford don,' someone would supply. Or she was 'on the West Coast now,' or she had remained in South Africa.

A few people knew Carol Barton and asked whether he knew her. 'Yes, I think she's still in Johannesburg.'

'Goli, hey! Good old Goli! Man, I still miss the place. Well Carol was a great gal,' as though she had partly died, 'just a great kid! I wish she'd come here.'

Why? Stephen wondered, why did anyone wish that?

He imagined that in New York there were such parties given by White Russians, Serbians, Spanish anarchists, Palestinian Arabs, Ghanaians and Czechs. All exiles, all dying. When all his oxygen was exhausted he would also relish thin gossip about South Africa and the people of his generation, become a comfortable exile, a cell in the specific tissue of exiles and cosmopolitans who had by now become organically accepted and integral in the American metabolism.

Ken entered from another room. 'There's a letter from Christopher. He says he'll stop by on his way to New York,' he told Janet.

'Good. When'll that be?'

'Any time.'

'Christopher's our son,' she explained to Stephen. 'He's

been summering in the Hudson Bay area. He says there are some interesting algae there. Algae are his thing.' She smiled fondly, indulgently.

The remoteness of these lives he saw in midstream pressed in on Stephen. There was none of his own air left, none of the spacious sunlight, naive and simple, by which he had learned to read the world. Here, existence was compounded into individual complex studies and specialised fields. Each man saw his own topic, noted its intricate interrelationships and structures and guessed at the intricacies known by others. In South Africa he had written music, it seemed to him now, like a child. He had composed as though he could pour sound simply into the heart of another man, a heart unobstructed by perceptions evolved to assimilate incommunicable knowledge. Here his communications were defined. He was a practising composer and an authority on the music of Southern Africa. He had become a curiosity devoted to curiosities, the speaker of an arcane language – composer, consequently, to no ear but his own. The longer he stayed the more arcane his music must become; it must breed into itself to retain the exotic worth that was supposed to give it value. It could not mate again with the sounds of his daily life, now American – that would breed an impurity into his sound, a new idiom into his voice. And then he would lose that now ghostly audience in South Africa who, when they listened to his music, thought that the earth sang and the cicadas chorused together and did not know that their unique earth was quaint veld, their noon remote from others'.

Each of these Americans with his intricate knowledge constituted one cell of this complex society whose function was a life other than Stephen's, whose purpose was something he did not know and could not, without destroying himself, adopt. If he did not adopt its purpose, America would shake him off as an intrusion, a piece of a foreign body, a cell or organ that lived by the principles of some other body born under the Southern Cross.

Something of Stephen's loneliness emanated through to

81

Janet. It prompted her to the courtesy that required her to turn the topic of conversation to her guest's interests rather than her own. She reserved the subject of Christopher and his letter for later, for that conjugal conversation whose even tenor is like the even conversation a man conducts with the sights and texture of his belongings and his people. She would deal with Christopher in a time and a language from which Stephen felt sealed off as if from the air of life. She asked him questions about South Africa while they sipped gin and tonic with wedges of lime – a drink he had never known in South Africa, even at the mixed parties of Houghton and Northcliff and certainly never in the shebeens. At last she came to the question that all these polite, interested Americans asked. 'Will you ever go back?'

'I can't. I got out illegally, without a passport. I'm a refugee.'

'You mean they wouldn't give you a passport. Why on earth not?'

'They've had some bad experiences with the wrong people getting out and making propaganda against the government overseas. We Africans talk too much.'

Ken liked his dryness. 'And have you talked too much here?'

'I've been on a lecture tour.' They laughed.

'Your topic's not very incendiary,' Ken pursued.

'No,' Stephen agreed, 'but I do some damage in ordinary conversations like this. And then, most Afrikaners, especially those who deal with us, are ignorant. They're afraid of people like me because I'm not a simple kaffir.'

'How did you get out?' Janet wanted to know.

'Oh, there's a sort of underground railroad and a refugee centre in Dar es Salaam.'

'Will you go back there?'

'I don't know what will happen to me.' After he had spoken he heard the passive helplessness he had revealed.

Ken heard it too. 'Why do you want to go back to South

Africa?'

'I don't.' But Ken ignored this reply. His waiting silence was as heavily palpable as a waking sensation that presses into sleep and breaks its integuments. And like a sleeper who begins to talk before he has quite shaken off sleep and talks as truthfully as in a dream, Stephen continued, 'I can't work here. I say to myself that tomorrow, or next week I'll be able to, but I can't. I compose, but it's all false. I can't bear to listen to it. I don't think I can write outside South Africa.'

'Then you must go back.' Ken spoke the imperative that Stephen feared. He brought into it the auditory reality of an American accent with a resolute inflection that Stephen would never have invented in his own mind, the instruction that, like the ground bass of a passacaglia, had sounded without interruption in Stephen's feelings for weeks. Stephen repeated, 'I can't.' Ken and Janet said nothing. 'If I go back I'll be in prison within a year – not a nice comfortable prison where people can write their memoirs. I'll be in a South African jail where people get beaten up and tortured and go mad. I've been in prison. A pass offender gets kicked around. Sometimes he's sent to work on potato farms where he wears a potato sack, winter and summer. Sometimes he's beaten for not working hard enough. They knocked the eardrums out of a friend of mine because he was a musician. Some people get beaten to death. In the jail they put ten men in one cell and give you one bucket that gets full long before morning. There are no beds. You sleep on the floor, as far away from the bucket as you can. And I'm not a pass offender. I can't expect such good treatment. I'm not likely to write much music there.'

'Then you must learn how to write here.'

'How? How can I learn anything like that?' Stephen breathed hard on his rage. These Americans thought they could solve everything. They had no respect for boulder weight, for things too heavy for a man to lift.

'I don't know. I guess it's easier to say than to do. Just give yourself time to hear what this country sounds like. You probably just need time.'

'Yes,' seconded Janet, 'after all, you haven't been here very long.'

Their unsuffering sympathy fed Stephen's rage. 'I want to write in my own language. In South Africa that isn't allowed. An African has to speak English or Afrikaans, a composer has to learn the sonata form and the instruments of the European orchestra. They are what he must write for. There's an instrument we have in Lesotho – a bow and a string and a gourd for resonance. It plays two notes. The person who plays it can hardly hear it himself, it's like a whisper, like a lover. In a world that's so quiet, there's room for an instrument like that. There are nothing but mountains and one bad road. It keeps the cars out. The people are too poor for radios. All they can afford is the sound of a gourd, like the earth, like the sunlight, like being poor, like being black. You can't hear it in Johannesburg – even the Africans are too rich there, or their being poor is a cramping vice. That bow and gourd says what I want but where could I play something like that in America? No one would hear it. Everything's so loud here, the cars, the radios, the fire trucks, planes. I can't hear anything human, alive. Even if anyone could hear my bow and gourd, what would they make of it? Two simple notes over and over, so monotonous. Not at all … psychedelic.' He smiled at this disparaged word of praise, as if to overcome squeamishness at having used it. 'I sound angry, but I'm not angry at Americans for being what they are. That's what they are. It's incurable. Like being an African. But it's at the other end of the world and I can't make myself learn what to be again, like a baby. I don't start from nothing. I'm a man already.'

Ken and Janet were embarrassed at this outburst. Their habitual withdrawal from involvement with strangers, especially strangers whose insoluble problems could grieve and fester in those whose pity held no power to remedy; an accepted training rooted in the manners of ancestors who knew that what is delicate must be protected (sometimes

84

by deliberate ignorance), who would not mention rape, drunkenness or money in front of women; and a traditional stoicism that would not weep but fastened troubles to the self like a brace to keep men upright – all made them withdraw from Stephen's demand.

Ken spoke first. 'I hope you'll take advantage of the musical opportunities in these parts. There'll be some interesting concerts in New York this fall and other things too. I've got a notice from Hunter College. I'll look for it after supper. You will be in New York, won't you?'

'Yes.' Stephen didn't tell him that he received his own notices, invitations, introductions.

'And I've got programmes for Lincoln Centre. I can often get complimentary tickets ...' Stephen saw how the problems of the boy Christopher must have been kindly finessed away until he grew up into, not quite a man – for he was allowed no human, intractable troubles, only those his society could digest – but an expert on algae.

Christopher came home that night. Stephen heard him arrive and the noise of welcome and explanation that a guest was sleeping in his room. 'Then you must go back,' Ken had said in an American voice with an unforeseen inflection. 'Then you must go back.' The initial staccatos of greeting sank into long blurred sentences and Stephen tried to fuse the reawakened rhythm of family discourse in his ear with the theme that had struggled forward during the drive through the mist, the song of playing with his brother in the morning. But he could not achieve the fusion and fell asleep again.

He met Christopher at the breakfast table. Ken introduced him to the bony youth. 'Steve's giving a paper on African music at Fenmore Hall this afternoon and going to New York tomorrow.'

'I think I'm in your room,' Stephen said tentatively.

'I'm only camping here,' Christopher assured him. 'I'm going on to New York myself.'

'Perhaps Chris can give you a ride down,' Ken suggested,

'unless you'd rather fly ...' During the meal Christopher accompanied firm gestures that reached for butter or toast on the well-known table with stories about his summer. He talked about what his expedition had accomplished. 'We collected hundreds of specimens that are probably new. How'd you like an alga named after you, mother?'

'I'd have to see it first,' she joked.

'I've got slides. Are you free tonight? Can we look at them?'

Janet drew him back to arrangements for the day. 'I've been waiting all summer for you to help your father clear out the cellar.'

'That'll be great,' Christopher assented before Ken could protest.

Stephen wondered whether his help would be welcome or obtrusive. No, he'd work on the location theme, even though nothing would come of it.

While he was sitting at the desk the boy Christopher must have used, Stephen saw them walking through the grounds. Sometimes they stopped to examine a change or permanence. The two men walking among trees, their heads flickering among bright foliage, who lived in that world inhabited by squirrels and jays that he had sometimes read about in northern storybooks, were indeed men, not plastic surrogates produced by a society that forbade suffering and wanted only organs of perception, units of intelligence, consumers. These two were men, father and son, archetypal and as mythical to Stephen as woods that harboured plentiful creatures, as strange as snows and blueberries and maples. Such familial affluence was unknown to him. His father had been one of the men who lived with his mother for a few years and then disappeared into the jails, into the labyrinth of townships around Johannesburg, or into the reserves. A series of men had played with him and the other children, in idle friendliness. Nostalgic for a life some of them had never known, they assessed him as a candidate for initiation and told him stories to inspire warlike heroism, sagas of Zulu impis led by Shaka and Dingane. But often they were irritable. The children seemed always underfoot, Sarah wanted more money to buy them clothes and Stephen was always wasting candles at night when a man wanted darkness and Sarah's hard breathing.

Stephen and his brother knew the world directly, not by the mediation of fathers. There were not discrete worlds, one filled with talking animals and fairies for children, another with money and taxes and politics for adults. It was all one world. Grown men as frightened as children of policemen who, as irresistible as witchcraft, might bang on the door in the middle of the night to ask for a pass, or dig up the floor to look for skokiaan. It was all one world. In an acid dawn as pink as millions of pounds, neighbours climbed on to bicycles and rode into the city; on the way to the long queue at the bus stop they stepped on the hoar that clung to wisps of dry grass and paper; some who had slept with braziers in closed rooms breathed the warm air too long and did not wake up in time for life. Nothing was omitted except this other world, inconceivable – the house set among wild trees and lavish grass, this world that the father and the son were revisiting and had never altogether left and this kind of humanity that grew among them. Stephen could never revisit his childhood. Now he must live in a world that his childhood had never guessed existed.

That night Christopher showed them slides of his expedition to the Hudson Bay. Beyond sight or sound of any other human life small villages grasped tight in dour friendliness. Granite boulders grew lichens like birthmarks and in their brief summer thronged with silky flowers that looked like Karoo vygies. Pane after pane of light offered visions that Stephen could understand – emptiness, light, virginity – where he had expected only more that was alien, unassimilable. In a landscape like this one could play an instrument with two notes. But he was afraid to think of what he saw. Would he go to the Hudson Bay to try another kind of exile?

Being driven to New York, he asked about the expedition. 'Didn't you feel lonely?'

'No. There were seven of us on the ship and we got to know some of the village people quite well. Strangers are very welcome. And it's not as if there aren't any phones. I called my girl in New York twice a week. It's not half as bad as it'll be next year when we go to Lake Baikal, if we can arrange it. We might go to Antarctica instead. What's Cape Town like? They say it's beautiful.'

'I've never been there. The government tries to keep us Africans out of Cape Town.'

'Oh, I thought most of the population was Negro.'

'In Cape Town there are a lot of people of mixed blood. They're called coloureds and are treated differently from us. Every shade of whiteness deserves a special degree of privilege.'

'You must be really glad to be out of it.'

'I am. Don't you ever get homesick when you go to these strange places?'

'I guess I've never been away long enough. It's no problem really. I could come back any time.'

They seemed to have come to a dead end. 'Do you ever get homesick?'

'Sometimes.'

'I guess people get homesick for the strangest things. One of our research team comes from Anatolia. He longs for sheep's eyes. Look for that in a supermarket!' Christopher laughed.

Stephen was silent.

'Mind if I turn on the radio?'

'Go ahead.' Sometimes they let the clamour of baroque music substitute for conversation. Sometimes they spoke through it.

'Why did you come to the States? To get out of South Africa?'

'Partly. People always told me I should go overseas to finish my education. They said my composing needed to be finished.' He smiled at the private irony.

'But your family's still there?'

'My mother.'

'Have you got brothers, or sisters?'

'Most of them died as babies. One brother grew up with me, but he died when I was in high school.'

'Your mother must miss you.'

'I don't know. I wrote, but didn't get an answer. And I asked someone I knew to look for her, but I haven't heard from him either.'

'Why don't you phone?'

'We haven't got phones. In the locations, only white officials have phones.'

Vivaldi gave way to Cimarosa by way of a commercial. How must it be to live in Christopher's world, where there was no sensual space, distance, silence, darkness? Stephen remembered reading that a night of darkness had come upon New York like a disaster. How must it be to live like that, deprived of any sense of the given light and the given earth's autonomous being? How would it be to live in America and lose all stillness, loneliness, man-otherness, to live in a world where the whisper of a string in a gourd could never be heard, imagined? Christopher could hardly be five years younger than himself, but Stephen felt old, old-fashioned, old as the chameleon who first allowed the news of death to be brought into the world, old as death, incomprehensible to Christopher. Christopher lived in the new world. Was there any music Stephen could write for him? What was there in Christopher's life he could understand?

'What does your girl do?' Christopher answered in sentences whose individual words were intelligible. It was the syntax, the meaning, that fled. When they came to New York, the road lost all connection with the shape or look of the land. It dived, swung, curved, twisted back on itself, over other roads and under them. Buildings crowded nearer and nearer as in a kinetic hallucination of suffocation, claustrophobia and spacelessness. The commercials between symphonies gave way to a long newscast about Vietnam, New York, Turkey, Israel, Lindsay, Rockefeller and people whose roles and names Stephen could not identify. As usual there was nothing about South Africa. From here it seemed an almost non-existent country. The few Americans who had heard of it refracted it, distorted it, saw it as an image of their own problems. If they cared at all, it was not for a country that had an independent existence, it was for a symbol of their own conflicts. The little of South Africa that survived had been absorbed into the bloodstream of another system. If he were to survive, he must learn who all these people were, must learn to become interested in them, must tutor himself in this system, this Vietnam, CORE, LSD, FBI, CIA, UCLA, this system of symbols and personalities in whom he had no interest. He must give up his self and must become a self who could subsist in this vast artefact that offered hardly a blade of grass he could recognise from his own life.

They drove through Harlem. The stores advertised foods he had never eaten. Children played games with rules and passwords he had never known. He had been here, in a black world as foreign as the white, where people didn't understand his English and stared at his strangeness, this black Harlem whose language was as opaque as Spanish Harlem's, as whiteness, as the intelligent assurance of a youth like Christopher.

They left Central Park behind them and the big stores and came to Stephen's hotel. When Andrew Mohone and Ester Matimba had come to meet him at the airport and offered to help him find accommodation, they had been careful not to take him to Harlem. Andrew wore a loose, flowered costume he had never worn in South Africa. He carried an airmail edition of the London *Times* under his arm. Later he explained that many had to masquerade to get a respect they could not otherwise achieve.

'Don't you feel funny to be an African pretending to be an African so that Americans will recognise you as the kind of

African they recognise?'

'What sort of game is that, man? You've got to do it. Believe me, there are lots of tricks to learn.'

Ester wore the expensive clothes of a performer offstage. Her bearing neither expected nor brooked contempt. In their aura, Stephen had been able to rent a room out of Harlem.

When Christopher left him, with vaguely friendly American remarks about being glad to meet him, Stephen wondered whether to phone Ester. Or should he wait until this sombre mood lightened? He felt lethargic, almost inanimate. He opened the window of his room. It gave on to a dark airshaft. In a corner a heap of crates and cartons rotted and waited for someone to dispose of them. Lights from other rooms in the hotel glowed anonymously. A pale sky sagged against the building's dark bulk. The city's flaccid roar sank towards the rotting corners of the airshaft. Its hoarse wheeze breathed into his face. The outside air, like the air in his room and in the passages of the hotel, had been used so often that an impalpable grime hung in it, like wear in the face of an old prostitute. Any man who took comfort in its warmth breathed dying, as if he slept in a closed room where a brazier slept with him.

He took out his notes for the theme of the game under the blanket. The whole affair seemed pitifully thin and worthless, but he tried to work on it. Every new idea seemed banal, false, either involuntarily reminiscent of a commercial, or masquerading like Andrew as an Africa he had never experienced, unnaturally bright and vigorous. Ai! the winter mornings had been cold, the air outside fierce, the water from the tap outside blinding. He and his brother in torn vests hid from the windy sun. Did Andrew tell stories about living in a jungle? Did he wear a different country in his memory and forget the location winters and the cracked European jackets of his native past? Stephen juggled the thin souvenir of those winters he dared not forget, devised harmonies and variations and eventually put the sheets away. He phoned Ester.

'Stephen! It's good to hear you, man. How are you?'

'Okay. How're you?'

'I'm giving a party. Come.'

'When? Now?'

'Yes now. I've got two people from Columbia who've heard your music and want to meet you. Have you done anything new?'

'No.'

'Well, they like what they heard.'

'Okay.'

'Are you all right, Stephen?'

'Yes. Why not?'

'I must be imagining. Too long since I've seen you. I'd like to see you myself, not just hand you over to those people from Columbia.'

'Drop the party and come with me.'

'I can't. TV people and journalists are here too. I want you to meet them, Stephen.'

'I've just come back. I'm tired. Some other time.'

'Stephen, you sound awfully depressed.'

'Goodbye, Ester.' He was surprised to find Ester giving a party. Parties were one of Andrew Mohone's tricks, a habit of the exile community. Ester was surely not one of these. She did not make a special, trivial virtue of being South African and different. She met New York on its own terms. She worked. She did not talk about how much she had suffered at home, how rare and sensational her escape had been. She worked. Ken worked. Christopher worked. That was how they survived. But he could not work. He had lost a gear. He had become junk. He was like the rest of the South African clique. He might as well not despise their party.

He showered and changed. He looked in the mirror cynically. What's the matter, man. He could still live. He walked through the airless corridor into the streets. Stores offered enticements to millions of people with incomprehensible needs. Windows showed copper pots and wooden bowls, dyed hammocks, coloured glass spheres, ceramic fungus, leather waistcoats, books about Zen, posters and records of Indian ragas. At best his music would cling to this sea ledge with other monstrous forms, curiosities, fads, psychedelia and would be heard by these bedecked hermaphrodites whose fantastic forms pressed past him with insinuations of contempt, either at his clothes or blackness. This transient hallucination was yet another world, another language. He was lost in an infinity of variations, unconceived possibilities. They all extinguished him. All pressed suffocation. He was nothing. South Africa was nothing. What he had taken as the world omitted a world, an infinity of worlds.

He mounted a bus and rode it passively until the driver told him that he'd have to pay another fare – the bus had completed its route. He climbed off and walked among shabby and indefinite stores. Some screaming children ran in front of him and were rebuked by a screaming woman whose words he could not interpret. He stopped to stare at a window that displayed a French Provincial dining room and bar. Then he walked on again. A man who might have been drunk leaned toward him and asked the time, brother, but he didn't answer and the man said, 'Fuck you, nigger.' He didn't answer that either. He was near another incessant highway. It roared without rhythm. He came to an overpass. He stopped to stare at the rapid cars, the inhuman speed, the implacable concrete legs of another overpass, the din of America. There was only one way. He would accept America. He would throw himself into it, into the breathless air, the machine light. He tightened his hand on the railing and pulled up. The freeway rushed and fled beneath him. He leapt into it.

Good Friday

Ruth rolls her overnight bag on the pavement, slowing and swerving for cracks and heaves in concrete and bricks, roots, flowerbeds round city trees, plastic planters and construction dumpsters. At the light, she waits, looking at the mobile sculpture over the T station. Its red sails dip and rise with the wind, blowing where it wills.

Her father will not feel breeze again. Soon he will not see light.

Red changes to green, the stream of traffic holds back and she crosses to the subway station. Escalators take her deep underground to the sculpture of lost gloves swept into a corner heap. Stray gloves lie stranded on the platform, spread-eagled, crumpled finger over finger. So many. Who would have thought loss had undone so many.

Some citizens complain that the sculpture of lost gloves evokes the Holocaust. That slaughter was not a Holocaust. No one offered the human sacrifice to God. Not Jews, not Christians. The victims, mostly, did not offer themselves.

Some did offer themselves. Edith Stein, her canonisation controversial. Maximilian Kolbe, another contentious saint, an anti-Semite who saved Jews. Always contradiction at the Sign of Contradiction. Dietrich Bonhoeffer. Not Catholic and so not canonised. There must have been others too, lost to history but written in the Book of Life.

As, surely, her father will be. But who can read the heart of the Lord who summons all to judgment.

She waits on the subway platform deeper than graves underground, among the bronzed gloves that fill this station with loss, death and slaughter trains. Journeys of the soul. A staring engine roars from the tunnel like a monster with red eyes, the station's concrete vault echoes its fanfare of hell, the beast rushes head first towards her, whines and stops. She lifts her bag and steps into its metal belly.

At the train station in Connecticut she takes a taxi to her parents' house, takes off her crucifix and puts it in her purse. Her brother's car is parked in the street and when she rings the bell her mother comes to the door and embraces her, leaving her brother Bernie at the dining room table with his wife and a lanky man who must be her father's cousin. Prowling the Net for genealogies, Bernie discovered him, the only one of her father's cohort to survive Hitler. The cousins have never met and now Saul has come from Paris to see her father before it is too late.

'Darling, let me introduce you,' her mother leads her towards the table where she sees tea served in the Russian manner, in glasses, with lemon, jam and cubes of sugar. She shakes hands with this fine-boned man who has flax-blue eyes like her own, wheels her bag into her childhood room, washes and joins them. Her mother, motioning her to the chair on her right, urges Saul to continue, 'I love these Yiddishe meises.'

He obliges in Yiddish: Yankel, a poor Jew in the shtetl, dreamed he would find a golden treasure under the Charles Bridge in Prague. Taking a shovel and food for the journey, he travelled to Prague, found the bridge and started digging. A guard asked, 'What are you doing?' 'I dreamed I would find a treasure under the Charles Bridge in Prague.' Saul shows how the guard clapped a hand to his forehead, 'Strange! I dreamed that at this bridge I would meet a man who left a treasure in his own backyard to come here.' Yankel picked up his shovel and pack, went home and dug in his own backyard. Under the plum tree, he found a pot of gold.

Bernie's wife applauds with plump hands and they all join her. Saul has evoked memories that bind them all to the people of the lost shtetl and their descendants scattered to the ends of the earth. The life that connects them is made by stories like this. Like the life of the Church, made one by the Word.

Ruth's mother offers Saul poppyseed cake. 'Just a crumb,' he takes a slice from the gold rimmed plate and the others follow suit though Bernie's wife gives him a warning glance. Ruth abstains. It is a fast day in Lent. Soon, Saul tells another story.

A community of poor Jews lived under the protection of a lord who used to extort whatever money they had to pay for – what else? – his wars and Crusades. One day, not satisfied, he said he would put the Jews to death. They begged. They pleaded. The lord said, No.

We are lost, the Jews told each other. Then one said, 'I have an idea. Let me talk with the lord.' Next morning, he went to the castle, 'Lord, if you let us live, I will teach your dog to speak Hebrew.' 'Hebrew! He can't speak at all.' 'I tell you, give us time and your dog will speak Hebrew. All the other lords will envy you.' 'How much time?' Saul strokes an imaginary beard, 'Let me see.' A phantom shtetl speaks in his sing-song, 'For a man to speak, takes two, three years. But a man,' weighing considerations, 'a man is more intelligent than a dog. Let us say …' stroking the phantom beard, 'let's say three years.' The price clear, his voice grows firm, 'Three years and your dog will speak Hebrew.' So the lord agreed to spare the Jews for three years.

Saul's voice modulates to the Jew telling the community. No fake wisdom now. Of course they are not satisfied. 'Woe! You will teach his dog to speak Hebrew! How will you do that? When he sees you have cheated him, he will kill us all.' 'Listen,' Saul's hands open in a display of honesty as old as the rocking of prayer and, seated at the table thick with cups and cakes, they all become members of that shtetl – her mother, cheeks swollen with grieving, Bernie balding and heavy, his jewelled wife heavy herself and Ruth, the youngest, the studious one. If she had not been born female, she would have seemed destined for the yeshiva. Here in America, she is the one who reads. She reads goyish books and has goyish friends and has slipped out of her family's world. And Saul?

He appears comfortable in the shtetl he evokes. 'Three years is a long time. Who knows what will happen? In three years, the dog may die.' He stops. 'The lord may die.'

It seems he has finished. Ruth cannot resist adding the ending a colleague once told her about the horse of the Emperor Diocletian learning Latin, 'The dog may speak Hebrew.'

Everyone laughs.

As Jews tell stories, the Jews are always poor. As gentiles tell stories, the Jews are always rich.

'My father loved these Yiddishe meises,' her mother says. 'But the real storyteller was Mottel, your uncle.'

'Ah, Mottel, on my father's side.' The conversation moves to who bore whom and who married whom. Ruth clears the tea things, leaving the intrusive sweeping of crumbs for later. She finds this genealogical talk as heavy as the begats in Deuteronomy and Numbers. She fills her mother's dishwasher. She will not accept physical birth as her sole identity. That was Hitler's idea. She is other than they would imagine. To Jews, an apostate. To gentiles, a Jew. To each an emblem of grudges.

When she comes back to the table, her mother nods thanks. Bernie is talking about what he has been finding on the Net, a lacework of marriages, children and deaths beyond imagining.

When silence follows Bernie's account, Ruth asks Saul, 'How long are you staying?'

'I must be back in Paris for the seder.'

The talk moves to photographs. Over the albums, her mother tells Saul names and he searches images of people he did not know for features that persist, like the shtetl in their stories, Bernie's fleshy nose from a dead uncle, her own cast of face and eyes from a grandmother. He tells Ruth she resembles his daughter, 'She's also a scholar. You teach art?' 'Art history. I have no skill myself.' 'Modest like her too.' Ruth smiles and turns to another page of pictures. Her mother knows only fragments of biographies. Bernie supplements with his research, but the family history seems a tatter of catastrophes and migrations.

In the seder at Bernie's house four years ago, they poured out the ritual drops of wine for the plagues, Blood, Frogs, Lice, Flies, Pests, Boils, Hail, Locusts, Darkness, First Born and Bernie added Spain, Stalin, Hitler. A theological muddle, but part of the bitter story her family holds to its heart.

Passover is a wary time. The Jews recall Christian stories, that Jews kill Christian children to make matzoh with their blood and real blood issuing from such stories. Christians read the Passion in which 'the Jews' hunt Christ down, perjure themselves at His trial, condemn him and refuse His life. When Jews tell the story, the Christians kill Jews. When Christians tell it, the Jews kill Christ.

Her father did not spill those last drops of wine at Bernie's seder. He would not participate in grudges and taught her, 'You can be born anything, come from anywhere, pray any way and be an American. That is why we are a great country.' If they had time, she would tell him about her pleasure in a parish whose members come from the ends of the earth. They will not have time.

Bernie drives them to the hospital, his wife, in the front seat, commenting. At the hospital, Ruth's father smiles at his cousin and Saul tells anecdotes. Her mother and Bernie, her trusted son, bowing his head with its black yarmulke, talk in the corridor with the medical staff and his wife arranges Saul's flowers. Ruth says little, holding her father's hand. From time to time, he slips her a glance. They don't need much.

Her mother and Bernie return and Bernie says, 'So, they want you here another few days.' Her father presses Ruth's hand.

Back at her parents' home, Ruth joins her mother in the kitchen. 'I'll do dinner. Spend time with Saul, Mother. I want to be alone.'

'He looks that bad to you?'

'And to you?'

'I see him every day,' a crack in her voice.

Ruth kisses her, 'Go to your guests.'

In the familiar kitchen of her childhood, she puts the chicken in the oven. He wants cremation. Perhaps his way to join the others who flew up as fumes and grit. She finds potatoes and peels them. Earth to earth. While the spirit returns to God who gave it. She checks the freezer for beans, her mother's vegetable of choice for high occasions.

Saul comes into the kitchen with French treats. Wine. Cheese. Paté. 'I brought some ham, from Parma. It's at the hotel. I can bring it tomorrow.'

'A few years ago we'd have loved it, but my mother's keeping a kosher house now.'

He looks round her mother's kitchen, not a cook's domain. The counters, cabinets, pots and range date to Ruth's grade school days and she recalls the kitchen always cluttered, as now, with grocery boxes, calendar, telephone, coupons. Saul sees the frozen beans and smiles at her, complicit.

Perhaps he assumes they share a civilised secularity where Jews eat ham without compunction. The world of her college and graduate studies, books and travels. A world where people hold memories they do not share, where differences can unite.

She hands the can of forbidden paté back to him. Would his dietary tolerance extend to accepting her?

At the table her mother is lighting the Sabbath candles, '*Baruch ata Adonai, melech ha alom …*' Ruth has never heard these words in this home. Superstition, her father would say. She feels betrayed on his behalf. Her betrayal is more shocking than theirs.

Saul notices that she eats no meat. 'I'm a vegetarian,' she confesses. She will not eat his paté or ham, but she accepts the French wine he pours, in spite of Lent.

When she was twelve, after a game of chess permitted during the Days of Awe, she asked her grandfather Mottel why he did not attend synagogue. 'You're almost a woman now, let me tell you. My father used to pray in the synagogue every day, and the people in the shtetl honoured him for it. Before Shabbat, he used to wear the Holy Day clothes when the shops were still open. The Jews, seeing him, would close immediately their shops and ran quickly to their houses to prepare themselves for the Holy Day. He used to speak only when strictly necessary on Shabat and only Hebrew. He gave his life to Torah.

'My mother was also pious, a good woman. I was pious, studying to be a rabbi.

'The War came, World War One. The Russians were afraid we wouldn't be loyal. They knew, the anti-Semites, what they had done to us and thought we would side with the Germans. Why not? All the Jews in the Pale were forced to move away from the war front. What could we do? We loaded our carts and walked. First rain, then snow. My parents got pneumonia. First my father died, then my mother, three days later. God allows this?'

Ruth recalls how he looked at her to see whether his granddaughter understood his argument. Teaching her, like a rabbi teaching a barmitzvah boy.

Seeing that she understood, he told more. 'At my mother's funeral, snow everywhere, I could not see the other side of her grave. After the prayers I wandered away where no one could see my tears. When I came to myself I called. No answer. I prayed. No answer. I couldn't find my own footprints in the snow. I couldn't tell where I was going. Snow-blind, I walked and prayed, walked and prayed. I walked till I fell down and still I prayed.

'When the storm was over, some Jews found me wandering like a wild beast and put me on their cart. I didn't know who I was. It was weeks before I knew my name.

'That was the last time I prayed. There is no God. And if there is and he permits things like pogroms and Hitler, I don't want to know.'

She nodded to show that she followed his argument, his

quarrel with God.

When Ruth wanted to go to school on Yom Kippur, her mother said, 'It doesn't matter if you believe in God. You must stay home for the Jewish people.'

That night, when the children were supposed to be asleep, her mother scolded Mottel, 'What are you teaching your grandchildren? God has nothing to do with it. Jews must stick together. If not, where will we be?'

Her father defended his father, 'We'd be like other people. Superstition would disappear but we would remain.'

'Tell that to Hitler. A Jew is a Jew.'

'The world is full of French Jews and Polish Jews, even Indian Jews. Why do you think I have blue eyes? We're in America, we don't have to copy Hitler.'

Unaware of Ruth, awake, in the small bedroom near the kitchen, listening.

Waiting for Bernie and his wife to arrive after the Sabbath service, Ruth gives Saul and her mother café au lait. 'You've been to France?' he asks.

'Eight years ago. Researching my dissertation on Matisse.' At his chapel in Vence, she prayed for the first time. In the room stripped of all but light and reflection she saw prayer filling the space and asked to be filled with light.

'A great artist ... You speak French?'

'A little ... Have you always lived in Paris?'

'I was born there ... My parents emigrated from Lithuania. They went to Prague, Budapest, Berlin – no work anywhere. In Paris they found something, not much, but enough. We were living in one room when I was born.'

'During the Occupation?' Ruth asks.

'My father said I was conceived in peace and born in war. My mother was taken in 42.'

'To Auschwitz,' her mother adds and they pause in silence. As when the lector reading the Passion comes to, 'It is finished' and Jesus dies.

'So you were left with your father,' Ruth's mother says.

'He was in hiding himself. He sent me to Normandy where they were keeping Jewish children.' He makes a grimace, 'It was a whole programme. They wanted Jewish children to baptise and they got some. The Archbishop of Paris was born a Jew. The French are dirty anti-Semites.'

Ruth says, 'They saved you.'

Her mother deflects conflict, 'And after the War?'

'I lived in a Jewish orphanage. It was wonderful. We were like brothers.'

Ruth collects breakfast clutter, pondering.

On her walk from Mass early this morning, she passed a runner stretching one foot out and leaning the other shoulder against a wall, ear to brick, as though listening. She wanted to ask, What does it say? but held her peace.

Will she ever tell them? Not while her father is dying.

In the living room her mother is telling Saul about her family, immigrants in the 1890s. Soon Bernie and his wife come and her mother sends Ruth to tell the goy next door who has offered to drive them to the hospital.

While doctors work in her father's room, they wait in the lounge, a corner room with a view of glistening buildings. The talk that covers their anxiety moves to scandals. Saul tells about French museum curators, 'They are all homosexuals,' who receive antiques and paintings and keep them as their own. An aide comes to suggest the cafeteria for lunch and Bernie herds them to the elevators.

In the cafeteria Saul catches her eye and smiles in spite of her soy burger. He orders a real hamburger and fries. Her mother also avoids meat. Not kosher.

Over Diet Cokes talk about the sins of others focuses on the Catholic Church, its homosexual and paedophile priests, sexist injustices, persecution of the Jews and treacherous motives in canonising Edith Stein. Saul tells about a procession of flagellants he saw in Spain, 'Thank God, no one knew I was

Jewish. It could have been like the Inquisition.'

Centuries of hatred crush Ruth. 'I don't know about Spain, but in America Catholics have given up anti-Semitism.'

'It's in their Bible. It says the Jews killed Christ.'

Soon she will hear the story read aloud. Tomorrow is Palm Sunday. But she says, 'Pope John XXIII stopped that accusation.'

'Believe me, I know Catholics. We live with anti-Semitism on every side. Believe me.'

She does.

Her mother sits at the side of a grey skeleton with blue eyes, everyone else, muted, near the foot of the bed. 'When you're better, we'll visit Saul in Paris,' Bernie says.

Her father's eyes meet Ruth's and she puts a hand on the bump that means a foot. Why pretend? She longs for truth. Though not the whole truth.

Bernie continues, 'Or, next year, you'll bring your family. No need for hotels, we've got a guest suite and have visitors all the time.'

Her father is looking at her. She is his child as Bernie is her mother's. They know each other and, when all is made open that is now hidden, he will understand.

The nurse dismisses them. Bernie and his wife set off for their home and the others stroll in the park where Ruth's father taught her baseball.

Ruth folds her blue scarf round her neck and falls behind. The sky is grey and the air sharp, but soon tender leaves, strong as fire, will break their sheaths and fill the sky with signs of resurrection. What about her father? He lived ardent for justice. The women who worked in his shoe-store wept when he sold it. They will come to his funeral and sit shiva with the family and then, year by year, forget him. Then they will die themselves. So it has been for thousands of years. Is everyone in the eye of God? Handmade, in this universe with all its galaxies? Each unique thumbprint, soul? If God sees it all why, all-seeing God of power and glory, do you destroy your own work? Why must my father die?

The evening meal, without paté or ham, passes with no talk about Catholics and Jews, but when she is lying in her childhood bed, she leans against a wall, recalls the runner this morning and hears groaning, heavy as bricks. Her grandfather Mottel takes her by the hand through the streets of the shtetl where the houses are shuttered, windows boarded up, even the window with broken glass on the corner by the market where he threw a ball when he was six. Mongrel dogs are sniffing in vacant lots strewn with bottles, scraps of paper and rusting cans. At the cemetery, graves are smashed open, Hebrew letters split hither and thither, bones and shoes tossed about and spattered with mud. A voice wails, 'Why have you forsaken us?' Mottel shields her, an arm round her shoulders. She cannot understand what he is saying in a voice like wind submerged in the hissing and wailing. He turns from her and the clamour of vituperation fades as he walks the vandalised rows toward distant graves. She cannot distinguish him, grey in grey.

In a moment when the others are talking to the doctor, her father takes her hand in his and says, 'That nurse did not endear herself to me. She said what I hear in my chest is my death rattle ... Ruth, darling, please forgive any harm I have done you.'

She kisses his face, grey as Mottel's, 'Forgive me.' She does not name the thing he would forgive.

The others come in, see that something forbidden has happened and look at her with disapproval.

At the lift, where she stands behind the others, Bernie falls back beside her and asks, 'What were you saying in there?'

'He was telling me how he's feeling.'

'What did he say?'

She knows he is angry to find her at her old younger-sister

game, holding something back, giving answers true only to the letter.

The lift arrives and when they come out at the lobby, Saul hugs her, 'Come visit us in Paris.'

She weeps through the ride home and other passengers leave her alone.

At the familiar church door the stockbroker who usually collects the offerings hands her a palm frond. She accepts and wheels her bag to a back pew.

She has been expecting 'the Jews' in the Passion but what catches her is Peter. Jesus warns that Peter will deny Him, Peter protests, never, even if I die with you. Jesus says, Three times before the cock crows twice. When He is arrested, Peter follows and remains in the courtyard. The night is cold and Peter warms himself at a fire. Three times people say, Surely you are one of them, Peter curses and swears, I know not this man. The cock crows. Peter weeps.

She does not take communion. How dare she?

At the church door, other faithful greet her – a Spanish student, a man from Nigeria, the widow of a Chinese professor. An Irish neighbour, seeing her bag, offers a ride home, 'How is your father?' This woman once asked Ruth to coach tutors working in the inner city. 'I'm pressed for time,' she refused. When they part, the woman opens the boot and hands her the frond and her bag, 'I'll pray for your father.'

Ruth takes the palm to her study, puts it over a photograph of the chapel at Vence, goes to her books and finds Ezekiel. He said the spirit of the Lord set him in a valley full of bones, very dry and asked, Can these bones live? He heard the Lord God say, Prophesy, and when he did there was a noise and a shaking and the bones came together, bone to his bone. The sinews came upon them and the skin covered them, but there was no breath in them. A scene for a horror movie. And the Lord God said, O my people, I will open your graves and bring you into the land of Israel and shall put my spirit in you and

105

you shall live.

What state of mind stands behind Ezekiel's account? Centuries of conventions clot the vision. If her faith has any substance, her father and grandfather Mottel and all those in the shtetl, in some way beyond anything she can imagine, will live.

'I'll pray for your father,' her Irish neighbour said. Taking him for one of her own.

Through her window, she sees lights in a remodelled house. When she moved into this neighbourhood it was a backwater by the drained swamp, a place for the dump, the almshouses, the orphanage, the blacks, the famished Irish, the lost French Canadians. Few such neighbours are left. The tumbledown houses sided with asphalt shingle and patched with tarpaper have given way to new windows and porches. Gardens hold roses where dandelions flourished only a year ago. Few students live here now. Who imagined, ten years ago, that millionaires would be commonplace?

Experience is full of the unimaginable that happens. A man like her father sees a woman on the subway and feels his whole life has changed, he must get off at her stop, he must meet her. They marry and Bernie and Ruth are born. His whole life has changed. Ruth herself, educated to scepticism and the civil secularity Saul assumes, has accepted baptism into a faith known for oppression and finds life in it, grace unheard of in her childhood's stories about Christians. And now her mother practises rituals abandoned during her marriage. Yes, she believes Ezekiel's promise, you shall live.

Monday, he seems stronger, her mother says. He sounds like his old self when she calls. But on Tuesday, seeing her principal, Ruth confirms that she will soon want time away though exams are coming up next week.

'We'll manage.'

Her message light is blinking. Saul, from the airport. 'Remember, we have Matisse paintings in Paris.'

Wednesday is her last chance to confess and the Holy Week pews are crowded with sinners watching for the moment to go towards the booth and the promise of pardon. It must be bizarrely uncomfortable for the man on the other side who hears the pettiness and neuroses, nastiness, misunderstanding, malice. How do they stand it, priests, shrinks, lawyers, breathing the bad breath, body odour and stench of sin? Is this really God's design? It seems of a piece with the whole foolish business where the will of God works through people who run out of wine at a wedding, gather in crowds without food and don't keep their vehement word. It takes miracles to make their projects work. It would take miracles for her family to forgive her. Her silence reads like a lie. What could she say? Dare she ask forgiveness without knowing how to avoid the next lie? She prays for better faith in this sardonic God.

If she could tell her father … She cannot.

He sounds cheerful and calm though weak.

Maundy Thursday, the parish priests wash the feet of twelve parishioners and she takes communion, praying, against experience, that the symbol will be true, the powerful will serve the poor. Her father would like that.

At the door, a smiling couple engage her in conversation. 'I always find this service so moving.' They ask after her father and the wife embraces her, 'Courage.'

Her mother says, 'His condition is stable.'

'And how are you?' Her mother's silence speaks. 'Take care of yourself, Mother.'

Good Friday, she leaves school early to attend the grieved service that has fed hatreds for centuries. This will not end in her lifetime, the two deadly stories aimed at each other, one blaming 'the Jews' for what Romans executed, the other blaming Christians for killing and killing and killing the innocent people. In a free fire zone, she follows the Stations of pain she saw scribbled in Vence, the innocent man unjustly sentenced, forced to carry the instrument of his death like

107

a Jew told to dig the grave where he is buried alive, falling like a Jew under Cossack hooves, spat on like a Jew, stripped, robbed, tortured, dead. Forgiving.

She is not the only one in this congregation who bears the pain of the church's sins. She worships with women who carried too many children and some shamed for abortions they saw no way to avoid. Speakers of Spanish and Portuguese had forebears converted at the edge of the sword. Blacks are still scarred by slavery the clerics condoned. All face One who commands, 'Forgive.'

She walks from the T station and its evocations of loss below, spirit above. A neighbour, gardening, greets her, 'Smell these hyacinths!' and invites her to the Easter egg hunt.

'Thank you, Emily, I'll be with my father.'

'I saw you trundling by last weekend.' Emily pulls off her garden gloves and comes out of her yard to hug Ruth.

Her blinking machine has no message. Her mother's number. So soon! She should have stayed. Bernie answers, '... four hours ago.'

So. Expected but beyond understanding.

'I'll come tonight. Can I speak to Mother.'

'Where were you?' The question startles her. 'At the school they said you went to church.'

'I'd like to speak to Mother.'

'What were you doing in a church?'

'Please let me speak to Mother, Bernie.'

'You converted, didn't you?' Her sibling, not to be deceived.

'Let me speak to Mother.'

'You don't deny it? ... You don't deny it!' Years of resentment load his voice. 'Don't come to the funeral. To us, you are dead.'

'Let me speak to Mother.'

Her phone clicks dead.

108

She rolls her bag through iron cold and descends to the lost gloves. A crowd waits. A light glares in the black tunnel. Body presses body, making room for her near an infant sleeping in a stroller. The air smells depleted. In the shoah trains, stench – fear, hunger, heat, cold, urine, faeces. Some protested, This isn't happening. This can't be real. It was real. It remains real even today, when her father has died and all is laid on Him and the pain of the world grinds like metal on metal.

Her father's pain is over. In the old cosmology, his soul is in heaven or destined there. In the new cosmology, heaven has no space and he no soul. In Judaism, he lives on in the minds and hearts of those who knew him. Yes, this is where he lives, in the communion of souls and in God who remembers all He has created, every face here in the subway, every body, every soul.

As her taxi approaches the house, its lights blazing, a woman carrying a cake box presses the bell, the door opens, greetings, embraces and the door closes.

She pays, walks the short path and three steps, presses the bell and hears its cascade of chimes. Bernie comes to the door, 'Have you no shame?'

'Will you fight with me now? He died only hours ago.'

'Is this a time to show your apostate face?'

'Let me speak with Mother.'

He is blocking the door, but people inside hear something happening. Bernie's wife comes to see. 'How dare you!'

A man presses forward, bearded, wearing a black yarmulke. 'Let me, Bernie,' he closes the door behind him and speaks in a low tone. 'You must be Ruth. This is a terrible business. Too much for your mother right now. Go home, go to a hotel, let her rest. It's too soon, shock on shock.'

'I'm her daughter. His daughter.'

'Have pity on her.'

This can't be real. 'And the funeral?'

'Perhaps you don't understand. By Jewish law you are

dead. We should have a funeral for you too.'

'I'm alive. It's my father who died.'

'Thank God, before he knew.'

She is willing to thank God for everything, but this … 'I need a taxi.'

'It is Shabbat. Go next door. They'll let you use the phone.'

The smell of the hotel will remain with her forever, the fluorescent light at the check-in counter, the bed filling the whole room, beige wallpaper, picture of trees, beige bathroom, small rectangle of soap, mean towel, hangers parting from hooks on the rod, implied accusations – people in these rooms will damage walls, steal towels and hangers, don't wash much. The hotel admits no responsibility for their unspeakable acts. An atheist hotel with no duty of generosity, a world without God.

Merciful exhaustion blinds her, though she starts awake again and again, replaying the scene at the door. In medieval cosmology, this is the night Jesus goes down among the lost. She is lost herself.

Faith is ashes. She is a traitor, incomprehensibly ingrate and duplicitous. She sees her mother blinded by a second pain that multiplies the first. Every gesture of love between them tainted. Why did she turn against her family and her people? What does she have to do with the church she could not defend to Saul? Her mother will be stared at, talked of, subjected to pity and curiosity. She will not go to the funeral. She turns and tosses. Every limb is herself.

And Bernie? The sibling spite of their childhood lingers still in both of them.

Although it belongs to infinity and eternity, the night ends. She travels home and at last reaches the T station with the lost gloves. Where the trinity of red sails move in the air, she grips the pull of her bag and walks like her ancestors forced from their homes.

Emily is out in her yard again. She looks into Ruth's face.

'Come in. Let me give you a cup of coffee.'

'I'm almost home,' Ruth's voice cracks like her mother's.

'I'll walk you to the corner. You haven't slept, I guess.' Emily stays with her until Ruth has a key in the door.

The answering machine has a condolence message from the principal. She weeps, washes, unpacks and the doorbell rings. A florist. Then Emily, bringing croissants, juice, coffee and Scotch, 'in case coffee doesn't do it.'

The doorbell rings. A florist.

Friends, colleagues and parishioners, hearing that she is orphaned, wrap her in bonds that pull her back from death. Her family is sitting shiva with those who knew her father, bringing food and talk to mourn and heal. Grafting the grieved back into life.

'Try to get some sleep,' putting a hand on her shoulder, Emily kisses her cheek, 'I'll come by later.'

From her bed, she sees a street tree, still a structure of bones. Soon it will show that it lives. She is willing to believe. She will hope for reconciliation though now it seems unforeseeable, like this morning's flood of care. Her mother will forgive her and Bernie will follow. Tonight she will attend the Easter Vigil. She is willing to believe in the Resurrection. She is willing to believe that the dog will speak Hebrew.

The Widow's Widow

As soon as the airline officials and I finished negotiating about my luggage, gone astray with my clothes for the wedding, I collected the rental car and drove to Hillary's house.

She hugged me, 'Come into the kitchen. Are you parched? Flying turns me into yesterday's toast.'

I laughed and we sat at the counter under her iron loop of copper pots and waited for the kettle to boil. Outside, chatter was filling the servants' rooms with a language I could not understand. It took me back to childhood when the sound of Magdalena talking with friends in the yard and my parents talking with friends in the house fused with everything else I did not know and could not imagine.

'I've got twenty lists.' Hillary sounded overwhelmed by the detailed dovetailing the wedding demanded. She's never enjoyed the power of administrative accomplishment. I wanted to show her I understood why she was handling the logistics on her own. Henry had to be away negotiating and could not change the timetable, not even for his son's wedding. Not now, when the whole country was waiting for the move everyone expected. 'The papers say De Klerk might release more prisoners before New Year's.' I was thinking of the most important prisoner, epitome of the change in my birth country.

Hillary's silence rebuked me for fishing. 'I'll just tell the maid where to put the wedding flowers.' She went into the servants' yard and stood on the concrete floor next to a concrete sink. I could not hear what she said but I heard her maid answer, 'Yes, Madam.'

When she came back, I asked, 'Where do you want me to stay?'

'We've been so busy we haven't had a chance to sell my mother's house. I hope you don't mind. The maid's still there looking after things.'

As I nodded, the bridal pair splashed into the kitchen with hugs and exclamations.

'Your gifts could be anywhere,' I told them. 'With the rest of my luggage.'

'But you're here. Tell us everything.'

I was thinking how lucky they were to live at this moment when the whole country and the world would see a change momentous enough for myth. How lucky to share their day of joy with the joy I had been hearing on the news as first one, then many prisoners were released and were met by singing and dancing. The last few months had been extraordinary – students put flowers in the barrels of guns in South Africa and crowds poured out of East Berlin. The land of my birth that had suffered so long, drought stricken and ostracised and the land of my parents' birth, also a prison, were full of people saying, 'Freedom.' They hugged strangers at the news. Every day anticipated the next with joy.

How lucky we were to have the wedding at a time that pinned our personal joy to joy in the world.

We didn't have much time to talk. Hillary needed to speak with her maid. I had to buy clothes and to call Karen.

I drove to the dead woman's house through familiar streets lined with plane trees hardly changed since the afternoons I had walked under them to my music teacher's, the same dapple of leaves and sun, the same mottled trunks, the same brick houses behind them. My music teacher, about the same age as Hillary's mother, had probably died by now. She had fled Vienna just in time and her stories fused with those of my parents about the persecutions in Europe. In my mind, they fused with the lives of the servants I heard in the backyard.

The maid, wearing a pink apron, was expecting me. She introduced herself as Rosemary and showed me to the room where I would sleep in the dead woman's bed. That was the first time I saw the floor to ceiling cast iron bars of a 'rape gate' between the entrance hall and the bedroom. At first I did not understand what it could be. Then horror of the fear it showed. How could things have gone so far that people would lock themselves into cages in their own homes. Would the country ever be able to recover from such insanity?

I did not believe anyone wanted to rape Hillary's mother, though I knew that some places had come close to civil war.

'I've got to have a shower,' I said.

'Would Madam like me to run a bath for her?' Rosemary asked. The offer took me aback. Even in South Africa, I did not expect such services. I declined.

While I went off to the bathroom and dressed again in the clothes I had worn since London, she made tea and when I came out she brought it to me on a tray and set it on a table between the two armchairs that filled the space between the widow's bed and the door. Almost nothing in all my returns had reached into my memory with such dense eloquence as this tray I had not asked for, with its embroidered doily, teapot, milk, sugar, water and a plate of tennis biscuits. My mother would have received the same tray when she asked a servant for tea. On the verandas of ocean hotels, on office desks and in the secluded space behind the shop counter where the owner has a chair, I had seen the same tray. When I visited Africans in their own homes and they wanted to do the proper thing, they would bring this tray. Pungent with familiarity, like the plane trees outside, it said, 'Nothing's changed.'

But everything had changed and was changing. I did not guess the extent of it until Rosemary asked, 'Would Madam like me to stay?' I did not know what she meant and she must have seen my confusion, 'My madam used to ask me to stay and talk.'

'Thank you, Rosemary. I can't talk now. I have to make a phonecall and then go out.' I did not tell her my clothes had gone astray.

I drank the tea, wondering what we could have to talk about. What did she and Hillary's mother talk about. Hillary? Perhaps Rosemary had children of her own and talked about them. Magdalena, who lived in my backyard when I was growing up, had two children in Bethal. They never visited and she did not keep photos in her room on the soapbox covered with an embroidered doily like the one on the tea tray. She kept a saucer with a candle butt there and her Bible and a red cigarette tin that, she told me one day, held coupons for the burial insurance she was buying. Her children hardly existed in my imagination, although the husband who came to be with her every second weekend was a real person and Magdalena sometimes took time to go to Bethal.

Years after she died, I went to the location there, but no one knew anything about Magdalena or her children and I drove away from the one-room mud houses, their rusting roofs held in place by big stones, knowing that I did not know anything of the life of the woman who had cared for me for eight years, or the lives of other women like her. All I knew was that they lived the way my grandparents had lived, needing permission for everything. But how it was without running water, how Magdalena pored over her Bible by candlelight while our house blazed with electricity, about that, I knew nothing at all.

Even the first time I did not accept Rosemary's invitation to talk I felt I was committing some wrong against her.

'How soon can you come?' Karen asked.

'I've got to buy clothes. The airline sent mine astray somewhere.' I'd need a nap. 'I'll take you out to dinner.'

'Don't be silly, darling. We want you here.'

At the shopping centre, guards stopped me to search my bag. Though everyone seemed to be carried away with talk of freedom, some things would remain. The inertia of institutions, the iron of habit, the mental cages and perhaps worse. The Reign of Terror in France followed a time when strangers hugged each other saying 'Freedom.'

Authorised, I bought the necessities of life for the next few days and then, stupid with weariness, drove back to the dead woman's home. Rosemary greeted me and offered me tea again and talk again and again I said no. 'I didn't sleep last night and need to rest now.'

Of course she couldn't imagine the exhausting flight. She had never been in a plane. She must have lived fixed as a tree in this place where she had worked years to serve a person and now to guard furniture and empty rooms. With her presence alone. This woman with her heavy breasts and belly, a body full of hunger going back years, perhaps to a childhood in a place like Bethal.

I half slept, floating through images of the unchanged trees and brick houses, of Hillary talking irritably to her maid and rumours that the day was at hand that would transform everything. Too soon, it was time to dress again.

Karen threw open the door and hugged me. Quickly, she led me to her living room, filled with flowers as always. Her husband Edward had founded a kindergarten where he would accept a white child only if the parents sponsored a black child too. A few years later, he declined children from fashionable families, to favour children of domestic servants. They were on a picnic the day he died. A sudden storm burst over the valley and he was running to scoop a child back to shelter in the farmhouse when a bolt of lightning found him, the tallest thing in a grass field.

Eight hours later, around midnight, her first night as his widow, Karen phoned me in America. Those calls over continents and oceans and time zones – they're supposed to make it easier to be so far away, but they feel harder. When Karen phoned from Johannesburg to say, 'Edward's dead,' the sky darkened. It must have been my pupils contracting with pain, but I thought it was the whole world going dark, Africa impoverished when his light went out. Just three months ago.

I was finding it hard to be in the room without him. She saw me looking round, feeling him missing. 'Come on New Year's Eve,' she said. 'We always used to celebrate alone but this year I want a few friends who knew Edward. It's such a terrible holiday here, everyone drunk for days.'

Karen grew up in Denmark and her conversation keeps the habit of seeing South Africa as an alien place. I was with her once when we saw a policeman twice her size dragging an old man by the back of his jacket. She stepped in front of them and scolded the cop. He was so surprised at this blazing fairy of righteousness picking a quarrel with him that he loosened his grip on the jacket and listened, bemused, while his victim fled. I was amazed. I didn't know a born South African who'd have delivered such a spontaneous scolding. We were too trained to acquiesce. We did not know and could not imagine the decorum citizens in a free country expect.

At the same time, Karen is passionately in love with Edward's country and filled their house with carvings and textiles that reveal her love. Now she is rooted in her past here and will not live in Copenhagen again.

'I can't believe he's really dead. He comes to me at night, in my dreams. Every night he's with me.'

As she was talking, Betty her maid came in and I greeted her. She did not use the servile third person form to talk to me. We talked about Edward. 'It'll never be the same,' she said quietly.

She has been Karen's maid for thirty years. By now, they move with the same light, quick movements and Betty knows exactly what needs to be done when Karen stages a party for parents and donors and they both prepare plates of finger food and edible flowers.

Betty served dinner and Karen and I talked. I said, 'It's so ironic, painful, that Edward isn't here to see the end of apartheid.'

'Who knows what will take its place,' she said. Foreboding from her. I was taken aback. 'Or if anything will change. Habits die hard.'

After we'd been talking a while, she said she was tired and we moved to her bedroom. She'd also had a rape gate installed when Edward died. Fear had found her, after all.

I sat in the carved armchair he used to sit in when she wasn't feeling well but still wanted people around. Where I used to sit, she had a TV now. A salve for loneliness.

When I was too exhausted for more talk, she asked me to call Betty from the kitchen. 'We watch TV together.'

So Betty was one of the family now. No, she had served the dinner but did not eat it with us.

I found her in the kitchen ironing panties. Panties! Freedom takes learned skills. My mind flooded with thousands of habits and decisions that people here did not know and could not imagine. Like Karen's instant outrage at that bullying cop. Who, in a free world, would choose to iron panties? To compose that fussy tea tray? To speak the syntax of servility? The old laws might be about to die, but my first country looked likely to survive as a widow with gestures and postures locked in place.

When I came back to the dead woman's house there was light in the room in the backyard where Rosemary lived, but behind the house next door the servants' rooms were bright and loud with music and the voices of men drinking. They were getting an early start on New Year's.

Rosemary was not with them. She was alone, locked in place, waiting for me. She came out as I walked to the front door, 'Did Madam have a good meal?' and walked in front of me to switch lights on so I need not go into dark rooms. I wondered what she did all day when there was no one to tend to and what she would do when Hillary sold the house.

I let my shoulders droop and jaw go slack to show that I was too tired for tea or talk. This time she did not offer, but I knew the pattern. I was wronging her, or had wronged her some time ago, long before I knew or could imagine.

Mulberries

Down the street a mulberry tree overhangs the sidewalk and now that it is full summer in Massachusetts and the berries are ripe and the sidewalk stained with those that drop, I stop to pick a few off the low branches within reach. Whenever I do, I am picking mulberries in 1960.

Four of us started early after Mass and before sunrise and when we drove high through the hills that cup Pietermaritzburg we saw the morning mist below. For us it was thrilling, in those days before flying was common, to come out of the mist and be higher than the clouds, pink, then butter yellow, then white, held like lumpy porridge in a bowl. We continued through the rising plain into green foothills and then higher into the sharp mountains that divide the coastal plain from the highveld, Drakensberg, Dragon Mountains, fierce and legendary. I grew up in Johannesburg, a city foreigners told me was ugly. I was too young to know anything else and thought they missed the character of the metropolis I loved. The Drakensberg were my first encounter with the kind of beauty that inspires people to see God in nature. 'I will lift up my eyes to the hills,' a devout friend quoted.

Pietermaritzburg was lush, different from crisp Johannesburg, different from the high peaks. In the hills that rise from 'Maritzburg on the Sweetwaters Road, people who still called England home rode horses, played polo and, I'd heard, hunted fox. In late winter, azalea hedges bloomed solid red and when we went into woods to pick mushrooms I felt the thrill of a city child doing country things I'd read about, of a colonial dressing up in the life of the metropolis that felt more legitimate and real than the lives we were living. In the mountains, I felt no doubleness of vision. The light was simple and clear, the air

119

transparent.

We were driving up to see a Dominican who sometimes preached vividly about the matter almost no one else would mention and we felt exhilarated as people do who share a truth that no one else puts into words. It would be twenty years before the Catholic Church would speak out clearly about apartheid. Our host gave us lunch and apologised that he would eat more quickly than us – the rule allowed him only fifteen minutes – and then we talked about people in prison in the state of emergency the government had declared when the world seemed appalled at Sharpeville. If not for the international reaction, the massacre would have passed like others, apartheid as usual. The international condemnation felt like our conversations with the Dominican, a relief to know that others saw what we saw. We had friends in prison and knew that none were dangerous. In any other country, we believed, their peaceful protest would have been legitimate. Not here where the slightest opposition seemed so lonely that to find another person sharing it felt like a light in darkness. Our friends believed everyone should have the vote and the country should be governed by law, not administrators with whims no one could question.

Secretly, I knew that with friends in prison I felt something like the thrill I hear now in America when people tell how they saw a celebrity in the drugstore lining up to pay the cashier like anyone else.

While we were up in the mountains, a quick snow squall touched the pastures, rare weather for us, and driving back we talked about the few other times we'd seen snow and about hailstorms we tried to treat as substitutes, about what it must be like abroad and about the beauty of the country we loved, the mountains, the highveld, the coast, troubling because we could not share that love with the people who lived around us and were not allowed to travel and could not afford to. Driving from town to town on country roads, it was common to see an African walking barefoot, sometimes with laced shoes too expensive to wear out dangling at their shoulders. Everywhere men and women in rags and naked, pot-bellied children showed what it means to have no rights.

In Pietermaritzburg the day had been hot and humid and we marvelled that we had passed from snow to swelter in a few hours. We stopped at the Girls' High School where I taught and lived and, while I was collecting a book from my room, the others walked near the tennis courts on a bright lawn punctuated by rose bushes.

Then we drove to the home of a friend who had not come with us. I recall others there, an Indian couple – the woman, a doctor, looking regal in her sari – and a Zulu schoolteacher. We talked again about justice, wondering what we could do about it. Our host had prepared dinner and invited us to go out into the garden and pick mulberries to eat with cream. Strawberries were exotic, rare and expensive and other northern berries wholly unknown. Our dessert was rich with colonial allusions and illusions, like Christmas dinner eaten in the heat of summer.

That is the main reason I stop under the mulberry tree to pick a few berries I may have no right to, though they overhang a public street. I think of Saint Augustine, whose *Confessions* I read that year, 1960. He examines a time he stole pears, though he could easily get better pears without stealing, and sees his thieving as evidence of original sin in himself. I felt that evidence in the celebrity thrill of knowing people in prison.

Until that day in Pietermaritzburg, I thought of mulberries mainly for their leaves. When I was eleven my brother collected silkworms in shoeboxes with punctured tops. They preferred mulberry leaves to lettuce and he sometimes procured leaves from a neighbour's tree. When the white worms wove their cocoons, he unwove them, holding the cocoon in his mouth and winding the thread on to a wooden spool he had made. Sometimes he did not let the worms weave cocoons at all. When they started laying thread, he set each on a four-inch square of cardboard he had fixed on a dowel. The prisoner worm would walk and walk, laying silk in its wake as it looked for a place to stop. My brother's cardboard square allowed no resting place. The worm walked, weaving its square of silk, and eventually died. Years after the craze, my brother still had the silk so remorselessly collected. I never learned what he imagined he would do with his harvest. Those worms fed into my sense that the powerful have no pity on the powerless and, in a gossamer way, into my decision to leave South Africa.

Here in America, I sometimes fear any object or experience can become a commodity. Not these mulberries I pick off a neighbour's tree as though they are my right. These mulberries hold a day that is mine alone. The old South Africa I grieved for is gone and the new suffers new miseries rooted in the old. My friends scattered long ago and there will never be another day that brings us together. The mist still rises in the valley's bowl, there may still be sudden snow in the mountains, marvellous to people who see flakes rarely. Another child may collect silkworms, another group of friends eat mulberries and cream and feel guilt at their pleasure in a world of pain. But that day remains in me, hidden. I know that everyone else also has days in their lives, hidden, some even from ourselves. Sometimes there's a glimpse in a gesture that may surprise onlookers, like my pause to pluck berries from the shady branches down the street.

Stompie

I almost stepped on the child's head before I saw him curled at the bottom of the stairs, the red hood of his jacket pulled over his head like a caul. He had drawn his knees up to his heart in search of a place in sleep warmer than the subway floor. I hurried on to the State House to see if I could vote in the Election the next day. I never met Stompie while he was alive and the last thing anyone expects is to step on the face of a dead person.

In the State House they were setting up tables for voting. The Consul talked like a bureaucrat who has worked things to a satisfactory conclusion. Even though I am an American citizen now, I could come back and vote the next day. For this Election they were making up the rules. I could live in two countries, beyond history and division, as though we were already in the ultimate state of the soul. For one day, the world in which I live far from where I was born would be one world and I could live like a suturing needle flying to and fro.

The Consul wanted documents to show who I am, so I showed my birth certificate. If I had come with no papers at all – if I had crossed a river of crocodiles and a reserve of lions – he would have accepted an affidavit. But I came to Boston years ago without trouble. The Consul wanted to hold on to my birth certificate. Perhaps he would take it to his expensive hotel to fax New York or Pretoria and ask who I really am.

Leaving the State House I walked down the granite steps and in to the Common. The few trees whose leaves had opened were slumping under rain. I went underground again, not recalling the child, barely noticing him asleep on the platform.

In Harvard Square I saw Lydia carrying her lawyer's briefcase. Thirty years ago we met here at a demonstration asking for the vote, but after a while we turned away to attend to our own lives. I thought I would forget the amputation that severed my worlds, though phantom limbs still ache.

'Are you going to vote?' I asked her.

'No. I don't live there any more and I won't go back.'

I called the man I divorced twenty years ago, 'You can vote tomorrow.'

'Are you sure?'

'The Consul said it's okay with both countries.'

The day we became Americans the court clerk told us to remove our gloves if we were wearing them, raise our hands and pledge allegiance to the flag, forswearing all others. I thought Pretoria a pain of the past.

His joy took me aback.

After the Civil War that followed the Revolution of 1917 my father heard that the streets of Johannesburg were paved with gold. In Vilna people talked about that golden world and about the world they knew, where Stalin did not like Jews. My father chose, promising his new bride he would send money and a ticket as soon as he could. That was 1929, the year that golden worlds crashed. It took him six years to earn her fare.

In their years apart my mother sang to her infant son about a land with raisins and almonds fit for the Messiah. She took her rosy child to the dairy and watched him drink a cup of milk. Sometimes she bought him a sugar bun and watched him eat it. Years later she would quote her landlady's chiding, Why don't you eat something yourself? Watching her son was luxury enough, she said. In her telling it seemed a sunny morning. Before the War. A golden time.

At the border a custom's official noticed a book bound in soft calfskin – Pushkin, a bourgeois luxury – and confiscated her high school prize. He told her he too loved poetry and complimented her on the child gripping her hand, saying he had beautiful eyes, like hers.

The ship stopped in Ireland. Her last sight of Europe was soft as white midsummer nights. When she walked along the Liffey, men smiled at her and her son. She felt pretty and proud and whispered to him about the father they would soon see.

Waiting for her those six years in Johannesburg, he was without English and without steady work, sharing a room with two other immigrants. He had one jacket and two pairs of pants. One night he woke to see a thief climbing out of the window with the jacket he had hung over a chair.

He often saw darkness in front of his eyes. Once he went to the General Hospital and lay there with his head swathed in white. She used to say she dreamed about him that very night, his face cut and masked.

They escaped Europe's savagery just in time and I was born where dust, thirst and lightning crack the earth and the people. Farmers burn dead grass in spring to purge each year of the one before. The scorched roots hold the blackened soil until the fields turn green with fresh blades tender as a child.

In Beit Street, where we lived in one room, I was sitting on the front steps when a boy led an ox waggon by, loaded with watermelons. A buyer answered his call and the sample he cut sparkled like sugar crystals. Like milk and honey, almonds and raisins. The melon and the oxen were huge, the other side of the street far away.

My birth certificate gives the name of the town as Doornfontein, a fountain surrounded with thorns. If the Consul faxed Pretoria, he would learn that's where I was a child. I had not expected to vote. The New England rain stopped and I went to walk along the Charles River. Cherry trees were in blossom. I wished for the pleasures of love. Towers glistened in the rinsed air on the other side of the river and the dome of the State House was shining pretty as liberty, like the beacon it used be. It's covered with real gold.

The mines where they open veins of gold are hot and take the men down like a child into fever. Every cell feels the press of deep gravity. All is dark except lamps and equipment, the miners' chests glistening like fish as they breathe the dust of gold and quartz until their lungs are caked with it. Their wives are far away. The children do not know their fathers. I wished I could vote for a world where children can know their parents and parents can know their children.

Five years ago they killed Stompie in scandalous circumstances. I never met him, but I heard how the little butt was stamped out. Those who killed him had learned the lessons of the country – that laws do not apply to all and any wanton wish may be acted in secret. The law accused a woman who carried herself like a queen when her husband was still in prison. To this day she claims innocence. She walked out of the courtroom defiant, holding her fist high, but her husband followed looking humbled by pain. Afterwards he said they would separate and put her out of his life as quietly as that man could. If I voted for him, I'd have to vote for her too. The slate of candidates allowed no choice. Perhaps there is never a choice, no world where candidates are innocent and revolution heals.

A Gem Squash

Thin as a weed, Derek brings his own food in a cooler and repacks it into Sarah's refrigerator, taking note of what she eats with disapproval. Sarah disapproves too. Food should be shared and bring people together, not say that hers is not good enough for him. He puts a bottle of Poland Springs on the section of counter she uses for chopping. No need to say anything now. She'll move it tomorrow if she needs the space.

'I notice you aren't changing filters as often as you should.'

'I've been told Cambridge water's clean.'

'You don't deny that it contains chlorine and chlorine's carcinogenic.'

If it's not the Special Branch, it's cancer. Sarah feels tempted to say, 'This obsession is so American.'

Nothing would insult him more. He has been damning Americans for thirty years and does it now, impatient to expose the iniquity, 'Did you hear the radio? About the police torturing that Haitian prisoner?' Of course she heard. It rang through her whole body and is ringing still. As though this is the only story, crying out to heaven with a voice of blood.

Her parents talked about such stories, awed by the evil and the terror. 'Just like the Nazis.' Of course Derek also hears the story ringing with others like it. The police committing torture. Shooting a black child. Or, this is after all America, a Mexican child. For the same wanton desire to kick and injure and be the beast on top they grew up with, 'Damn Americans.' Just like South Africa, the just object of his tireless fury.

One of these days, she fears, she'll lose it and tell him to grow up. For now she offers wine.

'Water. I've brought my own. My nutritionist says I must

drink a gallon a day.'

One of these days, she'll say, how do you think Moses or Jesus would see this obsession with food?

She hands him one of her blue glasses and a bowl of nuts, gestures to the white chair by the window and pours wine for herself.

'Are you going for tests this visit?'

'No. They say I'm all clear.' But not clear of trouble. 'I've got to see the tax people about going bankrupt.'

He sounds calm. Living on faith? For thirty years, running the Fund for Justice, he lived on little more and sent as much as he could to political prisoners. 'So you've decided to do it.' Last spring he was investing in a pyramid scheme he hoped would bring in enough to pay off his debts. He's a babe in the woods. Sarah wonders how, being so naive, he ever managed to funnel all that surreptitious money to its destinations.

'Can you keep your cabin?'

'I think so ... I brought you some ashes. You must tell me where to put them.'

'Thanks for remembering my garden.'

'Well, when you heat with wood ...'

'What time d'you see the tax people?'

'I've got to phone for an appointment.' Procrastinating? Maybe not. In need's tight grip he must count things like the cost of a long distance call. She used to.

He is leafing through her *Times*, stroking his beard and looking for iniquities. 'Another pillow?' Sarah asks, 'Okay. See you tomorrow. Take a shower if you like. You won't disturb me. Sleep late. It's your vacation you said.'

Throughout the night she hears his door swinging open and his steps to the bathroom. She sinks back into the dark water. A child is sick. No. She pulls to the surface. Her sons are grown and gone. She can sleep. Derek's in the bathroom and leaves without flushing. Fearing, perhaps, to wake her. How does he survive the dark months in Maine, alone, sick? Under the surface, water moving into an ocean. Blood, darkness, furling over each other. Time flowing away. Medium of this short life. He is going to the bathroom again. Like an old, incontinent man. Her father in his last days. No one by his side. Still a stranger in the country he came to. Also a babe in the woods. His immigrant incompetence used to infuriate her. She hurt him with scorn. A man of suffering. Why are some born to pain? Why is a Jew a Jew? A black, black? Can anyone change it?

Shipwrecks where schools of fish with dark faces open and close their mouths. Shuffling, streaming. Something monstrous there, beyond the crusted submarine, two men twisting another, his head down to his toes, yes baas. She cannot help.

Harsh crows announce dawn, a jay gives its fierce call. They are not angry. Soon finches will come to her feeder. Near Maseru, in a morning light, hoopoes courted on the yellow grass and frost flowed like threads of gold in the cream mountains. Heavy with the rocks someone hung on her back, she met the eyes of other people. Also heavy laden. They knew each other.

Sarah moves his Poland Spring bottle to make coffee. Last visit, he spread his stuff everywhere. Curbing irritation, she takes her cup to the patio where red geraniums parade like toy soldiers and begins to read. The Haitian prisoner is in a critical condition, his intestines torn. The policemen were raping him with a toilet plunger. Her parents' lament, Just like ... in Bosnia ... She puts down the paper. Enough. Looks at the red geraniums. Okay. Okay.

She reads again. A real estate deal. A manoeuvre against the special prosecutor. Recipes using tomatoes. Okay.

Walking to her office she sees the bathroom door closed and through the open door of the guest room that Derek, messy as ever, has spread pills and packages on the table, papers on the floor.

Something is missing. His shortwave radio. Where is the grey box he used to bring like a child, excusing himself every few hours to go off and attend to it, urgent for every detail? Last night, he did not even listen to the news.

She stares at her neighbour's maples. As long as she's known Derek, he has listened to the news. Even after the Fund for Justice dissolved in a spate of quarrels. Even after The Election, he clung to the news as to the voice of the Lord. He must know, know now, know who. Something is happening to him.

Sarah's heart rises in hope. Now that apartheid's over and there's nothing he can do for South Africa, something more gentle could happen.

She sees signs. The gift of wood-ash. Resignation about going bankrupt. Calling this visit a vacation. A shred of joy here and there.

She opens her email.

'Môre, miesies.' Derek pokes his head in her office door, smiling. He's always enjoyed a few words of Afrikaans with her. In the small office the minister at Harvard set aside for anti-apartheid work, where students met to plan a Sharpeville commemoration and denounce American imperialism in Vietnam, he said 'Voetsak' to her, smiling, the taste of home in his mouth. They were so homesick.

'I'll have coffee with you.'

'My nutritionist says, no coffee. But join me.' Becoming her host.

Sarah brews a fresh cup while he goes to the bathroom again, it's those eight glasses a day, sets a place and decides not to wait for him.

She is not accustomed to this coordinating any more. He has never been married, though a few years ago he talked about it. An American active in anti-apartheid work and of independent means. Then he stopped talking about marriage.

The paragraph about goals calls for a change in the paragraph about design and ...

Back in the kitchen, she finds him with the *Times* spread over the table, eating alternately from a large bowl of beige slurry and a black banana in his left hand.

'Americans don't know how to eat bananas. They should let them get black. That's when the starch breaks down into sugar and they get sweet.' He points to her bowl of fruit. 'You should never buy those yellow bananas. They're not ripe.'

Too much. To be preached at! About bananas! It may seem late to give up their friendship, though there was a long stretch of years when she despaired of South Africa and they hardly talked to each other, but if he carries on like this ... not that she'll close her house to him. He's too poor. But she won't open her heart as you do with a friend.

He stops eating to fold some of the paper away and she sits at the cleared space near his colony of bottles surrounding her salt and pepper. Camomile. Garlic. Willow bark. With sovereign properties she used to read about when she was writing her dissertation, *'Pearl*, a fourteenth-century mystical jewel.'

He picks up the banana again, takes a small bite, a spoonful from the bowl and chews. While he chews, she talks. 'Your garden giving enough for winter?'

'I couldn't plant much. With this fatigue ... But my neighbours said I must eat from their garden this year. People in Maine are so kind. When I had my operation, Mike looked at my woodpile and said, "You can't carry those big logs." He brought his sons and they split my wood into small pieces I could carry. Can you imagine? And Anne brought over such a pie ... but with very little sugar.'

Perhaps through neighbours like these he will see what she started to see when she gave up *Pearl* and recognised that people around her in factories and offices were also doing what they must, working to support their children.

'They sound like good people.'

'Not like most damn Americans ...'

Sarah wants to defend Americans. Not ideological, they build their world bit by bit. They do not seem to need a story that makes sense of everything. They take explanations handy enough for making soap and packaging and improving market share. They wonder how to pollute less. All caught in the web of capitalism.

Derek sees nothing in capitalism but mine owners in houses with brilliant flower gardens and lawns green during a time of drought, while at the hostels for migrant workers men shovel mieliepap on to enamel plates and push them at humiliated slaves. Capitalism is a miner who sleeps on a concrete bunk in a cell with five others, owning little more than one set of clothes. Capitalism makes migrant labourers everywhere, cuts husband from wife, mother from child.

Now, capitalism seems a neutral force to her. There is no other more merciful. There is need, work, capital, greed. Railing does not affect them. If anyone is ever to fly free, it will be by understanding what cannot be avoided, by something ingenious and not discovered yet, something you can't think of until you almost do it, like how to make steel fly lighter than air.

Derek has never worked for money. He's been a colonial Englishman all along, supercilious about the natives. In this case, Americans.

'Is Mike the man who arranged for you to get some preaching?'

His smile dims. 'He's got connections. Knows everybody.' Wistful. His own network gone. What does he do all day in Maine? Collect iniquities?

If he's going to rant on about Americans, they'd better not talk too much. 'I'm working today, but if there's something you want ... You can use this phone to call the tax people.'

'Have you got a telephone book?'

'In my office.' He follows her, she hands him the directory and he lingers, looking at her books. Not only about the moral universe where apartheid is the key pattern of evil, repeating in her own life what happened to her grandparents. And happens still. To the Haitian prisoner.

She will never lay down this weight but now the books in her office are about computers and genetics. When she learned technical writing, she started to see the world a new way, not only as the moral universe of suffering and courage. She saw an alphabet of utmost simplicity expressing utmost subtlety and another code, an alphabet for writing the words that make life.

The great work of her time is a human endeavour to master these alphabets. She began to be glad she was in America, near the heart of this work.

When she read about what was driving technology, she glimpsed yet another power to master. Communism and capitalism changed under her eyes from a choice of the poor against the rich, the suffering against the callous, into a choice of techniques. Both try to map and navigate oceans of desire and need. The code of that turbulence is still hidden, not yet like the digital code and the genetic code. She thinks, if I had another lifetime, that's what I'd like to learn.

For this lifetime, she believes, the moral choice remains, but wise choice must acknowledge the nature of things.

'Can I borrow this?' He holds out a memoir by someone from Kroonstad.

'Take it. I don't know when I'm ever going to read it.' He's stuck. Wilfully blind. Pitiful.

No. No! She is blind. His choice has also been the great work of their time. Justice is the great work of every time.

She hears him going to the bathroom again, probably reading and unaware of anyone else.

In the middle of the morning, she wanders back to the kitchen for a last cup of coffee.

'Do you want this article?' About sweatshops. 'I want to cut it out.'

'Go ahead,' ashamed of the rancid gesture that makes her rich, him poor.

The end of apartheid has stranded him here in America where an encompassing ideology seems strange to the temper of people. Two sermons a week. Two hundred dollars. For thirty years he gave every day to the cause, hundreds of prisoners depended on his work and now it is gone.

At The Election, he went back. No longer a political refugee, he gloated, 'I've got a passport for the first time in my life!' It must have been a complex visit for Derek, fulfilling a lifetime of longing and showing him, however that happened, that he could not go back. He did not talk of that decision. The main story he told her was about a man he sat next to on the plane from Cape Town to Durban. 'Aren't you Derek Wardell?'

'How'd you know?'

'I know you, man. I got your dossier. I'm with the political cops since 1965. I know you better than you know your own hand. No hard feelings, hey.'

'You still with them?'

'Retired. Just in time. Jirre! I never thought we'd meet this way.'

Sarah also wondered at the enigmatic coincidence. 'What a meeting, Derek! What did you do when he told you?'

'There we were, sitting next to each other. We had a beer … He talked about how the times are upside down and kept saying, "It's like the Bible says." He wanted me to tell him, as a minister, if it was the end of the world.'

'The end of his world, for sure. "I will cast the mighty aside in the conceit of their hearts and will fill the hungry with good things." Isn't that how it goes? You think he meant that? The prisoner would be president?'

'Those guys knew what was going on. They knew.'

'What was it like, talking to him?'

'Like meeting the Angel of Death and seeing liver spots on his hands. Twisted, but still human. Bald, a tremor in his right hand. He was my Angel of Death. He had my whole life in his records.'

'Did you hate him?'

'Not there in the plane.'

For Derek too, The Election must have been the end of his world, turning everything in his future upside down.

If God exists at all, it is as One Who Is invisible, present, everywhere hidden.

He has been leafing through the magazines by the white chair, making heaps of pieces he wants to tear out.

She faces him as she eases her shoulders, rolling them forward and back, 'I need a break. Let's go to the farm stand and get fresh corn. It's almost a sin not to eat it in August. Butter and sugar.'

'American corn is so sweet.'

Is that good or damned? 'As a kid, I used to long for mielie season,' she confides. 'Mielies and the first rain.'

'God, yes, the first rain.'

Her mother believed the children must wait for the first rain before it was safe to go swimming. After that blissful downpour streaming from hair to face they could go to the municipal swimming pool. Then, endless under the sky, blue and receding and near and blue, blue, the water, the sky, distant, pure, forever, as she floated and stared, the sun dazzling, the water tender, silent and happy, time without history, without smirch, without fear, simply being, being alive.

She has never seen such blue outside South Africa.

The fanatic for what should be, he exclaims, 'Children long with such passion. Can you imagine what the world would be like if we longed like that for justice?'

After longing for swimming, the children longed for mielies. The taste of butter and kernels connected them to Sunday afternoon drives to Hartbeespoort Dam and Parys and huge skies where cumulus clouds with heavy bellies pressed on the lower layer of air.

In dry Johannesburg their mother sighed for misty fields by

a river, mushrooms in the woods, northern berries, cucumbers, the white nights of summer and fresh snow where she would beat herself with birch branches after bathing in steam.

At weddings, there'd be a table where landsleit gathered. The children went off to find others, impatient with their parents' conversation.

He is willing to risk one ear of corn. She pulls the husks, leaving one layer over the seeds for flavour.

'Remember loquats?'

'We're like my parents with their landsleit.'

'What's landsleit?'

When she was growing up, at the dinner table in Yeoville, stories thickened around words like Hitler. At Purim her mother baked poppyseed hammantaschen and said Haman also wanted to exterminate the Jews. When Ambrose, the gardener, asked for a note with permission to come home after the curfew, her father told her Jews used to need permission to travel. Cossacks would tear up Jews' papers for spite and spit on parents in front of their children. The pogroms of 1905.

With Derek here today she is living in the pattern of her parents, half in Vilna, half in Johannesburg; half in South Africa, half in New England. She and Derek are creatures of the same species, amphibians under water with their nostrils in the air. Even if he becomes too impossible for friendship, they are closer than landsleit, relatives who last with each other when much else falls away.

Living in the North, she sees why people from the South feel misunderstood. She finds her friends among Americans who live now out of the places they were born to, gay men from Texas, journalists who have had their minds turned on Indian reservations. Her other friends are foreigners, Czechs who could not go home after '68, Chinese born in Hong Kong. She finds herself among people who have been colonised, who have travelled labyrinths, who know daily that they must live in a world where they will be misunderstood.

It seems more difficult to make friends among blacks here than under apartheid. Segregation happens here without the guns and laws of South Africa, or Eichmann's trains. Something makes American apartheid stronger. Capitalism?

Perhaps America really does reproduce apartheid, as Derek says, and she is blind here, like so many whites in South Africa. Wilfully blind. Perhaps she is too comfortable now. She has heard about the Haitian prisoner and read about him, but her day is full of pleasure. If she can live with such suffering and be calm after all, isn't she damned? How can anyone live in this world where there is so much suffering and where you can still go out on a sunny day to buy butter-and-sugar corn and take it home to eat with … a friend?

She has disappointed Derek. When they drove out for corn, he wanted a detour to buy a German beer he cannot find in Maine. Like the ascetic missionaries she knew near Maseru, he allows himself one daily indulgence, a beer, and gives the choosing and enjoying of it the attention of a gourmet. Of course it is not American and he drinks it warm. She feels this sensuality important and human. He is not a cold disapprover of other people's pleasures, not part of the bitter Christianity they used to see every Sabbath when every city fell silent before a frowning God. 'There's a liquor store round the corner.'

They find his favourite pilsener, but he wants to repeat an hour of companionable shopping in a discount store they visited last spring.

'Not today, Derek. I've got to work.'

'Isn't it only five minutes?'

'It is five miles. Twenty minutes at least.' Closing a gate that keeps him outside her work and place in this world. The day's abundance shrinks behind the gate. She is shut in a garden with brilliant flowers and a high wall hides the open world.

'Did you see the editorial about immigrants?'

'I did.'

'Damn Americans.'

'Derek, there's something funny about the way you see things. Millions of people wish they could be Americans. They risk their lives to come.'

'Don't you remember how they used the same argument against us in South Africa?'

'But here it's not like Africa, from greater misery.' Made by capitalists and colonial powers. She knows his script. 'People come from Europe and Asia, with talent and education. So many want to come to America. How can you think you know better than everyone else?' Deepening the personal edge.

'Because I do know better.'

'Oh then, well, of course, I have to agree.'

He leaves the room, his back straight, catching her eye. An Englishman does not bow to injury.

Dammit, why couldn't I hold my tongue? How could I talk to him like that? Such an old friend. Going through such a hard time?

When he comes back to the room, proud and smiling, he says, 'It's good we could make a joke.'

'Ag, man.' But she's drawn blood, she fears. What a mess. No one else shares all these years. During the treason trials they called each other. They were together when Verwoerd was assassinated, when the Portuguese gave up, when Biko was killed. He was the prophet who told her, 'De Klerk is a man of faith and knows what he is called to do.'

She is still repenting when he says, 'I'm off to the Divinity School to buy books and meet Clive.'

'Old haunts and old friends, hey? See you later, then.' Wanting to sound warm, not crotchety like before.

He bears his straight body with ease now and could stroll out to a game of cricket wearing that cotton shirt and the quiet decorum of men who know themselves masters.

No wonder America remains shocking to him. People must take as privileged what he takes as normal. Few can see the privation that is working in him like a yeast, making him tolerant and forgiving.

Sometimes she thinks God, if there is a God, will do anything to get a person straight, even if it means breaking every limb in his body.

Whatever God is up to, if there is a God, it remains inscrutable and she sets to finishing the proposal. The work engrosses her like pleasure and she stops only when the screen blurs. She stands and looks out at her neighbour's red maples, the flux of thought still moving muscles under her mind, until objects regain clear outlines.

When Derek comes in she is still working, 'I'll just be a minute,' and hurries to finish.

After the save command, she finds him reading the weekend magazine. 'Are you finished with this?' The piece on deaf Mexicans lured to New York and enslaved to sell trinkets on subway stations. Another iniquity.

'Have it.' After his life of sacrifice, this stinting poverty. South Africa and her parents' stories have taught her not to believe that wealth equals merit. Americans say, 'You deserve …' this house, this chocolate, not seeing that if all should get their just deserts, none would escape whipping. Derek believes that this world does not judge as God judges. She believes that, if God exists, the One Who Is is working quietly through a code more simple and abundant than anything Americans know. Or anyone knows. The one probable sign to the mind is paradoxes. And to the heart, love.

'Clive gave me a wonderful thing.' He has put it on the kitchen counter for her to admire, 'A gem squash.' A green ball no bigger than the globe an infant Jesus holds in one hand.

'Where on earth did he find a gem squash in America?'

'In his own garden. He smuggled in seeds.'

Her mother also loved gem squash and did not hanker to be in another place when she had it on her plate. 'What a treasure for you. He's lucky they don't train dogs to sniff the seeds in airports.'

'It's not cocaine.'

'If it was, you'd be able to buy it here.' Capitalism at work.

'He gave me two. I'm saving one, but we should share one.'

She resists the urge to refuse, to say that gem squash means nothing to her and so much to him he should enjoy it all himself. It is important to share, to give companionship as she takes the holy food. Especially today, when she has cut him and he is forgiving her. Choosing reconciliation, like a South African, she contemplates the orb enclosing the world he longs for. His pearl. A dark sphere without lustre.

'How should we cook it?' As they eat it, steamed, with butter and salt and pepper, the way her mother loved it, Derek tells her about his first year in the ministry.

'I was much younger than most ministers, you know. There was a good priest in King William's Town and he told me to go to university first, but I was so determined ... Then there was a crisis and they needed someone in the circuit near Thaba 'Nchu, so they asked if I'd go. They gave me a collar and permission to distribute the Eucharist. It wasn't really allowed for someone who wasn't ordained yet, but they did it.

'That was the first time I went into a township. There were two churches of course. A big stone one, almost empty. Six people came to the Eucharist. And another church in the township. So I went there. What a shock!'

He must have seen something like the crowded shacks of corrugated iron she used to see. Smoke. A chicken scavenging. Children with their fists in their mouths. Skeletons with swollen bellies.

Still in primary school, she watched two piccanins searching rubbish bins in the street outside, taking out half eaten mieliecobs. Outside the Coliseum with its starry sky and artificial scraps of cloud, she saw piccanins dancing for money. One played a penny whistle. They wore men's jackets gaping over bodies as bony as prisoners' in the newsreels of concentration camps she had just seen.

She never got used to it and then there was more. More. Always more suffering. At a settlement of tents on the banks of a dried out river, a child playing in a puddle next to the dirt road, the smell of urine, someone saying, 'They have to drink that, you know.' The next day at the mission hospital, her first corpse, a child dead of gastroenteritis.

Derek continues, indignant as though he is still in that circuit, 'And the church itself! Just a room of corrugated iron. The roof was rusting away. The rain was coming through. The floor was mud. People kneeled on that floor to pray. Their faith, their faith ...' His voice full of awe. Tender as a man in love.

That's what keeps him going. All the lonely years, this gold has been shining in him like a river of God. That's why he hates America. So much outward piety, so little of what he has seen as faith, hope, compassion.

'That wasn't all. After the service, a Coloured parishioner came to me. He said, "I know how little money they give you young ministers. I've been giving five pounds a month to the one who was here before you and I want you to take five pounds from me now." So there I was, a white man, taking charity from a Coloured. That was a shock, too.'

He relishes it, sweet as the gem squash luscious with butter. Nourishing him with something better than justice. 'The third thing ... It's not everyone who has the chance to know when they open a dossier on you, but that's what happened to me. I preached about the township and one of my six white parishioners came to me, worried. He was my age, working for the police and expecting to join the Special Branch. It was his circuit too. He wanted to warn me. If I went on preaching like that, I'd get into trouble.

'I had the whole country there. Everything clear in that one circuit.'

That country she knows as hers. Where she saw people at prayer and felt awed at their dignity. In a church in Ladysmith where her nanny had gone to die, women wearing blankets kneeled on bare mud, concentrating and still. Children of God. Their posture alone affirmed trust. Not railing about justice, they set aside the judgment of this world where victory goes to the bullies. They held such peace in their bodies that, looking at them, she saw why artists invented haloes to suggest that luminous quality. They could not know why they must live as the wretched of the earth, as Jews do not know why they are chosen and persecuted. Not for what they have done, the German notion, and not because they deserved it, the simple American idea, but by an inscrutable choice or by accident. If there is no God, working in the world in a subtle code, if it is all an accident and does not mean anything, there is no justice and no hope. But, even with no God, nothing can take from her mind's eye the dignity of those women praying. Her faith in their faith.

Derek's story brings back that morning when the veld was white with frost on the brittle grass and wind knifed through the church. Her hands burned with cold, her feet were heavy with pain. She did not know how long she would be able to sit on the chair one of the women had brought for her because she was white and must not kneel on the mud.

She and Derek came from the same place, grew from the same womb, were formed in the same code, like brother and sister.

In all these years far from her first home, he has been there but she did not know why.

'Thanks for sharing the gem squash with me. It was great.' The American word irks her like a lie, uneasy in the company of her gratitude that Derek has shown her where she is rooted and what she believes. She wishes she had led his life. Dedicated to serving these poor.

With this ending?

She has been like an American looking at his life and seeing that he is poor. But the God of the poor who calls him is, after all, the one who fed Elijah, renewing the meal at the bottom of the widow's barrel one handful at a time, and the oil drop by drop, until the end of the drought. Derek has enough.

Does his preaching reach to the heart like this in Maine?
Another country where people live one handful at a time and
understand that money does not reveal merit.

'Tell me about your congregations.'

'I'm afraid I may lose one of them.'

'How come?'

'I went to see the Berrigans and talked with them about
their protest at the nuclear submarine. I preached about the
millions, billions of dollars spent on military projects like that
without need, when there are so many people who do need. It
offended people in the congregation. Not the comfortable, but
the working class. I had to preach. It was just like my sermon
about the township.'

She cannot hold her tongue. She wants to protect him. She
wants to scold him. She wants to save him from the faith at the
core of his life, the faith she has just felt she shares. 'Oh Derek,
why do you have to be a prophet? You're a Jeremiah. They'll
stone you.'

She wants to stone him herself.

This Balkan Woman

'What's wrong with being unfaithful?' Patty hears Yelena musing at the sink of the communal kitchen.

'Are there children?' a colleague asks. He is gay, not available, and Yelena does not answer. Another conversation, about research on phages, has caught her attention.

The first time Yelena defended unfaithfulness in Patty's hearing she seemed still caught between the misery of arriving in the United States and the miseries of her Balkan homeland. There, a woman taken in adultery is put to death. Here, adultery seems an old-fashioned word and she can say what she likes.

Shapeless in dark clothes, she arrived at the Child Health Unit looking like one of the anonymous who throng refugee roads. She could have been a mother in mourning, moulded by grief. 'Sometimes I want suicide. The people I trusted don't keep promises. What is there to hope for?' She receives midnight calls about assassinations, cousins killed, a friend tortured and feels the burning and stabbings in phantom limbs as vivid as her own. Patty knows of such pains in amputees. She has not seen before how a brother or friend may be flesh of my flesh, blood of my blood.

What strength it must have taken for her to leave her mountain fastnesses, become a scientist, learn English and come to America. 'What are you hoping to find here?' Patty asks.

'Rest. So turbulent at home, you can't imagine. America has peace on its soil for generations.'

Patty bites her tongue on recent horrors in the national news. Nothing to compare with Yelena's sufferings.

Yelena's misery troubles the Unit. Patty senses her group like the mother of a vast family who knows the whole brood.

Days pass when she focuses on research. At other times she sees people avoiding this one, clamouring round that, a craned neck, a glance here, averted there. Her assistant summons her to eat birthday cake, hear announcements of success and settle people who are not getting along. She calls meetings, attends meetings, listens to problems and wishes, glances at mail slots, fax, water cooler, coffee pot and hears the rhythm of talk. Yelena is a rock in the stream.

Patty tells David, 'This woman from the Balkans is having a hard time adjusting. What will you feel if I invite a few people to come apple-picking with us? I don't want to single her out.' Though she has singled her out to him.

The Sunday hours are transparent as apple-juice. Patty's two girls taste fruit still alive and running with sap, run back and forth like puppies, notice new treasures with cries of conquest, collect proud hoards they can barely carry, their harvest heavy as heaven.

David shepherds everyone to cider and donuts, carrying Joan on his shoulders. Patty holds Claire's hand. They stand in fall sunshine between the fruit stall and the orchard full of promises. Others are picking and buying fruit, honey, pies, cheese, maple candies. Promises of infinite good spill from her daughters' greedy mouths like donut crumbs. She wipes them clean, almost ashamed to let a stranger see their confident American bliss. For the trip home, she sends Yelena to sit away from them, in front and, with one colleague in the back, shelters a daughter under each arm. It surprises her to feel their happiness so naked in the presence of this Balkan woman steeped in grief.

The children eat supper while the guests follow her in-structions to walk to the pond at the bottom of the road. David offers to go with them. She had expected him to stay. When they come back, he takes the girls to their bath. The guests drink wine, the girls say good night and leave for their story. 'They're dolls!' Yelena exclaims and Patty bristles. When David summons, she goes to kiss the girls goodnight and returns to everyone laughing at a joke she has missed.

'Another potato in the pot,' her mother used to say, inviting a waif. Talk flows from movies to customs like apple-picking. David finds their volume of Frost and reads the poem aloud. Yelena tells of her country's mountains and traditions that differ from valley to valley. 'In Serbian we say rat, brat. Like in French – guerre, frere. War rhymes with brother.'

As topics swerve during the evening, Yelena mentions friends in prison, her own interrogations, acquaintances in government, international organisations, artists, poets. Patty wonders at her first assessment of this woman. Yelena has cut her hair and washed it with henna. The whole long evening it shines like an unknown metal with copper glints. Through David, Patty sees that Yelena can look glamorous. She regrets bringing her home.

'Dessert,' she says.

'Have you tasted American ice cream?' David leans toward Yelena.

Patty finds her own dessert too heavy and sweet and sets it aside.

In a meeting about grants, Patty sees Yelena has given up mourning garb. She is wearing slacks and green sneakers with beige laces that exactly match the buttons on her shirt, a touch that must take hours of careful shopping.

She hears Yelena before a seminar, 'I'm thirty-eight, too old to find an unmarried man.' These public musings surprise Patty. She expects more discretion of a woman who has spent time in prison for her opinions and associations.

At the Christmas party, Patty makes her way among guests and colleagues, seeing that no one is left out. People smile and talk, playing their proper roles. Patty greets friends in other units. She enjoys this weaving and reweaving of familiar ties and registers the level of laughter, the pace of tides flowing between the food at one end of the room and drink at the other, who is talking to whom, the texture of the party. At a window a knot of fire draws people – Yelena, in crushed velvet scarlet as Santa's robe, with animation equal to the dress. Reflections in the dark window show the faces of people turned to her.

Moving through the party like a swimmer in a lake, feeling cold and warm currents, Patty keeps the window in sight. David's face appears among the reflections. She lets her conversation lapse, moves to his side, puts a claiming arm through his and joins the group reflected in the glass that holds darkness out. David moves his body closer to hers. At the story's punchline, they laugh as one.

Soon it is Christmas, with a dusting of snow on the firs. They postpone presents until everyone has a mug, chocolate or coffee. Patty finds a CD of Schubert songs they heard at a concert when David had just come back from the West Coast. The few days of separation had felt full of emptiness. Where was his voice, his breathing, the sound of a page he turns? Head on his shoulder, she allowed the music to carry her to spaces too complex to name. 'I'm not alive without you,' she said, surprised at the deep void of his absence. He said, 'You're alive in me. We're one life in two bodies.'

The girls tear at their loot – books, puzzles, marzipan, a tricycle for Joan, a bicycle for Claire. Oil pastels for Joan, magnifying boxes for Claire to show leaf, feather, insect, stone. 'I'm going to be a scientist, like Mommy.' Each finds a doll from France. While the girls weigh names, David opens his gift, a box inlaid with varied woods. She filled it with rosy shells, another allusion to a time alone, on the beach last summer.

This hour joins the concert and beach, a girder that holds the year and their lives.

After breakfast they walk to the pond, the girls skipping ahead and back to their slow parents. Ice covers the water's eye with the bleared gaze of a person who does not want to see. In the survivor's village, the men were told, 'Line up,' the women 'Lie down,' the children, 'Here. There,' the roofs set aflame. Patty draws her parka tighter.

'What's wrong?' David asks.

'Nothing.'

They take a customary weekend in mid-January, at an inn with cross-country skiing. After the vigorous outdoors, the grandmother who runs the inn will invite the girls to feed barn animals. Patty feels deep satisfaction that her children have this taste of rural life. David sometimes talks of a place in the country, but she wants someone else to look after her, especially when she feels as tired as she does this winter.

David will drive and comes for Patty at the Unit. Wondering why he is late, Patty takes letters to the mail and sees him with Yelena at the copy machine. She goes back, dons coat and scarf, takes her bag, looks round and switches off the light.

She finds them still in eager conversation and puts her arm through David's.

When the girls are asleep in back, she asks, 'What was Yelena saying?'

'That her grandfather used to tell her she's a cloud floating between heaven and earth and can't be fixed in one place.'

At the inn the girls, grumpy and whining in the car, revive and are promised a visit to newborn lambs. After supper, the girls safe in bed, Patty and David go out into the moonlit world where stars focus the heart's lens on peace and infinity.

Back, at the fire, reading, she finishes an article and stares at the flames yearning to be where they are not. David sets down his book. She sits on the arm of his chair and he caresses her back. 'What?'

'Remember that intern, years ago, who told me she had a brain tumour?'

She bought a velvet heart for the blind hours after surgery and wanted to know where to send it but when she called, the hospital knew no such patient. Before the intern came back, Patty told a friend, 'I must have gotten the hospital wrong.'

'She's been fired, you know. She's a pathological liar. There wasn't any brain tumour. We'll never see her again.'

Feeling humiliated, Patty threw the velvet heart in the trash.

'What made you think about her?'

David's trip to the West Coast has led to a new client, owner of a telecommunications company embarking on multiple mergers. 'I can't tell who we're negotiating with from one day to the next.' The client expects everything instantly and revised next day. Lawyerly caution must bow to brainstorms, hunches and paranoia. 'He's gross. Three hundred and fifty pounds at least.' There is drinking and more. David does not mention drugs but does mention prostitutes. She does not ask their sex or age. He does not feel free to let the firm down and comes home too late to find the girls awake.

His face takes on the impassive expression she knows as turmoil.

On Sunday, overriding Patty's doubts, Claire insists on cooking David's egg in the microwave. When it is done, she says, 'Look, Mommy,' triumphant and takes it to her father. He thanks her and taps the shell. Egg explodes over his face and glasses, the table, ceiling, everyone. Joan screams. 'Quiet, Joan,' Patty scolds. 'Are you hurt?' to Joan or to David. Claire is crying. David sits, his glasses blind with egg, his eyes closed. Patty slides his glasses off his face. He opens his eyes with a dazed look she has never seen in him. The eyes of a survivor.

'Joan, wash your face with cold water. Claire, drink some juice – you've had a shock.' She fills Claire's glass, then David's, 'You too.' He sips, obedient as a sick child.

Then he laughs and they all laugh.

That night, he says, 'I thought I'd gone blind.'

'I couldn't tell what you were thinking.'

He laughs. 'I guess I should be a lawyer.'

She has had a revelation but does not know what it shows.

'What can I do? If he's not married, he's a gay.' Patty's next step takes her into the Unit kitchen. Constrained silence follows.

'They are fighting again in my country,' Yelena says. 'Spring is the time for war.'

Driving in, Patty heard about the deadly jostling, the boy killed in crossfire, revenge to-and-fro without end. The Unit always has scientists from other countries and she knows how events there squeeze colleagues here. There is a coup or revolution, they come to work consumed, checking the radio and the Net.

'I hope your own family is safe.'

'Safe? Last week they came to my parents' house. My parents are simple people. They know nothing. The police asked about me. My parents did not know how to answer.' Her voice is harsh with hatred. 'They came to my apartment. They asked my friends about me. They could send someone here to kill me.'

'This is a safe country.'

'It has happened in the United States.'

'Let's make sure it doesn't. We'll talk after the seminar.'

The main thing is to calm Yelena. When they talk, she says, 'I don't want to intrude, but if you feel you're in danger ...' She suspects Yelena is missing the customary highs of her fratricidal homeland, hatred and fear.

'May I tell David? He used to do human rights work.'

Leaving the office, Yelena smiles, though her wan face remains pained. My life is so easy, Patty thinks.

David says, 'I think she's safe. I'll ask an intern to call her.'

'Getting attention may be enough, though what she says she wants is a man.'

David laughs.

She calls David at work. 'What?' he snaps.

'Did you remember the girls' school play?'

'We've got a closing.'

'I'll tell the girls.'

'Dammit. Don't sound so long-suffering. I'm working for you and the girls. For you, dammit ... Are you still there, Patty?'

'We'll talk later.'

'I've got to work late every night this week.'

He needs a break. She needs a break. She takes her lunch outdoors. The sun is mild and maple buds, red and swollen, strain upward in the shifting air. One pigeon chases another into sheltering shrubs. Walking towards the dark river, Patty catches the eye of a squirrel. It pretends to be inanimate and holds still, but when she turns her head it moves behind a tree trunk to hide from her. She keeps the trunk in view, but the squirrel remains hidden. She knows it is there. She stops. Who will move first?

Last week, a colleague put a finger over her lips, looking at Yelena. Another time, one reached to touch Yelena's arm. Forgetting the squirrel, Patty walks to the river. Inaudible water glides between rocks. If the city fell silent, she might hear its rustling and enigmatic movement, drop by drop shaping valleys, seas and lakes, holding this planet blue and dear, unique with human life.

In the Balkans, they are spilling human life. Fury streams from one to another, bodies fill ditches and ploughed fields. Were the killers children? Are they parents?

In *The Princess and the Pea* the girls glow, their eyes shine. Stage and audience share a fever. Her children are hers and not hers in a world that makes this one dull. Who knows what they understand. Sometimes no pretence can persuade them; other times they can be bought with ice cream and cake like this, after the play.

'Have you tasted American ice cream yet?' What is happening to David? Does he want this life, missing his daughters' play for the money he earns for them?

Last year she moved Joan's birthday party for a meeting at the Unit. At the postponed celebration Joan said, 'It's not my real birthday.'

While she warms their supper, the girls play outside. She sees them flying on swings in the late afternoon light. Do they dream of being birds on streams of air, buoyed over clouds and mountains? Do they long to be human and not human at once? To fly with strong wings like angels?

When she calls them in they are warm and rosy, soon fed and ready for bath, story and bed. Too secular and soft to be angels. She kisses them, breathing baby powder. She misses David.

She eats alone, reading about AIDS in war zones. Statistical and harsh, the report focuses on Africa, prostitution and a myth that sex with a virgin – usually a child – cures AIDS. What about the Balkans?

She looks at her daughters' drawings on the refrigerator and goes to their rooms to hear their safe breathing.

If David were here …

Hours pass. She checks doors and alarms, prepares the house for sleep, turns on the news and goes to bed, not attending to the stories of murders and fires. Under the comforter, she remembers the squirrel, knowing her movements, keeping his invisible.

David comes in, 3.10, red digits on the radio face, and she sighs as though she has been holding her breath in sleep. When his weight balances the bed she turns and touches him, but he breathes as if sleeping.

Next day, feeling drugged, she notices a higher pulse in the Unit as if everyone is acting or watching. Passing Yelena's office, she hears her confiding, 'Last night I was in ecstasy,' and when she glances in, sees that she is beautiful today, a flower open to the sun. Seeing Patty, Yelena comes to the door and when their eyes meet, quick as a cat's, the curtains of her irises draw closed. 'I heard a wonderful talk last night about healing children's trauma by songs. In refugee camps with an actor friend, I saw it. I have something to take back to my

152

country now.' The pinhole in each grey-blue eye is black. Her hips confront Patty.

She wasn't talking about a lecture.

At her own desk, Patty sits numb as though egg has exploded all over her and her world.

If she hears happy chatter from the girls, she will burst into tears. If she hears whining, she will scream. She calls the sitter, please keep them later than usual. Home, she slumps into an armchair and stares at the leafless yard. Time passes, she summons strength and walks out and, in the fading light, sees her home as though its roof has been set on fire and its walls burned to skeletons.

How could he? And with that woman! – promiscuous with lovers, themselves probably promiscuous, perhaps infected with HIV, a firmament of sexual transactions. Her mind floods with numbers and maps of the pandemic, one spark then the whole world. That woman, transmitting her hatreds and unbridled appetites, searing their home, destroying their children's haven. What if David infects the girls? Don't let Daddy kiss you. Don't let Daddy put on that band-aid. How could he? Is he mad? Infected by his lascivious West Coast client. He has lost hold of what is good, what is true, what is steadfast. She despises him.

At the girls' swings, she sees a blur on the ground and stoops to pick up Joan's doll, its face spattered by rain. Poor doll. A woman of the gutter. Carrying AIDS. 'What's wrong with being unfaithful?' Patty grinds the doll into wet grass and dirt, rips the red dress, tears out dark hair, finds a stick and scratches out the eyes. Clutching the doll, she is a child again, weeping, howling, cast to the ground, beating it with her fists, still clutching the stuffed rags.

A spring rain patters. She rouses herself and looks at the victim in her fist. Arms pimply with cold, she goes to the house, slides the glass door, stuffs the doll into a plastic bag and that into a bag of trash. She climbs to her bathroom. As hot

153

tears fall over her, she thinks of raped women trying to wash themselves clean. It can't be done that way.

Her rage distils. She says nothing to David but avoids his touch. Work presses on them from waking to sleep and she pretends not to know that she gives no early kiss, no night caress, no touch taking his body as her own.

He calls, 'I'm working late tonight. I'll come home to see the girls and go back.'

'Fine.'

The poison is dripping, hardening her vital organs. Turning to stone, she will die to find relief.

She must not die. She must defend the girls.

At the Unit she maintains calm. She hears conversations about work, movies, sports and a family trip to Disney World. One group is working on clinical trials for a malaria vaccine. If they succeed – they are one cell of an international effort – millions will live. The momentous consequences hypnotise all and work flows through the Unit like a plasma. Yelena's group focuses on inoculations for newborn refugees. Her cousin has died in the epidemic of crashes on Balkan roads. A colleague complains that Yelena is 'high maintenance'.

'I'll talk to her.'

No time here for her personal disaster.

David's new client demands a weekend meeting on the West Coast. 'As soon as this is over we'll all take a vacation,' he says, as though only his schedule constrains. Is her life so flimsy to him? Not enough to withstand breasts under velvet, hair glistening like water. How can conjugal love, worn with daily use, survive this allure, forbidden and unfamiliar?

On Friday night Joan screams in a nightmare and when Patty goes to hold her, cries and cries, still in the grip of terror. Claire wakes and will not go back to sleep. Joan cannot find words for the horror in the dream. It's leaking from me to them. The news is HIV blood sold to hospitals in Asia and

Africa. Proliferating calamity.

She takes the girls to her own bed and reads stories. When their minds and hearts are cleared and they sleep, she switches off the light. Her phantom marriage is burning. One pain in three people.

She stuffs the weekend with pleasures and reassurances, movies, meals with their friends, a puppet show, the Science Museum, but Saturday and Sunday Joan has nightmares again and again they all sleep in one bed.

No wonder millions fear foreigners and want to wall the country off like a gated community. She could stand at a border now and shoot every person trying to cross. One by one. She would like to kill. She would like someone to rape Yelena. Someone with AIDS.

But the work of the Unit must go on and smoothly. Patty smiles and recognises Yelena at the staff meeting.

People who endure torture without breaking must know how to fix on one point and feel nothing else. She fixes on Joan, weeping at a nightmare too bad for words and Claire patting her younger sister's back, saying 'There, there.'

David opens the door when she turns into the driveway. The girls scream with joy, 'Daddy, Daddy.' He takes them into the house, Joan on his shoulders, 'You're getting too heavy for me.' Claire hangs on his arm. He deposits them and comes back to the door looking for Patty. She is still at the car, taking out child gear and her own bag.

He puts arms round her and all she is carrying. 'Let me.' His voice and pace tell her he knows the world is hanging askew. He puts an arm round her shoulder, they come through the door together.

'You look tired. I'll give them supper.'

Lying on the familiar bed at an unfamiliar time summons a day in childhood when she did not want to go to school and faked illness, her mother's concern sweet and horrible. Tears wet the pillow. She will not leave him if he will not leave her.

She will live degraded in her own mind. She will not ask him anything he does not want to hear. When did she become so craven? Willing to expose Joan and Claire to infections he brings back from other women.

'Don't wake Mommy,' Claire tells Joan, the older sister enjoying authority.

She comes to reluctant waking again when his hand touches her face. She keeps her eyes closed, 'You've got a fever. Take this.'

She swallows without meeting his eyes. If she dies everything will be solved.

Later he wakes her to put a thermometer in her mouth. A bustle follows and she wills herself into blindness. Nothing hurts.

He is drawing her shawl round her. He says something to someone in the living room. He is leading her to his car, fixing her seat belt, driving. She will know nothing. Everything will be as it must. She does not love him.

She cannot live without him. If he died, she would throw herself on his pyre. One life in two bodies. If bigamy were allowed, she would accept another wife. If he has other women, she will become one concubine among others. She has no pride. She has no life without him.

And the girls?

He leads her through doors and answers gatekeepers like a hero with spells from a wizard. They say, Tests, not knowing she has failed, she is craven, her face in the dirt. She does not care that she is weeping. He is with her.

People apply equipment to her hand, arm, torso, breasts. She has withdrawn from everything except his hand. When he moves, she clutches it. A newborn's reflex, grip. If you're falling, grip.

The hospital finds exhaustion and orders rest. David works at home. The babysitter finds a teenager to come afternoons. Patty naps, wakes, looks at the sky, sleeps.

The girls are playing on the floor, sunlight gilding hair and jewelling eyes. Seeing her looking, they come to kiss her. They lie on each side, she reads and they look at the pictures together. The story ends, she says, 'I'm tired now,' they slide off the bed and leave. A universe of time is hers. She lets herself expand into an infinite that is now, luminous and intimate. Life and everything that has happened is good. She has gone through a sewer of hate and despair. Of her own will the misery of the world became hers and will never leave her. It is infinite. But prostituted children still live. They live, she lives. To live is bliss.

She is an atom of gratitude in a stream of light.

David comes in, holds her hand. 'Will you come down?'

She does not need help walking and they take the stairs slowly.

After lunch, the girls play outside. 'What's today?'

'Friday.'

'When can I go back?'

'Monday, if you like, but you have to avoid stress.'

She laughs. 'Doctors always say that ... Before I forget, I love you.'

'Before you forget?' He strokes her cheek.

'What's happening to your client?'

'He's happy enough. We've proved this: if you insist, you get vacation.'

On Saturday, she says, 'Does this mean we have to change our lives?'

'I was also near collapse. We'll work it out.'

'Has Joan been having nightmares?'

'No. They're both fine.'

When she sees Yelena again, she smiles at the other concubine. Yelena professes concern for her, but seems preoccupied with suffering of her own. Patty does not investigate.

Weeks pass and she thinks, I imagined it all. Yelena remains downcast. She applies for refugee status but says, 'I don't like

America. The way people are.'

'We'd like you to stay. You are doing good work here.'

Yelena's eyes swim with tears.

'There, there.' She has suffered so much. No wonder she grabs for love, legitimate or not.

Tears in her own eyes, as though they suffer together, Patty is astonished at the tenderness she feels.

At the dining room table, she is writing notes to people leaving at the semester's end. David sits, picks up a card, reads it, sets it down. She looks at him, he says nothing. She continues. After two more notes, he asks, 'Will Yelena stay? I suggested a petition for asylum.'

'Oh ...' She looks at him, 'I thought you asked an intern to speak with her.' Words and rage tingle like a rash breaking out all over her body.

'It seemed simpler. I'd met her ...' She knows that her eyes are weapons. He drops his. 'She's one troubled lady.'

'What do you mean?'

'She's consumed. So many people she knows have been killed ... She's a fury, ready to spike kids with bayonets and shoot men right in the face. Such hatred. She's secreted so much, it's like armour now. Nothing else can get in. If there's anything else in her, it can't get out.'

She has also secreted hate. How dare he criticise Yelena after what he has done? The squalid treachery of men, brutal with desire until sated, cold with contempt after. David disappears in an indignation as large as the world populous with raped, seduced, betrayed and infected targets. She sees her hands on the table, clenched. Nails bite her palms, teeth of the beasts he has brought into their home.

She masters her voice. There is no avoiding this. 'She has applied for asylum. She's calming down.' Her voice cold as a blade.

'She won't be calm near you. She's too jealous.'

'Jealous?' She looks at her fists on the table, the pen sticking out. She sets it down. He will speak and break the skin of silence that has made life possible these last weeks. She is afraid of his words and every pustule is bleeding.

'Apple-picking, seeing our lives, nearly killed her – peace, work, beautiful children, nothing to fear.'

He is blaming her! This is too bitter to be borne. She raises her eyes to challenge his. 'How do you know?'

'She told me.' And what else? Her fists and his hands flat on the table.

'Did you sleep with her?'

His silence is worse than anything foreseen. 'Once.'

'I hate you.' She unlocks her fists and presses palms to the table to feel its inanimate, indifferent calm. She has already fainted under pain. Then there was that hour of light when she knew pain as a face of life, inseparable. 'How could you?'

'It'll never happen again.'

'How dare you use that lying cliché?'

He covers his eyes. Each minute a block of silence between them. He folds arms on the table and drops his head to them. She can see the back of his neck.

She was willing to die on his pyre, accept his concubine. She cannot bear his humiliation. She touches his elbow, 'David.'

He lifts his head and then his eyes. A dense branching of things they could say grows between them.

The Man of God

During the pregnancy, following hard on scandals about other celebrity ministers, Eliot took Ada to Tucson. She knew no one there and neither did he. The press would not notice his doings in the background if he maintained the flow of stories they were used to in the foreground – incendiary comments on the news of the day and appearances with celebrity allies. He flew to Paris. He had himself photographed in Oslo and implied a role in Nobel peace nominations. He mediated a civil war in Africa and spoke with executives of oil companies in Colombia, dined with a mayor, visited a massacre site and paid homage to a dying poet. In Tucson, Ada waited for the pregnancy to come to term.

A poet herself, she had come to Boston to accept a prize for writers showing unusual courage and to teach classes for a few weeks. Eliot had been on the selection committee and after dinner with the committee and two editors, each wondering whether to vie with the other for a book of her passionate lyrics, he took her to his favourite bar for a glass of wine.

It was her birthday, she said.

Though she had heard gossip, 'His third wife's a waitress. Tells you something, doesn't it?'

But she had not met him then and didn't take much notice.

Neither of them expected the pregnancy, though on that day she chose to call her birthday, the years closing in and her chances pinching, she had prayed for a baby. Her atheism had lapsed. Neither Marx nor Lenin could comfort her. Nor the Prophet. In any case, she did not believe and wrote as a woman who did not believe the Koran supports patriarchy. Someone or something might hear her prayer that she would not die barren. In her memories, in her family and her family's friends, her grandmother's village, even in Alexandria, a barren woman was accursed or wretched. Her high school atheism was no match for this judgment, old and wide as the sky itself.

What's more, on a reading tour in Turkey she had escaped an earthquake and walked the ruins while radios still sent news and songs to bloom in the rubble. A complete fuck-up, though rescuers were still searching for survivors. She resolved to have a baby and refute death with life.

She had already had two abortions, one in her second year at university, another in her first year of marriage when her husband said, 'I can't afford another mouth to feed.' A young lawyer building his career, he refused to be swamped by premature fertilities. A month later, she discovered his affair with a secretary in a ministry charged with saving antiquities from vandals and art thieves. After the divorce he married the other woman, but meeting Ada at a film festival, he invited her to dinner. She fed him spoonfuls of custards, he toyed with the possibility of marrying her again, but sense prevailed. At this stage, he could afford only one wife at a time.

Eliot and Ada met for dinner again. Again. Again.

It was a week after her birthday that he called the florist for his usual order on such occasions. Red roses, of course, now mixed with white hyacinth. She was a poet after all, roses a cliché.

Ada felt herself charged with honey like a hive at the end of summer and next morning in a café she caught her reflection in the glass door swinging in and back and men's eyes when they saw her. Everything swelled with sap and pleasure. She was beautiful and everyone saw it. Still toying with her croissant, she started a poem about bees and their dances, opened her purse for her pretty notebook and gold pen and wrote phrases – how a bee grasps the organ it seeks, the flower's glistening moisture, the bee nuzzling deep, the hairs, the nectar. Her mother believed bees brought good luck and she was sure she would see one this sunny morning. In the meantime, it was a pleasure to sit being beautiful, holding her red book and gold pen and writing phrases in Arabic, French or English, whatever came, emotion recollected in tranquillity. In her hotel room, the flowers were waiting for her.

Eliot nurtured his virile enchantment. He was on fire and it was fuelling his eloquence, preaching and writing. Colleagues applauded his annual lecture at the seminary, the press featured his conference at the Peace Centre and more invitations came in to his speaker's bureau.

She wanted him to see the tape of a television interview but when it started on the VCR, he turned from image to substance, 'You're beautiful,' exploring with hands, mouth, nose and every other organ of delight and power.

Power was what he liked most. Her breathing, her cries, his control, his timing, his interpretation.

A week passed. Another. He would find a research position for her at the Centre for International Peace. His lawyer would help with her visa. His brother, on sabbatical in Europe, would let her live in his house.

She cooked dinner for Eliot and when he saw what she had done his eyes glistened, 'No one's cooked for me since I was a child.'

'No one takes care of you. Look,' she stroked his arm, 'dry. Like a stone in the desert.'

She massaged him with warmed oils. 'Now you are alive, a palm tree.'

In restaurants, he normally ordered steak, cheeseburgers, ribs. She had prepared chicken soup with bulghur, zucchini stuffed with chicken, rice and pignola nuts and pastries soaked in honey. He ate and it was good but when he left, citing work, he went to a greasy spoon and ordered sausage and eggs.

She wrote a poem about the dry stone and the erect palm tree. Next week, in peace after intercourse, their feet playing with each other, toes walking up calves, sliding along thighs, suggestion and postponement, he confirmed the job

162

at the Centre. 'A year-long appointment. The visa will be no problem.'

The day the test showed her pregnant, she stopped drinking coffee. She had forgotten her moment of weakness and faith, did not thank God and dressed carefully to meet with one of the editors interested in her book. When he suggested a drink off site she joked, 'You'll make me famous and if they hear at home that I'm drinking alcohol ...' Nothing need excuse the glow spilling from her like light from a door opened for guests. She savoured her secret and tender breasts.

Afterwards, she went shopping. She had shopped in American-style malls in France but here, in their native habitat, they won her anew with easy lighting, wide spaces, glistening displays and asexual invitations to browse and test. This was the future, where she could shop free and anonymous, free in a free country, like snorkelling without sharp sun and shadow, without glare, dust and heat. She did not have to sidle and press through crowded and winding streets. Men looked at her with appreciation and desire but without insinuating glances, hands, bodies or cajoling calls to touch their wares. Without bargaining and its seductive exchanges of silence and power she could reach consummation at her own pace in a transaction smooth as ice cream, almost too melting to taste. When she yielded the object of desire it came back to her hands veiled in wrappings that made it her own, like a wife, with written proof like a marriage certificate that secured her from questions. Shopping in America she could feel like a man. She bought a soft green robe.

Refreshed by the mall, she visited a middle eastern market and relished anew the play of question and answer, nuance and implication, drawing shopping into intercourse. She bought a large cobalt glass amulet against the evil eye and Ahmed, behind the counter, knew it must be for a special friend as surely as if he had seen the sparkle of a diamond ring. She couldn't wait to give it to Eliot.

163

She did not drink the wine he had brought and he drank bourbon while she served lamb and eggplant with cinnamon, feeding him first with a fork, then with her fingers.

Afterwards, rising from bed, she swathed herself in the soft green robe, picked up a package on the bureau and brought it to him. Uneasy, he unveiled the gift.

'To hang in your car or your office window … Against the evil eye.'

A Baptist minister does not hang amulets in his car or office. A Baptist minister does not believe in superstitions.

To avoid words – this was not the moment – he kissed her but she stayed his hands, 'Wait. Let me tell you.'

'What?'

'Why I want you safe.'

She might as well have shown him a dagger dripping in blood. 'You must get rid of it.' Dazed, she knew he had said this before. 'You can't get pregnant.'

'I am pregnant.' She sat far off, at the foot of the bed, swathed in that robe.

'I can't afford this.' She looked at him coldly. He tugged his goatee.

She walked to the mirror, saw herself, another fuck-up, and his reflection leaving the bed. She heard him taking a shower and she was wilting like a cut tulip.

A small rage stirred in her belly and she started to brush her hair with hard strokes, counting. Her mother had told her Cleopatra brushed like this. She opened her cosmetics box and salved her lips with crimson like the roses he'd sent. She marked the centre of her lower lip with a glossy highlight, outlined her eyes with kohl, glossed her eyelids with blue, opened a jar with her palm and closed it with three fingers, dabbed, smoothed, brushed and checked with sure gestures, her rage blazing now. She opened a perfume bottle, pressed wet from its lips and touched behind the lobe of each ear, the pulse in her throat, knees, ankles. She resumed her vigorous brushstrokes and when Eliot came from the shower, dressed, she set the brush down and reached up to undo the buttons of his vest. He caught a glimpse of himself, his goatee, his widow's peak, white shirt, black vest, the piquant resonance he cultivated of nineteenth-century Satans. Why not? They would discuss this business again after tomorrow's trip to Minnesota.

When they met again, the temperature rose quickly, 'Are you mad? Get rid of it or get lost.'

'You are talking about my daughter. Your child.'

'How do I know it's my child?'

'You dog,' her body shaking, her face dark and sharp. When he touched her shoulder, she spun away.

'Look. I can't have you pregnant at the Centre. I haven't got any money.'

But her breasts were warm and he stayed the night.

So it went, like a game where the same cards appear again and again in different combinations.

He gave her money and the publisher gave her a small advance for an anthology of Egyptian poems. She visited the Centre, making him uneasy, but she wasn't showing and also wanted to avoid scandal. Her parents would suffer gossip and ostracism and perhaps, in these fanatical days, worse. Her brother might kill her, citing honour. She threatened to leave for Paris where she had friends. Eliot had forgotten that. She was not like other women he'd known.

A woman poet on the selection committee became Ada's confidante and sent her to a lawyer. 'That sex-starved old biddy wants to crucify me.' He would be burdened for years.

Ada didn't seem to understand, he had a wife to support, alimony for his second wife, car payments and, now, bail for the son born barely after his first marriage and soon abandoned, arrested a week ago in Georgia on a drug charge. Everyone was hounding him. First that Greek woman he'd met last year. Now Ada. He loved too much. His wife understood. If he opened his heart, he opened it. He ministered. He hugged people. He wiped away their tears. God would not condemn him. The God of Israel, David and Solomon knew about wives.

But Ada was engrossed with her daughter in a soft world inside her body, a secret second heart beating under her breast. She wrote a poem to her daughter, 'You pulse with the thrum of my mother's heart, heard before I was born.' She daydreamed how her daughter would play in the sun and dance with other children, solemn country steps with handkerchiefs and dazzling whirling. She bought CDs at the Middle Eastern store and Mozart and Schubert – her daughter could hear in the womb. She told her daughter what she might see one day – the stout man at the fish store, Ahmed at the bakery, her father's widow's peak, flowers and 'words I am writing for you, my comma becoming a name'.

She called home. Her father, long sick, was neither better nor worse. Her brother's furniture business was thriving. Her mother asked when she would come home. Ada talked about the anthology. 'You've met a man.' 'Yes.' 'Is he serious?' 'Yes.' 'Is he circumcised?' 'He's Christian.' 'Your brother will kill you.' Ada smiled. Her mother's tone changed, 'What is going on with you, my daughter?' Ada sent the question to the heart beating under her heart, the sentient brain, the arms and legs – What is going on with you, my daughter? 'Only good … Tell me about Fatima's wedding.'

She wrote about the village feast her mother described. Words colourful as silk embroidery flowed from her pen, processions with drums and children distributing ataif in the streets. Roasting lamb. Rosewater. Then, evening swallows weaving through dusk. Then, dawn and a heron stalking the marsh. Then, a heart beating under the bride's heart.

His brother in Europe asked, 'Is she really pregnant.'
'Her breasts … she's pregnant.'
'Take her to your own doctor. What if there's a problem?'
His own doctor ordered a sonogram, he went with her and

saw movement. His heart tightened and expanded. He turned to look at Ada, upright as a cedar of Lebanon, and reached for her hand.

She poured Eliot's bourbon, 'I spoke with my mother today.'

What did he have to do with Ada's mother, a woman who covered herself head to toe outdoors. Illiterate. Ahistorical. By now Ada had confessed she knew neither her birthday nor age – no one in the village noted such things. More than centuries yawned between him and that world. How could it be that this swamp was threatening to entangle and trip him? 'What did you say?'

'I want us to visit them.'

'You're mad.'

'We'll pretend we're married.'

She massaged his head and kissed his forehead on each side of his widow's peak. Scented and warm, she described a trip up the Nile to the heart of Africa.

Each needed a story. He agreed to Alexandria. She agreed to Tucson. They would rent an apartment. He mentioned Reno but he could not afford another wife. He needed a new car.

Anxious at his entangling, he bought clothes in Newbury Street where the assistants knew him. They brought him reassuring suits, shirts, vests and the tailor for finishing details. 'So how's life, Sulaiman?'

'Can't complain.'

But Eliot wanted to complain. His brother told him to write another book. He called his speaker's bureau.

It was a relief to accept solicitous attentions in the air and, in hotels, to slip on his public persona, comfortable as that green robe Ada liked so much, to charm strangers and fellow ministers in their bumbling goodwill. But Ada's hovering constrained him. He couldn't look at women with the usual invitation.

She wanted a ring, 'for my parents'. Let her borrow one from the confidante who had sent her to a lawyer. She made a scene of weepings and melodramas like the rants in Scripture. People tore their garments and poured ashes on their head.

At the jewellery counter, seeing her fluent hand marked with his ownership, he kissed the palm.

'When I was married I never wore a ring and now that I'm not married, I do.' Amused, like him, at what they could pretend. 'Now, wedding cake.' They stopped for coffee and mint tea and she devoured the chocolate cake with greedy speed. Seeing his surprise, she put his hand over the secret still hidden under her clothes, 'My daughter wants it.'

He had not found a right time to discuss the child's future or faith with her.

'Eliot! What the hell are you doing in Alexandria?' His school friend looked at Ada with appreciation.

'My interpreter,' Eliot explained, 'I'm writing about monotheism.' His friend winked.

Ada smiled, 'But if my family hears …'

They would spend only a weekend in a hotel near her parents' apartment, a place of doilies and brass and copper ornaments. After that, the upper Nile.

Perhaps the Egyptian sun was getting to him. He would not fight his destiny. He would acknowledge this child.

In Tucson, they rented cheap furniture resembling her mother's. She hung a pink-tinted mirror in the living room and bought matching rose pattern linens for bedroom and bathroom. He bought a wide screen TV and DVD player. They opened a bank account in both their names. He bought her a used Ford. She asked for his schedule, citing emergencies, but he refused. His office knew how to contact him.

She cooked for someone accustomed to her kind of food and every day he went out to read the newspaper and eat a real meal. He read about monotheism but did not discuss ideas with her. He was tired of how she puffed up her Marx for their fights. She didn't believe the slogans she used to show her independence. What independence? He was paying for everything.

Ada's biddy back east introduced her to a new confidante in Tucson. Ada was asking when he would divorce his wife, how much he earned, whose voice had left a message on the machine. Jealous as a wife, she threatened to search the trash for mail he discarded.

The more she wove her women's magazine domesticity round him, the more he relished the tolerant indifference of hotels, their stocked minibars and gifts of luxury toiletries. Often, his hosts sent fruit, champagne, chocolates. But the child, a daughter as Ada had said from the first, drew him back and held him. By now she could live outside the womb and must have fingers, hair, eyes able to see. She would see him. He would see her, his second chance. When his son was born, he was too young for awe. Now he was preaching about the fatherhood of God and his congregations were shouting Amen! Alleluia!

The world was charged with anger and fear. He flew to Paris and offered to mediate. A peace group asked him to keynote an interfaith demonstration in Berlin. Ada worried about her visa and asked again when he would divorce his wife. He had never promised what she assumed.

Little more remained between them than lying in the same bed, coming together when hunger overcame caution, but sometimes she was a rose.

The baby was born when he was in Cleveland with another woman. In a dark predawn Ada called a taxi to take her to the hospital. During the labour her friend in Tucson warmed preserves Ada's mother had sent, fed them to Ada and talked about women's traditions. By the time Eliot arrived, twenty-two hours later, there was little for him to do. He saw that he was excluded and resented, but at sight of Sahara, the rush of tenderness knocked everything else aside. Her face, still creased, pitiful and miraculous, drew him with power and when he dared to touch her cheek, his eyes swam. She grasped his finger like a bird and overcame him with fear and glory. In another age, in Alexandria, he might have cast himself to the ground and covered his face. In Tucson, while a nurse tutored Ada on breastfeeding, he sat watching in the state mystics call union.

Ada's friend Peggy preceded him home to prepare for mother and child with clean linens, diapers, salves, wipes, powders, flowers, juices and, when Eliot came supporting Ada and Sahara, opened doors and disposed Ada on the couch. Before leaving, she gave Eliot a list and he took it, the torrent of his tenderness overflowing into gratitude. Ada accepted his gentleness with relief, joy and a hairline of bitterness. Still in his trance and dazed by interrupted sleep, he saw the apartment transformed with baby equipment in every room, Peggy every hour and Ada's mother installed in the room he had thought of as his study. All the women except Sahara took Ada's point of view, mute but critical. He replenished his Christian forbearance in Tucson restaurants and the one tolerable bookstore on the main street.

Frank, returned from Europe, had an idea for a video tour of America with stories illustrating Eliot's sermons. The series should secure Sunday slots and mean significant money. With Frank, Eliot felt sane.

Not in Tucson. There he was a tolerated foreigner, ignored and dissed by Peggy's New Age farrago of Asian and local superstitions stirred with survivals from Europe's Dark Ages. Peggy cast Sahara's horoscope and declared Sahara an old soul who had lived many lives. Ada's mother supplemented these superstitions with amulets for car seat, crib, blankets and jackets, a bag of weird baby clothes and head bands with pink flowers that disfigured Sahara into an alien child destined for servitude and seduction. Ada controlled the situation. While she nursed Sahara, he had no rights. No one asked him what Sahara should learn to believe. Ada's mother, nominally Muslim, had no more idea of monotheism than Peggy, now adding to the apartment litter with fake Navajo kachinas.

Eliot had once thought himself broadly tolerant of other cultures and faiths, but he was coming to hate these practices and the baleful ignorance of these women's claims. It was like living in Hell, except for Sahara herself. He burped her, rubbed her back, poured endearments on her, sang to her, dandled her and, when she looked into his eyes, saw the wisdom of another world, the direct mystery of God. She would be a queen, president, dancer, sculptor, poet, scientist, 'anything you want, my darling, my pearl'.

Ada had a different story, 'My poor daughter will be unlucky, an illegitimate child.'

His restraint broke. 'Don't tell her ugly stories. They come true if you believe them. You should know. You're a poet. Sahara is a child of God.' Though he wished she had a Christian name. Sahara evoked an unpropitious desert.

Ada snorted.

'The whole concept of legitimate is feudal and bourgeois. She's an American citizen. People risk their lives to be so lucky.'

'You're living in another world.'

'You bet.'

Their other fights were about women. Ada told Peggy and her mother and their silent criticism deepened round him.

He bore it to hold Sahara and see her mastering life day by day. She was not becoming more human. She had been human from the first instant he'd seen her, a soul from God. Her fuzz followed a widow's peak, her eyes and eyebrows repeated his family's features, her chin and mouth seemed her mother's. Biology and history shaped her like clay shaping a pot, but she was unique, unparalleled in all time since life appeared on earth, in all time to the extinction of life. When she yawned, sneezed, opened her eyes; when she closed them, sated, he knew the infinite hazards that had surrounded her sure growth, himself among them. Now that she was alive, tender, needy, hands covered to protect herself from herself, he could kill to protect her. Something to notice when he preached on peace.

He never confided his musings. His public prayers spoke to public policies. When he'd first met Ada, years ago it seemed, he had imagined her poet's insight braiding with his stream of private reverie, the true substance of his being. She had never been his complement. But Sahara, his child, was extending his being, showing him to himself and knitting him like bone to bone, knitting him to human history, other fathers, parents. She opened books and epics to him and showed him what had been there all along while he was blind: the highest good for everyone, their children. Here beat the precious pulse at the heart of ethnic wars. Good and evil twisted into each other, a mystery to theology. The women acceded to his right to pick Sahara up and croon to her, to bend from side to side holding her, to show her how to move in a world swept in cross currents.

His hours with Sahara stained light everywhere.

His brother guessed. One afternoon in his basement studio, editing an episode in Plains about Jimmy Carter and other Baptist peacemakers, Frank said, 'I need a break. Can't drive myself like you.'

'Money, bro. Got a daughter now.'

'Proud Daddy, hmm.' Frank was childless and, like Eliot, three times divorced. Eliot touched his arm. Consoling? Commanding? Taking charge, claiming a father's role, leaving Frank the unencumbered playboy, junior.

Ada's mother left for Alexandria. Peggy visited, but Ada spent days alone. She went shopping and bought gold earrings, dresses, shoes, a new purse. She carried the car-seat through glaring parking lots that reminded her of Alexandria and strangers stopped to say, what a beautiful baby. She accepted the homage. Single as a saguaro, she knew this empty state, prelude to writing. Hours slid by with no sound. She dreamed, looking at Sahara, flesh of her flesh, nourished by her milk, a miracle, an answer to death. Mothers on TV screamed, tearing their hair, and her own body cramped. How can women live after such pain? She had saved Sahara from everyone, especially Eliot. Poor fatherless child.

Every day a new wonder, Sahara smiled, waved her arms, could hold up her head. Learned to turn over.

The paediatrician declared her healthy and praised Ada's mothering. Ada fell on the praise like a ravenous wolf.

Sahara began to coo. One day she chuckled in sleep, a deep satisfied amusement.

The sun swung slowly from one side of the living room to the other. Egypt, Greece, Paris and places like dunes without coordinates sifted through her hours. Day and night bled into each other. She slept with Sahara, listened to her breathe, looked at her dark lashes and, when Sahara stirred, roused herself to nurse, change the diaper. Some days she brushed her hair a new way, played with cosmetics and jewellery, dressed herself, dressed her daughter like a princess and drove to where she would hear her daughter praised. She bought geraniums, parsley, basil and mint in pots, set them out on the apartment balcony and watered them. Sahara's sisters, they needed her. She flipped through women's magazines but the American life they showed seemed strange. Peggy had returned to her own family and Ada declined invitations to drive out and visit. Torpid, listless, she wanted this suspended honey time, these long, still days.

She was not writing and excused herself to herself, too busy with Sahara, but at times her own rebukes rose from sigh to shriek. She was wasting her life here, an alien and a whore like her brother said. She recalled the knowing laugh of Eliot's school friend and reviewed her marriage in Alexandria and her husband's infidelity. Other men had left her. She reviewed her mistaken decisions. She could not go back to Egypt. She would not survive in Paris. She was stuck in this country she did not like. Even the desert, saguaro, cactus, was not her desert. No great civilisation rose here. What was she doing here? She had fucked up her life.

Eliot came seldom and soon left. He said he was busy with the documentary but she knew there were other women. He saw she had been spending his money but her baubles cost less than one vest on Newbury Street, not worth her histrionics. Sweet Sahara was beaming at him now with toothless joy. He tossed her in the air and caught her and she screamed with pleasure. What a lover she would be.

Ada roused herself. When would he ask his wife for a divorce. She needed more money. As a teenager he had held the world at bay with a boom-box. Now he glanced women's complaints aside without hearing.

She threatened to fly to Paris. He found her passport at the back of a drawer in an envelope with a card the woman from Cleveland had sent him and a statement of earnings from his speaker's bureau. He pinched his nose, thinking, and tucked only the passport into his briefcase.

He'd seen her furtive at a can of tea and pulled the metal top open. Hundred dollar bills. He laughed. Why not under the mattress? He'd been so wrong about her.

His lawyer said, she can't take the child out of the country without your consent.

A TV producer agreed to view the documentary. He and Frank were working at the top of their form but he needed privacy and rented an apartment in Boston. When Ada called in a rage that he'd abandoned her and her daughter, he cursed the carelessness that always accompanied a tranche of intense work. The landlord had sent a letter to Tucson; cheques he'd written on their joint account had bounced. He put down the phone and poured himself a bourbon and when he picked up again, Ada's tone had moved to abjection. She'd been thinking about her life and would end it, hers and Sahara's too. He set the slopping glass on a table and told her to stop. She stopped.

'I'm coming to Tucson,' quiet as ice. And with rage, a barely

174

visible reflex from the past, 'Please keep Sahara safe.'

He called Peggy, said Ada was having a nervous breakdown and asked her to call the police if necessary. 'I'll come to Tucson as soon as I can.'

'She thinks she can lasso you,' Frank said, 'and jerk you around.'

'I'll have her locked up.'

'Whoa!' as much admiring as astounded.

Peggy called. Ada and Sahara were installed in her guest bedroom.

'I'm working to deadline. I'll send you a cheque.'

'Money's not the point.'

'She's talking bounced cheques.'

'Tell her to look in her tea canister.'

He told his lawyer Ada had proved herself too unstable to be trusted, but his lawyer advised no court would give him custody.

He flew to Tucson during a work lull, flattered Peggy with celebrity attention and, in her living room, stroked his goatee while Ada did her dervish dance of rage. When Sahara woke, he held her feet on his to walk and dance. She had two teeth now and clung to him, wordlessly complicit. He knew she wanted him to get her away and he would, but it would take time. Meanwhile, he kissed the soft soles of her feet and the palms of her pudgy hands.

Flying over the weary geology between Tucson and Boston, he wondered, was his pain heartbreak. An attendant stopped by his seat. Bourbon? Champagne? He noted her body, but unexpected grief occupied him. He must protect Sahara from her lunatic mother. He recalled that reflex, Keep her safe.

Ada was praying too. That he would die. That he would become impotent.

She returned to the apartment. A bow tie, his books. Artifacts of lost life. A letter reminded her, the lease must be renewed or cancelled.

Her confidante out east wanted her to come back to Boston.

She was afraid. He had threatened to take Sahara away, 'if you behave like a lunatic'.

For want of another idea, she packed a bag, threw out Sahara's furniture and toys and flew to Boston. Solicitous attendants surprised her with an extra seat for Sahara.

The apartment she had rented sight unseen simulated space and light with mirrors. 'Why am I saving his money?' She called a realtor.

Day by day she retrieved her footing. She saw a doctor and he prescribed calming medications that would not harm Sahara through her milk. A psychologist recommended day care but she was not ready to relinquish Sahara and said Sahara was not ready.

Eliot called. Peggy had told him her number. He wanted to see Sahara.

She would not have him in her apartment and they met in a park. He pushed the infant swing and, holding Sahara, slid her down the plastic slide. She touched his goatee. He could have shouted his love to the whole world.

Ada sued for child support. Half his earnings, his lawyer guffawed.

'I didn't know she was a gold-digger.' He had been so wrong.

But he was seeing Sahara every week and noticed that Ada dressed carefully for every meeting. She wouldn't get him in the sack again, not now.

Indifferent to the curiosity of the other parents and the condemnation of Ada's biddy, he attended Sahara's birthday party carrying a gift the store attendant had suggested. Guileless Sahara sat in his lap and fed him cake. Her mother said, 'Kiss,' and she held her face ready.

Soon after, he called Ada to cancel their next meeting, 'for a doctor's appointment', and she asked after his health with credible concern. 'I need surgery.'

'Oh no!'

He accepted her invitation to visit. She offered wine. 'I shouldn't. Just a little.' He stayed long after Sahara had fallen asleep and sealed their conversation with a brother's kiss.

She told her confidante, 'I prayed for him to die and be impotent.'

'Don't worry, you're not that powerful and God doesn't listen to prayers like that.' But her friend did not know men and Ada was not sure she knew God.

She called him and they talked a long time again. Mulling over this judgment on him, she felt pity. She would shame him with her nobility.

After the operation she brought Sahara to the hospital and met Frank. Sahara held up her face for kissing and Eliot gave her a Get Well balloon. At 'Bye-bye' she blew him a kiss and Eliot met Frank's eyes, 'Okay. She's stolen my heart. It's grace. She's providential.'

He went on vacation. Where, Ada did not know. With whom? No money came that month, she despised her pity and her ire rose to high tide. She called her lawyer.

Eliot was not returning calls. Her lawyer said, 'All communication must go through the lawyers, now.' He had betrayed her again.

At his Peace Centre, people smiled and exclaimed at the child in her arms, neither surprised nor outraged.

In court, he did not greet her.

'He feels I can't touch him,' she told her lawyer, bitter that the court would not give her sole custody and humiliated by the pitiful sum it assigned. She called a journalist – her family would believe a marriage and swift divorce – but other stories commanded the headlines.

Eliot returned and they started the visits and alternate weekends.

Sahara started to speak words. Eliot said, 'You should talk English to her.'

'Two languages will confuse her.'

'Will you lock her up in a harem?'

'Fuck you.'

Every week he came to fetch Sahara and take her away. He returned her calm as a queen. Ada's therapist said she should wean Sahara. No one needed Ada alive. When she opened her red book, it read like the litter of gaudy toys underfoot. She was not ready to work. She feared to pray.

But with Sahara in her arms, assurance filled her like mint tea with honey.

Eliot agreed to help with a visa. She started a poem and toyed with it. What else could she do?

Sahara was walking now, getting into everything, driving her mad. Her therapist suggested day care. 'She needs to separate from you.'

Fearful, she took her daughter to the church hall and relinquished her. Sahara crawled to a toy another child was banging and did not notice when Ada stole away. Alone at home, she sat with her heart bare and dry.

At day care, she met another single mother and invited her to tea. The children played on the floor around them. Each woman told the other a story. The other mother also wished for more money, a husband, a home, a father for her child. 'Would you get married again?'

'I wanted something better than my parents' lives.'

'How'd you think our children will see our lives?' She would tell Sahara an epic romance, but if she tilted her life, the opal went dark and became a cracked cinder, a fuck-up.

The day care teacher asked to meet all parents. Eliot called, 'We'll go together. I'll drive.'

The teacher addressed her as his wife and did not seem to know he was a man of God.

In Court

They began as adversaries.

Karl Meyer liked tennis – the dedicated field of action marked with clear white lines that defined where to stand, where to serve, to answer, to run; in a world made human and sane by rules; the dedicated clothes, white, formal and fit for action; the dedicated language, slightly arcane, historic, precise and shared in the comradeship of the courts.

On a Saturday afternoon, when the sun shone crisp on the cleared space of hours, he walked towards the pavilion where friends waited. Birds with melodious notes sang in the trees, bright flowers edged his path. The racket he held at the leather shaft and delicate neck felt poised with promise. 'Hello, Karl.' Jamie, Willem and Herman waved greetings. They offered a few sentences, like wine poured to the ground, and then they were on the court, bouncing, running in the dense dance of air and light, movement and control.

Scraps of conversation survived the trance of concentration, the sky, the net, the lilt of serve, bounce, run, rally. Movement with grace, effort with joy. 'They're destroying the country.' It was always surprising to Karl that Jamie, built so burly and tall, spoke in a thin treble. 'There'll be nothing left here but a ruin,' and Karl knew what he meant. He had driven past burned-out oil tanks. The news had too many scenes of rubble, soldiers and the higgledy-piggledy of shoes and shopping bags and hands.

Karl disdained politics as a game not worth its prizes. Too many politicians swelled as their names appeared in headlines. Time on TV pumped them smooth like brown paper bags schoolboys puff and explode. Bang. The class laughs and the teacher swells with anger.

But the conversation in the tennis pavilion wasn't politics, it was patriotism. Soldiers sent from borders with other countries to borders within the country. Battlefields all over the land. Law and order lost. In milk and wool country, in wine and orchard country, in factory and mine country. Students. Unions. Church groups. Unruly and incessant. Coordinated. Cumulative. The peaceful country of his childhood was now at war on every hand and in every field of action. 'Total onslaught,' Willem said. Willem liked to use phrases ready-made by the press and politicians. Karl watched the spotted guineafowl he had brought from his farm pecking on the lawn between beds of yellow, orange and red cannas. The sky, a deep blue Karl had never seen anywhere else in the world, held its peace. Doves were talking to each other in a dialogue one did not have to understand, like the Saturday afternoon talk of servants in the backyard. Karl wanted to be done with war and talk of war.

Bella set the tea tray on a bamboo table and departed, the bow of the white doek at the nape of her neck a small bird in flight.

'They're talking about big trials,' Jamie looked meaningful.

'You think that'll do it? I don't.' Herman crumpled his embroidered linen napkin and dropped it in the centre of his plate. 'They spin out these trials for years. As far as I'm concerned, it's just expense and waste.' Herman always liked the role of critic and sceptic. Nothing ventured, nothing lost.

Karl wanted to disagree with the narrow greyness of his safe position. He wanted to say something in sympathy with the passionate cannas and the elegant spotted fowl wandering so calmly among them. 'We've had incompetents handling them. People who don't know how to keep order in court. The case dismissed last week – it was a travesty. People don't see what the country's facing, don't understand what's going on.'

'You think a good judge could keep a political trial short?' Herman scoffed, recognising Karl's subterranean challenge.

'Why not? If I had one of these cases, I'd have it wrapped up in two months, I tell you.'

'You would?' He couldn't tell whether Jamie was impressed or jeering with Herman.

'Why not?'

'We all know these lawyers are clever and paid by foreign money. The international anti-apartheid set.' Jamie's younger brother, a reporter on *Nuus*, had recently joined that set and the chorus of carping that wore out the nation's pride as its critics travelled abroad and made safe names for themselves as foes of apartheid. 'It's the fashionable thing to give money and from the lawyers' point of view, why not? The longer the trials last the better. Maybe you don't know their tricks, Karl. You've never touched a political case. They know how to make delays last years.'

Karl was almost speechless at this patronising lesson. 'They wouldn't trick me.'

'Come on, Karl! You don't know anything about politics! The last time you attended a political meeting you were a student.'

'That was enough.'

A lilt of township jazz wafted from the servants' quarters next door. Saturday afternoon. A time for relaxation and licence.

They were on the courts again before Bella returned to take the smeared and crummy plates, the sugar bowl where orbs and scabs formed when a careless guest took sugar with a dripping spoon, the delicate stained cups.

On Saturday afternoons, Themba prepared for funerals. He was often asked to talk to the mourners at the house of the bereaved and in the ceremony by the grave. Sometimes it was a long drive to the township. Dusty roads, hovels made of mud and plastic and sheets of naked iron. He honed his spirit to give heart. Let the mourners leave with songs in their mouths, confident in their strength. Victory was certain. Their cause was just. When he spoke and the elders nodded assent, he felt as though his father had just smiled at a good report from school.

His three companions were enjoying the idleness of passengers, joking with each other and talking about who would make what power play at the next regional meeting. Themba listened. He foresaw a harsher future than they. It could only be a few days now before the police came to the office. Or soldiers. Or worse. He listened with professional attention to the youths' speculations. When he spoke for these young men and to them, they would raise their voices to cheer: Viva! Amandla! resolved to fight until the struggle was won. He must know how to sustain courage in their hearts.

Themba swerved. A mother had pushed her child forward to cross the road. He honked and shouted at her. How dare she set the child in danger before herself! His heart raced as the mother restrained the shoulder of the girl with a pink bow proud in her hair.

Themba's own Magdalena was nine days old today. This morning when he dandled her, her chubby feet, still creased and soft, had danced on his hand like rain. Her toes had not touched the earth yet. When he put his finger in her hand, her fingers furled around his index with a soft bird grasp he would never escape. He looked at Lily with proud despair that they were both caught, servants of love. Lily did not meet his eyes.

She was hiding something from him.

He was feeling unbearably thirsty, tormented by the blue smears of mirage dancing on the road ahead. False promises.

At last week's funeral, police in yellow vans parked under eucalyptus trees watched the proceedings. Some walked about, talking to each other on walkie-talkies, thinly disguising a disrespect for the dead and the mourners Themba found brutish.

The mourners barely had time to scatter earth on the coffin when the police warning came. Before older people had time to get away, choking smoke. Some of the youths covered their faces with wet rags. They had prepared, sure the police would shoot tear gas. They were growing more canny about violence, less careful to avoid it. Experience. Common sense. And forewarned provocateurs? It was getting more difficult to know who was what. He must talk with Kunene about provocateurs pulling mass action towards riot. It had never been easy to inspire hope without turning people's confidence into impatient rage. After last week's funeral, there were two more dead. And after this week's?

He focused on the emotion he wanted to create, concentrating and planning as he had learned in childhood. Teaching gardening, the teacher said, first, you prepare the soil. When the soil is good, everything grows well. When the soil is poor, everything grows sick. What was the right soil here? The youths in the car must also learn to listen to old people who remembered the past and had learned wisdom, and to adversaries, to hear how they would act. They must hear people's fears and calm them, hear hopes and bring people together. Their listening and self-command would prise open the jaws of the state and release those mangled by its teeth. Meanwhile, the government was still taking hundreds into detention and threatening more political trials.

They would take him. The questions were, when? Charged or simply detained? If charged, with what? If detained, how long? Some of these political trials took years and the leadership on the ground was dangerously thin.

He turned on to a side road. Golden dust followed them like a dwarf pillar of smoke. It would not do to think too long. He saw no way to evade the police with dignity. At first, he and Kunene had avoided the authorities. Dressed like servants and delivery men, they seemed invisible. Rallies and meetings continued. After some, people turned from outrage to stoning and burning. The President accused the organisation of treason and blamed it for terrorism. With Kunene, Themba prepared a press release. It warned that the police and army were tormenting people beyond endurance. The government's unjust policies and officials were responsible for the country's violence. Their own organisation was non-violent. They did not criticise supporters who became provoked, or turn a back on those in exile and prison who had lost hope in non-violence and chosen armed struggle.

Yesterday, he had gone to the office and worked through a pile of correspondence. They had to show that their organisation acted within the law and in good faith. The authorities knew where to find him and Kunene. They would come.

But, holding Magdalena to her own body, Lily would not look at him.

He was thirsty. The road turned towards a low bridge over a muddy stream. Rolls of glistening barbed wire blocked the bridge. A handful of soldiers patrolled with guns tucked between chest and arm. Dry eucalyptus leaves whispered and their shadows skittered along the road. On both sides of the bridge, army vehicles flanked the road. Young men sitting in trucks, under arches of khaki canvas, looked out with bored faces. They would rather be playing soccer or joking with girls. At their age, Themba had spent Saturday afternoons rehearsing with the choir. 'Jesu, joy of man's desiring.' The older choirboys snickered about other joys of man's desiring. Across the muddy stream, behind the glittering wire, a metal sign, Coca-Cola, rusted from the corners where it had been bolted to the wall of a country store.

A small winter wind shuffled through dry grass, husks of a summer past.

At the arraignment four months later, Karl did not notice Themba. His eye was more caught by the publicity director, Kunene, showing off for the gallery. Kunene did not plead a simple not guilty, like the others. He took the occasion to make a little speech on the justice of their cause. That kind of thing would have to be stopped. Also the Anglican priest who insisted on blessing all present before the proceedings could begin. He would not allow them to turn the court into any more of a circus, with policemen at every door, the dock, the bar, the stand and the gallery. The opposition press were relishing the pictures they were getting, subversive suggestions that the unarmed prisoners held the state in terror, while the government, armed but ineffectual, could not withstand the righteous virtue of their cause.

To these reporters, Karl knew, he was the guilty one. He would show them. He would not let this trial run for years, a punishment before sentencing. He would not allow bias on either side. He had gone out of his way to be fair and they would have to admit it.

Jamie could not understand why he insisted on inviting Nico Veenendal, a known liberal, to assist in judging the facts of the case. Sure there was Ben Marais, a reliable country magistrate, on the other side. Why complicate things? But Karl believed in fairness. Fairness visible to all was the only way in this case.

Nico would bring to the case wisdom, the prestige of his career and the strength of a God-fearing life. Nico was an old friend. He had been Karl's professor in law school. Principles he had instilled still guided Karl in thorny cases. Nico and he respected each other. When Sipho Ncube could not find anyone willing to rent him office space, Karl insisted on fairness – if a qualified lawyer, even a black, wanted to practise in the city he must have chambers like anyone else. Nico was almost the only other lawyer who agreed. They both convinced the municipal authorities to make space available.

Things were better since those days. People were heeding the advice Nico had been giving for years. There was even a new constitution. But now Nico had moved out on a limb again, asking for more. For all. Too fast. Neither blacks nor whites were ready yet.

But Karl had found it good to invite Nico to dinner. After the food and wine, in the mellow time after the meal when Nico accepted a small cognac and swirled the golden liquid with appreciation, contemplating the beauty of the Cape wine country and of its oaks imparting character to this magnificent brandy, after a silent toast, Karl said quietly, 'Well, Nico, could I invite you to sit with me in the Matthews case?' He saw surprise and pleasure in Nico's eyes and found it good to be reciprocating Nico's invitation, years before, to join the faculty of the law school.

Robed for the arraignment, with pudgy Ben Marais on his left, Karl felt Nico's presence on his right hand like a guarantee of probity, a gold standard. It would be a good trial. The lawyers for the defence were the best in the country. They too were champions who had dedicated their lives to the law. Karl was eager to watch how they handled the rules and the play of wit and stamina that would shape history in this dedicated field. He waited for the ceremonies of opening with bridal nerves. Let the real trial begin.

He did not notice Themba among the twelve defendants in the oak dock.

Themba observed Karl. Seated in the centre of the bench, robed in red as though he dressed every day in fresh blood. The lawyers manoeuvred. The court recessed and met again. Days passed. Weeks passed. In late spring, when jacarandas were blooming outside the prison, Lily brought Lena to court in her carrycot. During the break Themba saw her still sleeping with clenched baby fists, a born revolutionary.

Soon fallen jacaranda blossoms browned the streets. Summer heat glared from building to building. Themba enrolled at UNISA, but found it difficult to concentrate on economics and sociology. He thought about the case. He thought about Lily. She did not come to court like the other wives and rarely came to prison. A few newspapers noted the first anniversary of their imprisonment. One afternoon Kunene's wife broke off speaking in a low voice when she saw Themba. He thought she looked at him with pity and curiosity.

At Lily's next visit, she would not meet his eyes. He asked

gently, 'Are you lonely?'

She bent her head and turned it askance.

'Why don't you look at me, Lily?'

She looked at the hands she held in her lap like an empty boat.

'Where's Lena?'

'Your aunt's looking after her today.'

'Why don't you ever come to court?'

'I can't bear to see you in their power like this.' Her mouth twisted like a child's about to cry.

'Don't come then, Lily darling. Don't come to court. But come here to see me. And let me see Lena. This trial could take years more. I won't know her when I come out.'

The defence lawyers were angry. The judge was denying every petition. He's trying to be fair, Themba thought, appointing Nico Veenendal. He saw that the judge feared the lawyers would outwit him. They knew him as an addict of fine music and fine wine, of books and paintings and Persian carpets, a connoisseur who travelled to Europe every year, a proud man impatient of weakness, a self-made man who believed that every man could make himself. A man comfortable with the way things were and ready to dismiss critics as ill-informed or ill-willed. He believed they would try to trick him. He would not let himself be tricked.

Themba wanted him to see something else: their cause was just. They would not challenge the law's legitimacy. They would not appeal to a higher law. They would not defy. They would argue, as they had always done, that their organisation was lawful and they had always obeyed the law. Let the judge see that they respected the law although they opposed specific laws. The new society they worked for would need the law's protection. Let him see that they were not terrorists, careless of the future. Let him understand that they respected his office and his choice of life. Let him not fear. Even when their cause was won, the new society would need fair judges.

The new society would be Lena's. 'He's got a daughter, hasn't he?' Themba asked.

'She doesn't live at home. She preferred boarding school to living in the same house. Even his wife can't stand to live with him. She spends most of the year in Europe.'

In the panelled chamber where they took tea, Nico listened to Karl talking with Ben Marais about the news of the day – more violence, boycotts, strikes, multiple dangers to the state posed by a total onslaught. Ben expressed opinions with rustic certainty and in a moment alone with Karl, Nico said, 'I'm troubled by that kind of political talk. It might prejudice the case.' Karl flushed deep red until his face seemed as bloody as his robe. When he regained his voice, he said, 'Thank you, Nico. I know how to run a fair trial in my own court.'

Nico dropped the matter until Karl seemed more calm.

A stubble of frost grew daily on winter's jaw. The prosecution presented its witnesses. Themba observed the judge's impatience, straightening his papers with meticulous long fingers, leaning forward to ask the clerk for a reference or exhibit, leaning back to listen. He aimed at a judiciously inscrutable face but his attention quickened when senior defence counsel spoke. Although they addressed him as M'Lord, it was he who respected them. They disliked him. Every few weeks he brought cake for the defendants. 'Stale leftovers,' the lawyers scoffed. 'The slave-owner wants to feel good,' Kunene said.

Themba also suspected the appearance of generosity, but there was more to the judge than their sceptical disdain admitted. When one of the younger defendants asked permission to train for and run in a marathon, he granted permission with admiration for the young man's spirit. When it came to the law, he thought, this man would be scrupulous and judge by principle. He began to feel some hope. They had always acted within the law.

In the cage of a police van hurtling them towards prison,

Kunene said, 'I am not going to say anything to discourage you. You are a man of discernment.' Themba felt trapped as if inside a bullet targeted to kill.

The prosecution finished its parade of witnesses in time for a summer break. The defence asked for a recess. In the panelled room, afternoon sunlight was sloping on to the table of heavy oak where Ben pushed aside the dirty teacups. 'It's a strong case. More than a hundred witnesses.' Ben had been more of a support than Karl had expected, but as he set his briefcase on the table to pack his papers Karl noticed his new double chin and popping buttons. Too many good lunches and teas. Ben should play more tennis. Or something.

'I don't think they'll call the defendants to the stand,' he said. 'A scruffy lot.'

'Oh, I don't know,' Nico said, 'some make a good impression.'

'You think so?' Karl sounded more amazed than angry.

'I do.' Calm and firm. 'I think they've got a story to tell and will use the court to tell it.'

Karl remembered Kunene's impudence at the arraignment. Well, he'd shown he wouldn't put up with nonsense in his courtroom. Nico was wrong. 'I bet you a bottle of whisky they won't take the stand.'

That shut Nico up. He looked upset and left the room.

During the summer recess the pains around Themba's heart increased. They took him to the prison hospital. They prescribed rest. Themba slept during the day and dreamed of times on the run when he drove all night and slept in strangers' houses by day and of a childhood time of illness when he had slept in the room assigned to his aunt, a servant in a white suburb. The dogs had learned not to bark at him. His aunt interrupted his naps with cups of steaming tea and soup. The mornings were strangely silent, except for the sounds of birds and occasional footsteps and conversations in the concrete courtyard behind the house. It felt like a time of unaccustomed solitude, ease and care. At night, when she slept head to toe on the same bed, he felt her body offering comfort through its simple being and warmth. He dreamed of her now and took the interruptions of nurses and orderlies with a patience they did not expect from men unless they were very ill, least of all from men reputed to be fiery leaders with dangerous views. When friends brought Lena to visit him, he chuckled at her inquisitive prowling about the ward.

'Like father, like child,' a friend said. 'She wants to know everything that's going on.'

But Themba's appetite for knowledge had dimmed. When the visitors left, he just wanted to sleep in the clean bed of the prison hospital, opening his eyes from time to time to see that the sunlight had moved across the room.

When Jamie asked how the case was going, he did not rub in its length, nearly two years now. Karl was doing a good job. Other high profile cases had either collapsed or were also proceeding slowly. The gang of defence lawyers who took on these cases had mastered the law's delay.

Among the white lines of the courts' defined rectangles, they ran and hit and leaped in harmless play.

Sessions resumed when the late summer fruit was coming in – hanepoot grapes, Kakamas peaches, Granny Smith apples. The defence laid out its argument. The prisoners would take the stand in their own defence.

'I hope you bought that bottle of whisky a while back,' Nico could not resist. 'The price has been going up.' Karl despised him for the weakness of the jab. Next morning he had his clerk take the fifth to Nico. He saw no point in talking.

The case ground on. Themba took the stand and, led by his lawyer, presented his childhood poverty and the indignities inflicted by police, extreme and, he claimed, shared with many.

He spoke of listening to his people's pain and of his work to give them political voice, of his faith in eventual victory and negotiation. He spoke modestly and, Karl thought, truthfully. At times, he almost acknowledged that violence might not be avoidable but denied that his organisation was responsible. He looked beyond, to reconciliation in a unified country.

Karl noticed Themba's quiet acknowledging glance when a dignitary entered the courtroom during his testimony, his fingers setting pages straight when the lawyers handed him papers and other exhibits, his meticulous grey suits. The man bore himself calmly, like a leader who knows that others wait for his words. They did. When he spoke, the crowded courtroom fell still. During intermissions, Karl knew, dignitaries crowded round Themba and Kunene as though they were already leaders of the country, their ambitions fulfilled. During sessions, Karl listened and took notes. Occasionally he interrupted, disgusted that the careless prosecution did not understand Themba. They were not dealing with an unprincipled demagogue like Kunene, a communist revolutionary or one who claimed a right to pick and choose which laws to follow, which to break. No. This was a man who respected the law as a safeguard of decent society, concerned for the future. A man they should have on their side.

He dreamed he was playing tennis in the courtroom. Themba was his opponent. Or, sometimes, his partner in games against Jamie and Ben. The walls of the court gave way to walls of forest, like the thick green valleys near the coast where indigenous hardwood hung with vines gave shelter to white rhinoceros and birds of purple plumage and brilliant song.

He woke, rose and went to the bathroom, but the harsh light hurt his eyes. He drank water and felt relief. He slept again and dreamed. The dry court was vast as a desert cracked with drought. They played from a tense distance, hardly bridged by the ball spinning at their blows. Lizards slipped into the cracks between them. Grass thrust up and spread with spider arms in all directions. The country cracked into rubble, the concrete split like a broken fruit and thick blood poured slowly from its skin.

Themba sometimes thought he would faint on the stand, but he summoned his strength and stood with a straight back like a free man. This was what he had lived for – the right to declare himself and speak for all who spoke through him. They had given him courage and purpose. They had entrusted him with hope, to speak for their old age, their children. He spoke and saw his words move the prisoners with him, supporters who filled the gallery, the press, diplomats come to represent their countries' concern, church officials come to show God was listening, celebrities drawn into the trial's wake. Even the lawyers. Even the judge.

From time to time the judge lost patience with the prosecution. Couldn't they do a better job? He asked questions, followed up on cross-examination. Sometimes it seemed he wanted to convict. Sometimes it seemed he wanted to protect.

The lawyers noted his interventions. If he found against them, they would appeal, saying he had intervened not like a judge but like a prosecutor.

They kept Themba on the stand for three weeks. Karl developed a slight tic of the cheek under his right eye. His doctor suggested sleeping pills, but Karl refused. He promised to exercise more and sleep more. In his dreams now, women cried out in terror and triumph, guns clapped open the sky, smoke obscured the lines and the ball became a rock thrown into store windows and schools. Themba, inside, ran like a shadow from classroom to classroom, hunted. It was Karl who was hunting him. He tried to wake but sleep held him. He had to play another interminable set.

Kunene observed his perturbation with a sardonic eye. 'You're giving him nightmares,' he told Themba.

When they turned to Kunene, Themba sat with relief on the foam pad friends had brought for the men consigned to the dock's hard oak. He saw that the judge looked worn. His clerk was doing crossword puzzles at a desk set so far under the bench Karl could not see what he was up to.

Jacarandas were blooming again as the defence summed up. Karl interrupted senior counsel, 'But why didn't they protest the violence? Why? I am really troubled by this question. How do you answer? Wasn't it their responsibility?' It did not occur to him to look at Themba or Kunene in the dock.

Themba's lawyer bowed slightly, as if in courtesy. He had no intention of exposing his clients through unwariness.

The question, he said with deference, raised new issues not proposed in the indictment. He asked M'Lord for time. The law's delay. The trial was now in its third year. Karl was sick of it. He wanted it to end. He wanted to go to Europe, to a concert, to read a book. The country's turmoil had grown ever worse during the years that kept him prisoner on the bench. Although he had stopped reading newspapers – the trial consumed all his time – headlines and brief talk with old friends were enough to show him the trial had accomplished nothing to bring order.

In the panelled room, behind closed doors, Nico said, 'They can't be held accountable for the violence others committed while they were in prison.'

'You've always shown you're on their side,' his irritation erupted.

'Karl, for goodness sake, what are you thinking?'

'I haven't been able to rely on you for anything. You've been partisan from the first. They just can't do wrong in your eyes.'

'You're insulting me, Karl, and I demand an apology.'

'An apology. Are you crazy? I had no idea I was asking for unrepentant prejudice when I invited you to serve as adviser.'

'I demand an apology, Karl.'

'Excuse me,' Karl picked up his briefcase, walked past

Nico to the door and closed it firmly. Nico looked at Ben, who avoided his eye.

'What do you have to say about that?'

Portly Ben replied, 'I wouldn't take it too seriously. Karl's tired. We all are.'

'Do you think I've shown prejudice?'

'I'm not going to get into it, Nico.'

'I'm not going to let him get away with it.' Let Ben tell Karl.

It took Karl nearly two months to write the verdict. He worked on the farm. After a rapid walk through the fields each morning, he settled down to writing and did not stop until the late evening radio programmes turned to Schubert and Mozart. From time to time he looked out at the golden sweep of grassland, the peach orchard and the guineafowl pecking in the grass under the trees and felt his love for the country swelling like a wound. He turned his back and focused on the soft scratching of his pen on paper.

On the day he read the verdict, a man two blocks from the court aimed his gun at blacks in the street, shooting to kill them one by one. A hawker wrestled him to the ground. Although police clustered thick around the court, it took a while to reach the scene. Some recognised the gunman, a past member of the force. When the clerk said, twelve dead, eighteen wounded, Karl covered his eyes with his hands. An involuntary gesture.

Security in the court, tighter than at the arraignment, presented him with a small audience of luminaries. He explained the issues. He cited precedents. He described the historical context. He analysed the evidence and the arguments. He could not read his whole decision in one day. On the third day, after all his explanation and care, the verdict was met with a gasp. What had they expected?

In the panelled room where he did not look at Nico, he did not speak to Ben. He was spent.

He wanted nothing but sleep, blessed extinction, but the telephone rang incessantly. He was astonished. When Jamie called and commented in his treble voice, Karl said, 'I don't understand your reaction.'

'I don't understand you, Karl. Don't you know what's been going on in the country? Don't you read the newspapers or watch the news?'

'You're not asking me to interpret the law to conform with politics, are you?'

'Karl, you're a baby.'

If only he could sleep like a baby.

'What's this I hear about Nico bringing a suit against you?'

'Nico's crazy.'

'You've done yourself a lot of harm, Karl.'

He poured himself a whisky and remembered that Themba's younger brother had just died. Cirrhosis. For a moment he looked into a lifetime of pain and numbing drink. He closed his mind's eye. But not before remembering that damned wager with Nico. Whose dark life had he looked into? He drank the whisky like medicine, not caring for the taste.

The President did not call him, but what was it, if not a signal, when he pardoned ten other political prisoners? Karl wondered whether to defy him and invited Jamie to dinner.

Afterwards, they drank and talked about the world situation and the situation of the country.

'You've been too busy with this case to appreciate what's been happening,' Jamie said. He swirled the brandy in his snifter and held it up to the light. 'Best in the world, I'd say.'

Bella entered quietly, took drained coffee cups from their end tables, asked, 'Anything else, master?' and left them alone in the large house.

'It's the end of an era,' Jamie mused. 'We're in the last years of our history, you know.'

'That's absurd.'

'No man, Karl. From now on, this country's history will

be written by those men you had in the dock. Didn't you see it? Didn't you see who the press came to cover? Who the diplomats talked to?'

Karl felt as if his skin had been torn off.

'Bear it in mind, Karl, when you sentence them.'

The President pardoned more political prisoners. Everyone said what Jamie said.

The case went to appeal and the lawyers brought up his whisky wager with Nico to show that Karl had been prejudiced against the defendants. They brought up his criticism of Nico. The press was publishing stories about hit squads led by police he had trusted and cited in the verdict. By the time the appellate court heard the case, Karl knew how the verdict would go. Colleagues passed him in the corridors and did not stop to talk. Even Jamie could not join him for tennis this year. He was not surprised when the prisoners were released.

He went on with his work – a labour case, a land case, things as they had been before. But now he was alone as he had not been since the bitter days of childhood when other boys scoffed; he kept his nose stuck in books and no girls.

The prisoners moved into the centre of public life again, their pictures under newspaper headlines, their opinions in interviews on the television still controlled by the state they had defied.

Karl planted oak trees on his farm. Let them know, after a hundred years, that he had done something right. Then he saw a programme that decried planting imported trees instead of fine indigenous varieties. Sometimes Karl considered work in Europe or the States, but these were just dreams. His tic grew more constant. His doctor told him to drink less and to rest, but work was still a comfort, so he ignored the doctor. Violence throughout the country multiplied and now it seemed no one could control it, not even those who had invited it. Karl planned a rose garden to replace the tennis court.

Themba wondered how the man who had condemned him saw things now. At odd moments in the car, in the bathroom, he found himself thinking about Karl. He wanted to speak with him. The wish grew. He did not want to answer questions about why he wanted to see Karl. They would not bump into each other in the ordinary course of things. Where then? The wish slipped into darkness, like the wish to spend more time playing with Lena.

Karl threw the invitation into the wire wastebasket under his desk. A poplar's uneasy leaves by the stream bed caught his eye – silver coins slipping through merchant hands. All judges in the area must have received the invitation. An opportunity to hear leaders newly returned from exile or released from prison, on the judiciary of the future. He had heard enough and feared the worst. Kangaroo courts, show trials, venal and political judges, officials running petty tyrannies, indulging personal tastes, sometimes perverted. The rule of law would follow the sad script of the rule of power. A few lawyers of the recent generation who had protected defendants with the rule of law might stave off darkness for a year or two, but even they would find that politicians they had protected, once in office, understood opportunism, not principle.

Silver leaves shuffled through gambler fingers quicker than the eye. The poplar seemed still untouched by drought. Doves called from branches that showed no sign yet of the drought branding the continent from north to south. A little wind rose, twisted dust round itself like a dog making its bed and lay down. The doves had nothing to say. A dry time. A dying time. If he went ... He did not need to court the simulated sightlessness of colleagues who would not care to be seen talking to him. He turned to other letters in the meagre post.

Falling into a nap after dinner, he swung his racket to meet the ball's parabola. In a quiet court white rules held them until the lines inverted like photographic negatives turning opaque transparent, light dark, dark light. In a pliant, electric game he served and ran and rallied in a space wider than the sky, waiting for the deep hit of ball on string, still, hold, swing, hit, his opposite dancing to the same beat, run, leap, swing, hit, deuce, love, love, deuce, deuce, game.

He woke to the discomfort of his body slumped in its chair, his neck cricked and a moist stain on the cushion. His teacup was gone. Bella had taken it while he was collapsing on himself with open mouth a-dribble like an old man. He walked quickly to the bathroom by his study, washed sleep out of his face and found work on the labour case he must decide by the end of the month.

About to set the cap back on his pen before a nightcap of brandy, he pulled the wire basket from under his desk, found the invitation, accepted, tore a stamp from its sheet, pulled it over the damp sponge and fixed it in its corner. He screwed the pen closed, no word in his mind. He could have been asleep, walking.

He bore the evening's slights with numb obedience, colleagues who did not greet him, a past clerk who waved from a distance and took no nearer step, a moment when both the barrister on his right and the magistrate on his left were turned to other conversations and he saw himself talked about at the other end of the table – a glance in his direction before a bite of fish confirmed something, a nod and answering grin, another bite and chew. He felt immune, a patient under local anaesthetic who sees the surgeon expose and cut his intimate thigh without hurt, only nonchalant curiosity.

After the ice cream and speeches, the guests moved to the hotel lounge for coffee and brandy. Small groups settled in armchairs. A few lingered near the cups and urn of coffee.

He saw Themba in the flux of people. He had put on weight. As Themba turned from the table, a steaming cup in his right hand, Karl caught the moment. 'How are you?'

Themba stopped and looked at Karl. 'No, things are good. I'm very busy.' He moved another step away from the table.

'You're active again, I see. I expected it. You'll be playing a big role in the country's future.'

'Yes. You said so in the verdict.' Neither moved now. 'I appreciated that.'

'You understand, I had to sentence you. I did think you broke the law.'

'No, man. I thought you were struggling.'

'I was.'

They fell silent as though they had lifted a heavy beam together and now stopped to rest. In the uneven knit of conversations and ting of teaspoons on saucers, a quiet ring around them felt like the moment Karl had seen himself discussed. He looked at a silver bowl on the table piled high with decorative fruits and realised he was waiting for Themba to take the lead.

Someone brushed by them. Themba said, 'Your timing was unlucky.'

'It wasn't really my timing.' He was thinking of the lawyers and the headlong rush of events he had not seen, catching him blind.

Themba heard unaccustomed helplessness, bitterness. A course of self-destruction. 'No. History was moving its own way.'

Seeing something, Karl recognised, beyond the range of his own eyes. 'I heard you were ill again in prison. Are you better now?'

'No, all that's over. I'm fine.'

Karl could not stop. 'They say, conditions on the Island have improved a lot.'

Themba, also aware of people watching, heard Karl's pleading undertone and laughed sadly, 'Who says so? You should go yourself and see. Spend a night in a cell. Eat cold mieliemeal and samp on a tin plate. Live without rights for a day. Even one. A judge should know these things.'

Karl did not see how to continue.

Themba did not want to end with rebuke. 'This time, yes,

the authorities were trying to treat us right. I mean, the leaders, not ordinary prisoners. They're still in misery. But we had newspapers. TV. Books. Sports.' He smiled, knowing his man. 'Kunene taught me to play tennis in prison.' He laughed.

'I play tennis,' Karl heard his own confessing, astonished.

'I know.' Their eyes met. 'My wife left me, you know. She couldn't take the fear, the long time alone.'

'I heard.' He raised his eyes to Themba's. 'You've got a daughter. Did she go with her mother?'

'No, I've got custody, but Lena's still learning who I am.'

Karl nodded, grave. 'She lives with you?'

'I'm too busy. Too much travelling. She's with Kunene's children.'

Karl did not want to talk about Kunene. Voices from other conversations flew against the net of attention between the two of them and Themba's stance showed Karl what he had not seen in court – careful listening, the wellspring of his activism. As though Themba could answer and speak for him too, he bared his fears. 'What do you see happening in the country? There's all this violence. Do you think ... How do you think it'll come out?'

Themba did not answer. Wary of his recent adversary? Then, 'I don't know. The younger people don't always listen to older leaders now. Our organisations were almost destroyed while we were in prison. We lost leadership on the ground, where it matters.'

A plum in the silver bowl, Karl saw, had ruptured and was oozing, broken by its own ripeness. He straightened his shoulders. 'Will you be able to bring order into the situation?'

Again Themba paused.

'Well, your silence answers me.'

Taking a step away from the table to show he was ready to end their exchange, Karl gestured towards the fruit and a platter of cake.

'No, thank you.' As friendly as though the half-hidden exchanges of sympathy and accusation had never happened,

Themba continued, 'My doctor says this must go.' He pointed to his shirt stretched tight, like Ben's. 'More exercise, he says.'

The roomful of talk fell away from Karl. 'Would you ... I, er ... We could ... Well, why don't you come over ... We could play a game of tennis.'

'Thank you, but, you know, my schedule's really heavy.'